SEASON OF THE HEART

Ann Hammond

A KISMET™ Romance

METEOR PUBLISHING CORPORATION
Bensalem, Pennsylvania

For the Sanibel Seven

who helped me discover the joy of island living, and
fellow writer Pat Kay, who convinced me I could translate it to paper.

ANN HAMMOND

Ann Hammond's experience as a hospital respiratory therapist helped put her in touch with emotions necessary to write about people, and her "on call" status for helicopter rescue gave her plenty of time to plot a romance. After years of writing for her own enjoyment, family and friends encouraged her to actually submit a story to an editor. A native Floridian, Ann hopes readers will discover the beauty and charm of "old Florida" through her work.

ONE

This is what hell must be like, Lane Stafford thought wearily as he continued to place one foot in front of the other. It had to be. A never-ending journey down a road leading to nowhere. A stretch of black-topped fire shimmering under the noonday sun with such intense heat Lane could feel blisters forming on the soles of his feet.

He glanced down at his shoes. They were Italian, a luxury purchase made two months ago.

Expensive.

Good-looking.

Damned impractical for walking any great distance. They might as well have been made of paper for all the protection they offered from the scorching pavement.

The side of the road was little better. High grass made walking there no easier than hacking a path through the Amazon jungle.

A city dweller all his life, Lane wasn't about to explore unknown territory by tromping through the weedy undergrowth. Every so often he could hear a slithery rustle skittering away from his presence—confirmation it was much better to let the road fry the first layer of skin off his feet than risk encountering a snake or whatever else thrived on this miserable stretch of nothing. He struggled to resurrect lessons from his college zoology class. Alligators preferred the marshy inland areas, didn't they? Of course they did. Anyway, what animal in its right mind would be out in the middle of Dante's Inferno.

A sting of pain brought Lane's hand slapping at the back of his neck and he checked his palm for evidence of a kill.

Nothing.

No bloody-black smears to confirm the suspicion he was quickly being eaten alive by that most deadly predator of all—the mosquito. Yet his body was a testimony of abuse. Every exposed area of skin, and some that weren't so readily accessible, was a stinging mass of minute red welts that itched unbearably.

He thought mosquitos chose their victims as the sun set, not in the middle of the day, but there was no denying that some insect invasion had descended upon him like Japanese Kamikaze pilots after an aircraft carrier. It did Lane's fraying temper little good to realize he had yet to settle the score a bit by killing even one of the blood-sucking little beggars.

Well, Jerry had told him these islanders hated tourists in spite of the money they brought with them. Killing them off was certainly one way to make sure they didn't come back.

Bone-tired, Lane sat down at the side of the road, his legs drawn up so that his arms dangled limply over his knees. He squinted toward the hot, wavering fireball that was the sun. "Okay, Rod," he called aloud. "Show yourself. This is the *Twilight Zone*, right? And I'm this week's episode."

There was no eerie music to confirm this accusation, only a small rustling sound to his left indicating his voice had scared some poor creature half to death. He hoped it was a mouse.

He told himself that he wasn't going to die right here in the middle of Caloosa Key. Eventually someone would come along and give him a lift, although he'd yet to have one car pass him, so Lane wasn't really sure just how he knew this would happen.

He was twenty-eight years old and in fairly good shape, he reminded himself irritably, not some three-year-old kid separated from Mommy in a shopping mall. Even in off season the island was inhabited by a handful of locals who kept the place running. Though he'd been on the island little more than an hour, Lane knew there was a town of sorts up ahead. Maybe a mile. Caloosa Key was long and narrow, information that had been furnished by his soon-to-be-ex friend Jerry, who, when Lane thought about it, was seldom right about anything outside of business. But surely, Lane reasoned, he could walk the length of it in one day.

Still, he hadn't counted on the heat. A drought, for God's sake! The hottest June in Florida in thirty years. And here he was, stuck in the middle of it. Why hadn't Jerry warned him?

Lane thought longingly of the past three weeks spent in Amsterdam. Cool. Crisp. Every flower glistening wet with spring rain. Heaven on earth, though he'd been too busy to realize it at the time.

He decided he was going to murder Jerry Carlisle.

The man had gotten as much mileage out of this friendship as he was ever going to get. No more favors. Let Jerry find himself another architect. Carlisle was rich enough to afford the best; now all he had to do was find someone stupid enough to come down to this Devil's Island.

What had possessed Jerry to buy property on such a dismal little sandbar? Crazy. The man had been peculiar in their college days, and obviously the inheritance of all that Carlisle money hadn't made him any more sensible. If Lane ever got back to Chicago alive, he was sure as hell going to tell him so.

And then he was going to kill him.

Something large and noisy strafed his ear, and Lane slapped it away. A deer fly as big as a golf ball zigzagged out of range. "Coward," Lane muttered, and smiled evilly at the thought of Jerry's demise.

Slow and painful, and somehow . . . hot.

"You're not gonna start crying, are you?"

Since that was precisely what her fluttering emotions had in mind, Maggie Rose James marshaled her features into a vague smile of denial and whirled to face her younger brother. "Of course not. Why should I?" she protested brightly. She was chagrined to hear her voice betray her by breaking midsentence.

With an economy of motion, she jumped onto the floating dock and looped the boat's cast-off line around the anchor cleat. Harlin Walker, Caloosa Key's ferryboat captain, made a move toward them, but Maggie waved him away. The load they had brought back from the mainland was not heavy, merely cumbersome, and she and Robbie could manage it alone.

"Well, you didn't say a word all the way across the bay, and that sure ain't like you." Robbie scowled at his sister's lack of response. The very fact that she failed to correct his English or rise to his teasing was a bad sign. Typical of twelve-year-old boys, Robbie had little patience for feminine frailties and threw Maggie a look of impatient disgust. "Come on, Mag. Snap out of it. You said yourself, the worst part is over."

"It is."

"And Mom made sure we'll have some money."

"There'll be enough for a while."

She did not want to be drawn into further conversation about the future. Not today. When the wounds were still so fresh. Hoping to distract Robbie, she set off across the crushed-shell parking lot, her arms filled with assorted packages. Together they managed to transport the rest of their purchases from the small boat to the station wagon.

As Maggie slammed down the hatch, Robbie came up beside her. She could read the determined sparkle in his eyes. He wasn't going to be sidetracked. "It's not bad living in the cottage. You can practically spit on the inn from there, so it's not like we never see it anymore.''

Maggie's lips twitched into a smile. Sweet boy. He was trying so hard to help her through this transitional period in their lives. The least she could do was pretend everything was all right. She sighed and held up a forestalling hand. ''Okay, you can stop preaching to the choir. Those are all the same things I pointed out to you six months ago. Remember?''

The boy offered a relieved grin, and Maggie felt her heart catch at the similarity between Robbie's gently sculpted features and the tanned good looks of their father. ''Yeah. It's just too bad I was the only one listening.''

She reached out quickly to issue a playful swat of affection which Robbie avoided with practiced skill. ''Get in the car, you little brat! And mind your manners. It's not too late for me to send you to Great Aunt Mildred to raise.''

''You wouldn't do that.''

''Try me,'' she threatened in the most menacing tone she could summon.

Unaffected by his sister's words, Robbie laughed and bent to retie one sneaker. ''Nah. Give up the chance to run my life? I figure you already got the next thirty years planned for me.''

''Certainly not,'' Maggie replied with an affronted sniff. Then with mock innocence she added, ''By the way, how many children would you like to have? I think three.''

''What!'' Robbie yelped, and suddenly the past six months were sliding away. They were carefree kids again, laughing and dodging away from each other's grasp with taunting ease.

Oblivious to the heat, they chased each other around the ancient station wagon. Cornering Robbie between the open car door and the front seat, Maggie laid siege to her brother's hair, mussing it into a hopeless silver-blond haystack, and Robbie retaliated by tickling his sister unmercifully along a well-known sensitive area just below her rib cage. At last, panting for breath, their youthful exuberance spent, the two collapsed ungracefully upon the car's front seat.

"Whew!" Maggie gasped, blowing a strand of her own silvery hair out of her eyes. "We haven't done that in a long time."

"We haven't done anything in a long time except—" The boy broke off, his face coloring with a guilty flush. He hadn't meant the words to come out sounding like a complaint.

Maggie swung her head to eye her brother sharply, immediately gauging the boy's thoughts. Poor kid. Robbie could be so adult sometimes it frightened her, as though he were forgetting how to be a child. And then suddenly, he was just a boy again. With all the childish worries and foolish pranks being twelve years old entailed. She hated the changes taking place in their lives and wished she knew some magic to make this easier for him. They needed normalcy now, to get out from under the shadow of pain and death that had dominated so much of the past three years. A sudden fierce sense of her responsibility for him washed over Maggie.

"It's okay to be resentful, Rob. It hasn't been an easy time for either of us."

The boy was silent for a long moment, then his voice came across the short distance separating them, a low whisper of anguish. "I miss Mom, Mag."

"I do, too, honey," she replied softly.

Remaining perfectly still, Maggie waited for Robbie to continue at his own pace. The boy was still young enough to resent the coddling of females, so she made no move toward him, fearful lest he withdraw into himself once more. In the eight months since their mother's death from cancer, not once had her brother voiced his feelings on the matter. It concerned and frightened her, making Maggie feel painfully inadequate to be his legal guardian. A surge of pure relief gripped her that at last Robbie seemed to be coming to terms with what had happened.

The silence that spun out between them was almost palpable.

Maggie squinted through the dusty windshield. The air was hot and motionless, the wild, tangled growth of the island as still as a landscape painting. Above the drooping limbs of a late-blooming Royal poinciana, a red hawk circled lazily. Maggie watched Harlin Walker tinkering with his boat's engine. There was nothing wrong with it. Harlin always tinkered. As Caloosa Key's only official link with the mainland, he took his responsibility seriously, even if the ferry only ran back and forth to Fort Myers twice a day.

She tossed a glance toward her brother. Scrunched amidst the seat's thick padding, the boy's face was barely visible, yet she could sense the tension within him and knew him well enough to hazard a guess as to his thoughts.

"It's going to get better, Robbie. I promise. Now that Mom's estate is settled, we can put everything behind us. You believe me, don't you?"

A long pause. Finally, with a sigh, "I guess so."

There was more in those few words than the boy was letting on, and Maggie slid near him, covering one of his thin arms with both her hands and tilting her face toward him. "Tell me what you're thinking, Rob. I can't help you if you shut me out."

The child kept his face averted, and for a moment Maggie feared he meant to stonewall her. Then, with a muscle at the side of his jaw clenching and unclenching spasmodically, he said quietly, "Every time we go to that lawyer's office, I get mad at Mom, Mag. I don't want to, but I can't help it. Mom shouldn't have sold . . ." His voice trailed away quickly.

He was afraid he'd said too much, afraid his sister, who probably never had a mean thought in her entire life, would think he was some kind of monster. He could feel the tears clogging his throat, and he hated the thought he might cry in front of her. After all, Maggie might have legal say-so over him, but he was still the man of the family now. His mother had told him that before she'd died.

Maggie's heart ached for her younger brother. She could see he was striving for control, could feel the immature muscles in his arm bunching beneath her fingertips. Curiously, she felt no unsettling panic as to how she should handle the situation; her own thoughts had not been so far removed from his.

It pleased her when he did not flinch as she reached out one hand to stroke his hair. Like her own, it was thick and, oddly enough, fine as cornsilk, a shimmering blond shade they had both inherited from their mother.

"Robbie, I thought you understood why Mom sold the inn. She knew the cancer would cost a lot of money to treat, money we didn't have, and she didn't want to see us burdened with a lot of unpaid bills when she . . . afterward. You know that since Dad died, the place was slowly falling down around our ears. The three of us barely kept it open before Mom got sick, remember? So how could just the two of us manage? She was just trying to make life a little easier for us, that's all."

"But you love the place. Aren't you mad at Mom for selling it?"

She favored him with a forthright smile of regret. "A little, maybe. Mostly because I think we could have managed somehow. But I guess I'm just sad, really, because that's where I grew up and where you were born. There have been so many good times there, Rob. Maybe you're too young to remember them, but there were. When Dad was still alive and before Mom started to get sick. Lots of people were always coming and going, important people—"

"Like Grover Cleveland," Robbie offered.

Maggie laughed. "Well, that was a little before Mom and Dad bought the inn, but yes, like Grover Cleveland and others. But that's only a part of what makes the place so special to me. It's also the love and care Mom and

Dad put into it. The history. The way people came to feel about the place when they stayed there. Remember the lady in England who always asked Mom to ship jars of fig jelly to her at Christmastime? Just think, people in England eating Mom's homemade jelly!'' Maggie settled back in her seat. With a pensive sadness, she remarked almost to herself, ''It's hard to accept that a part of our life is over, never to return.''

''You could do what that lawyer Mr. Drummond says. I heard you talking to him.''

Maggie's brow lifted. ''What was that?''

''Go to court. Tell the judge Mom wasn't complete when she decided to sell the inn.''

''Competent,'' Maggie corrected patiently. ''And if you heard that much, then you also heard him say we didn't stand much of a chance of winning. Mom sold the place *before* she got too sick, so, whether I like it or not, Mom knew what she was doing. Besides, I don't think you and I want to see her name dragged through the mud in public by saying she wasn't mentally capable of making that decision. Do you understand, Robbie?''

''I guess so.'' After a long moment, the boy sighed heavily. ''Why doesn't that rich guy do something? The place is gonna fall down if he doesn't fix it up soon.''

''I don't know what he's waiting for, Rob,'' Maggie admitted. ''I guess Mr. Carlisle is a very busy man.'' Her voice lacked conviction. The fact that The Caloosa Key Inn was still vacant—six months after they had vacated the manager's quarters—did not bode well. But for Robbie's sake, Maggie tried to be cheerfully optimistic. ''Just wait till he gets around to restoring it. It's going to be so beautiful, honey. Just like in the old days.''

The boy gave his sister a tight, skeptical smile, but he was astute enough to catch the unsteadiness in Maggie's voice and wise enough not to comment on it. ''Better,'' he declared with sudden confidence. ''We won't have to do any of the work.''

Maggie's mouth quirked with humor. "No more painting."

"Or cleaning the pool."

"No more making twenty beds every day."

"Or listening to crabby Old Lady Endicott complain about her arthritis all winter."

They laughed together, a clear, hearty sound that helped to restore their flagging spirits. Maggie was relieved to see Robbie's good humor return. Like a sudden squall, the boy's mood could change without warning.

Unexpectedly, his hand, small and slightly grubby, reached out to capture Maggie's fingers in a gesture of quiet empathy. "You'll see, Mag," he said softly. "It will be better."

It was such an un-Robbielike thing for the boy to do that Maggie's eyes immediately filled with tears. Blinking rapidly, she drew him toward her in a fierce hug. She was suddenly aware of just how deeply she loved Robbie but how poorly she had guided him through the past few months. The boy's vulnerability was painfully obvious, yet she had allowed herself to fall into a moody, dreamlike rhythm of listless malaise. But no more, she vowed silently. Her brother was depending on her. She couldn't let him down. They had a home and enough money to keep them for a time. The shop in town had been modestly successful last season. They had each other; they were still a family. That was the most important thing.

There was nothing to be done about the inn. It was lost to them now. She and Robbie had left behind the shards of so many of their parents' hopes and dreams, but at least they would see the inn returned to its former beauty, once more the shining monument to southern hospitality Robert and Tyla James had always envisioned. Though she had never met him, Maggie was sure Mr. Carlisle would not stint in the restoration. She and Robbie would have to be satisfied with that. No matter how much it hurt.

Robbie was struggling out of her arms, the look he

threw her one of amused exasperation. "Don't do that. Suppose Harlin sees and tells the guys?"

Her laughter held a sharp edge, but it was genuine. "Sorry, I wasn't thinking."

Feeling somewhat heartened by her new resolve to take more control over her own life, Maggie slipped the car into gear and bumped it on to the two-lane road that led home.

Lane watched a column of ants march up and over the top of one shoe, thinking the little devils must be the hardiest of all creatures if they could manage an outing in such an unbearable inferno. *Maybe they're just killing time waiting for me to die so they can pick my bones clean,* Lane thought. *Greedy bastards!* He shifted his toe out of their way and rose slowly to his feet.

He was immediately aware of a floating disorientation coupled with a hollow rumbling in his belly. It occurred to Lane that he was still suffering a bit from jet lag and that his last solid meal had been yesterday in Amsterdam. It was something more than simple hunger, though. Beneath the slick sweat of his wrist, his fingers found his pulse. It was rapid and pounding, and the sudden unamusing thought struck Lane that if he didn't get out of the heat soon, he just *might* succumb to sunstroke. A pretty embarrassing way to go, but dead was dead, after all.

Imbued with new energy and a sense of urgency, Lane lifted his shirt from the waistband of his trousers, unbuttoned the front, and used the tails to fan himself. The action did little but stir warm air back and forth. He needed to cool down, and quickly. There was a small stand of pines off the road about three hundred feet, and though he didn't relish tromping through the high grass to get to them, they at least offered shade. He could rest a while until his temperature was under control, then begin his trek to town once more.

He had just put one foot off the pavement when he heard it—a car motor. Not really expecting rescue to come from the direction of the ferry landing, Lane shaded his eyes and strained to see in the opposite direction.

Nothing.

He swiveled to look back the way he had come.

Still nothing.

The road was arrow straight, with no car in sight. Had he only imagined the sound?

And then suddenly Lane saw it, rising out of the wavering heat of the road like the monster out of Loch Ness.

A big, beautiful car.

Coming his way.

Coming fast.

Passing him by if he didn't snap out of it!

"That guy's crazy to be out walking today," Robbie remarked as he caught sight of the man standing up ahead at the side of the road.

"I don't think he's out here because he wants to be. That was probably his Mercedes we passed back there. Shall we give him a ride to town?"

"No!" Robbie said sharply.

Her brother was seldom so uncharitable, and Maggie glanced his way in surprise. "Why not?"

"I just don't want you to," he said, and then because he knew Maggie wouldn't find that an acceptable reason, Robbie added, "You're always telling me not to talk to strangers. Well, he's one. He could be a maniac."

"Robbie! What a thing to say!"

The vehicle was almost upon him before Lane realized this might be his only chance for rescue. He stood at the side of the road and stuck out his thumb in his best-remembered pose from eight summers ago when he'd hitchhiked his way around Europe. Imploring, but not too aggressive. It was obvious he was a fellow motorist in trouble, not some psychopath who'd chop a good samaritan into little pieces just for the fun of it. Frankly, it never occurred to Lane the driver of the car might pass him by.

Someone should have told the driver that.

The car—an old, beat-up station wagon—*did* slow down. He caught a glimpse of blond hair, a female at the wheel and a small boy in the passenger seat, and had actually taken a step toward the door handle when the wagon suddenly increased its speed and left him standing in the road, wide-eyed and slack-jawed with stunned surprise.

Lane reacted instinctively.

His palms tented into a prayer and he shouted after the vehicle, "Aw, come on, lady! Have a heart. I'm dying out here!"

The appeal apparently fell on deaf ears, if, in fact, it had been heard at all. The station wagon kept going.

Lane swung around. His anger was so great that if he could have found a rock big enough, he would have kicked it into dust. "Heartless witch!" he cursed. How could she *not* stop? His situation was so obvious it was almost laughable. Whoever she was, she must be the most unfeeling, uncaring woman who ever walked the earth. If he ever saw her again—

His tirade ended abruptly when he heard a car motor, and his head snapped up hopefully. To his surprise and immense relief, Lane saw it was the same station wagon that had passed him by only moments ago. Evidently the driver had suffered a change of heart and was coming back for him. He straightened, ignoring the dizziness assailing him. He wasn't about to let the driver get away a second time, even if he had to throw himself over the hood of the car.

The station wagon pulled level to him, and Lane saw that the driver was a young woman. Pretty features, hair pulled back into a ponytail. He noticed she had a nice smile, which she offered to him somewhat shyly, as though embarrassed.

"You don't *look* like a maniac," she commented hesitantly.

Lane shoved his shirttails back into his pants, then lifted

one hand. "Lady, I swear on a stack of Bibles, I'm not."
With sudden inspiration, he withdrew his wallet, flipping
it open with a twist of the wrist to allow the accordion
folds of the credit card section to trickle downward. "I've
got American Express and Diner's Club. Would a maniac
have those? Would you like to see them?" With rescue
close at hand, he could afford the generosity of good
humor.

She smiled at him again, this time with genuine friendli-
ness, and Lane felt the warmth of that smile enter his
senses like a sip of dry red wine. The woman really did
have the most delectable mouth—wide, generous, the deep
pink of a summer rose.

"Sorry I didn't stop the first time," she apologized, but
offered no further explanation. "Get in. Robbie, slip over
the seat to the back."

Lane didn't waste any time thinking it over. A moment
later he was beside her in the front seat of the car. Levering himself to face her, he extended his hand. "I'm Lane
Stafford, and right now I think you're the most wonderful
person in the whole world."

The woman laughed as she swung to face him. Her
voice had a light, musical quality that struck a strong
answering chord within Lane's body.

He'd been right about her looks. Upon closer inspection, his savior had an extremely appealing attractiveness.
Besides that lovely, definitely kissable mouth, she had an
exquisite pair of large, cornflower-blue eyes, made all the
more startling by the fact she was darkly tanned. She had
a chin that suggested a stubborn nature, tempered by a
nose modeled in gentler lines, slightly upturned at the tip
with a pert youthfulness. Her hair was a silky blond,
streaked with silvery highlights that might have come from
years of exposure to the sun. It was long and thick, with
a springy body, which was probably the reason she had
yanked it unceremoniously to the back of her well-shaped
head, capturing its fullness in a white satin ribbon.

Lane was caught by the sudden desire to set it free and

watch it cascade around her shoulders like a silken cloud. He could well imagine what her reaction to *that* might be. If the woman was at all nervous about picking up a stranger, she'd be screaming her head off if he made any attempt to touch her. Still, the idea of seeing that sleek, lustrous mane unfettered was intriguing.

"I'm Maggie James," she said, clasping his hand in brief, cool contact. "Welcome to Caloosa Key."

He felt his smile stiffen a bit, and hoped it wasn't too obvious.

The Maggie Rose James of The Caloosa Key Inn? Lane couldn't believe his luck. She wasn't at all what he expected, although he had nothing to base a mental picture upon. But he doubted there could be two women with the same name on the island. Remembering Jerry Carlisle's warning that the previous owner of the inn was not likely to roll out a welcome mat, he wondered what she'd do if she knew just who he was and why he was here, then decided he didn't want to find out. There was no way he was going to let himself be turned out onto the road again.

"This is my brother, Robbie," she indicated with a wave of her hand in the direction of the backseat.

Lane levered his body around to say hello to the kid. He was surprised to find himself face-to-face with a skinny, towheaded boy who regarded him with open and sullen dislike. "Hi, Rob. Sorry to steal your seat, but believe me, you two are lifesavers."

The James boy mumbled a reply, and Lane wondered what he had done to get on the kid's bad side so quickly. He decided he'd best leave well enough alone and turned back around in his seat.

Maggie James was concentrating on maneuvering the big wagon into a U turn, and Lane watched her covertly as she instinctively swung her head around to check the road, making sure no traffic was coming.

She had a long, graceful throat, and Lane decided he liked the way it met her collarbone, the flesh there barely visible at the modestly exposed neckline. He noted she had a good figure, too—high, firm breasts covered by a thin linen blouse of turquoise, a nipped-in waist, and tanned, coltish legs encased in crisp, white pedal pushers. Lane realized the last thing on earth he wanted to do was leave this stunning creature, no matter *who* she was.

Not caring for the swift, riveting interest he seemed to be developing for a total stranger, Lane marshaled his feelings into order. Hell, he didn't owe this woman any explanations. He was here doing a favor for a friend. It wasn't his fault her mother had sold the inn, and hopefully she'd made her peace with that by now. It was as simple as that.

Still, he didn't offer any further information to indicate her name was not unknown to him.

"Was that your Mercedes I passed?"

"A friend's. Too delicate for this heat, I guess."

"Do you know what's wrong with it?"

"Busted radiator hose. I don't suppose there's a garage on the island?"

"No. But our one and only gas station keeps a few items handy. They can probably fix you up with what you need, if you don't mind doing the job yourself."

"Guess I'll have to. How about a car-rental agency?"

"Nope," Maggie responded with a laugh. "You really are getting off to a bad start, aren't you?"

"You're the only good thing that's happened to me since I arrived on this sandbar."

Something in his voice brought her head swiveling toward him, and for the briefest moment, their eyes met and held. He could read the uncertainty in their clear blue depths, tinged with just the slightest bit of curiosity, and Lane wondered if she felt the same swift pull of attraction he did. The air between them fairly crackled with a primitive anticipation, sharp and exhilarating. The heat of desire skipped along his veins like quicksilver, not an uncommon reaction for him in appreciation of an attractive woman, yet he *was* surprised by the intensity of the feeling, how suddenly his interest had been caught and held.

Unconsciously his eyes traveled downward, fastening on the sweet vulnerability of her mouth. Maggie Rose James offered him a small, hesitant smile, and unexpectedly in this day and age of feminine assertiveness, she flushed scarlet. Her gaze returned to the road quickly, and the moment was gone.

The silence stretched between them.

And then, Maggie said in a businesslike voice, "Tell you what. You come home with me to help unload this stuff," her thumb jerked backward to indicate a jumbled assortment of bags piled neatly in the cargo area, "and I'll take you to Ernie's to get a hose. If he's got one that fits, I'll take you back to your car. How's that for island hospitality?"

"Maggie . . ." The boy in the backseat groaned his sister's name, and both Lane and the James woman gave him a quick glance. Robbie's features were wreathed in displeasure. "I can unload this stuff without any help." The kid's attitude had deteriorated into undisguised hostility.

His sister frowned. It was clear she had no better clue than Lane as to what had gotten into her brother. Her delicately sculpted brows descended in a single warning scowl meant to improve the boy's disposition before she favored Lane with an apologetic smile. "Robbie takes his 'man of the family' role very seriously, Mr. Stafford, but I'm sure he didn't mean to sound so unfriendly. He'll be glad for the extra help."

There was a sound of protest from the backseat, but before the boy could voice further complaint, Lane said, "It's the least I can do. Just one more thing . . ."

"What's that?"

"Does this car have air-conditioning?"

She offered him another heart-stopping smile. "Sorry. It broke two summers ago and we never saw the need to get it fixed."

"You've got to be kidding."

"No. Really. The heat is bad this summer, but you get

used to it.'' Her blue eyes narrowed. ''Say, are you okay? You look pretty beat and your face is flushed.''

''I'm not ready to run any races,'' Lane admitted, ''but I'll be fine.'' He did not confess that the same feeling of disorientation he'd felt earlier was back, nor that he could again feel his heart pounding in his throat. *Sweetheart*, he thought wildly, *if this is you doing this to me, I'll marry you.*

''Look, forget about helping us with this stuff,'' Maggie said reasonably. ''Why don't we stop by Doc Holbrook's place? During the season he treats a lot of tourists for sunstroke. You've probably got a touch of it.''

''I'm not a tourist,'' Lane responded tersely. He was beginning to feel slightly embarrassed by her concern. ''And the only thing I am is thirsty, hungry, and tired. In that order.'' Afraid his tone might have seemed a bit abrupt, he added, ''Besides, you'll damage my macho male ego if you continue to imply I can't stand up to a little heat. Especially when you sit there looking as cool as a cucumber.''

There was a squawk of annoyance from Robbie, but Lane ignored it, preferring instead to concentrate on the delightful sound of Maggie's laughter.

The untamed wildness of the island gradually began to give way to civilization. They passed long stretches of stately sabal palms, orderly plantings placed along the roadside back when the first settlers had come to the island. The tangled undergrowth and scrubby palmettos became less evident as more and more residences came into view. It was obvious that professional landscapers had made a fortune on Caloosa Key. There were glimpses of carefully groomed lawns behind high privacy walls, over which trailed thorny bougainvillea. Fragrant but deadly oleander lined many driveways, but there were few glimpses of the homes beyond.

Interested in the architectural design, Lane struggled to see past the veil of foliage cleverly planted to screen most of the homes from view. Some of the residences were older, displaying a Spanish influence popular in the twenties: lots of pink stucco and red-tiled roofs, black iron grillwork, and circular towers. There were a few monolithic California moderns with sharp angles and plenty of windows. Several newer-looking houses were Early Victorian replicas, favoring screened porches, widow's walks, and an overabundance of gingerbread trim. And looking very expensive, but sadly out of place amidst an oasis of palms, sat one English Tudor mansion.

"Nice neighborhood," Lane commented dryly as they passed a long row of exceptionally large homes.

"Our permanent snowbirds. Anytime the weather gets rough up North, they fly down here to escape. We won't see them again until December." One finely sculpted brow lifted, and she cocked him a serious glance. "Do you have a place to stay on the island?" He could see her mind working quickly, pulling the pieces together. Her passenger had come to the island in a Mercedes, and in spite of his present shabby appearance, she was knowledgeable enough to recognize expensive clothing when she saw it. Lane smiled inwardly. Only the James woman's natural reticence kept her from the same blunt questioning he had endured from the ferryman.

"Nothing as grand as these places," he responded. "My friend's made arrangements for me." He did not add that those arrangements would be the manager's apartment at The Caloosa Key Inn. Along with road maps, the ferry schedule, and the Mercedes, Lane had also been left the address of the island real estate office that would supply him with keys. He stole a glance at her profile, so clean and beautiful, and realized he could not drum up the courage to spoil the easy friendship budding between them by elaborating further.

Before they reached the town of Caloosa Key, the station wagon left the paved road and turned onto a curving shell-and-sand driveway bordered on either side by trespassing seagrapes that threatened to pull the car into their midst. The road looked as though it had been hacked out of the undergrowth.

The drive widened into a clearing, in the center of which stood a small house—a cottage, really—one and a half stories high, with a tin hip roof and white pine siding. Concrete block piers lifted it three feet off the ground, and there were four long, wide steps leading up to a screened porch. The house was typical of Old Island architecture, and Lane hazarded a guess it had been built in the early nineteen hundreds. It was holding up surprisingly well, although there were a few signs of disrepair, and an unattached building, probably a garage, was sagging badly. Still, it was an appealing little structure.

The yard area had been cleared but not planted, although there were palmettos and Spanish bayonets clustered around the base of the house like petticoats peeking out from under a Victorian lady's skirt. There was little grass. Most of the compound consisted of sabal palms, gumbo-limbos, and one majestic banyan tree with long fingers of vine trailing to the ground.

Maggie brought the wagon to a halt in front of the sad-looking outbuilding and they got out. Finding his knees a bit shaky, Lane stood quietly beside the car waiting for his pulse to settle while he admired the simple, unassuming design of the Jameses's home. Banyan House, a small sign proclaimed over the screened door, and Lane thought for all the grandiose mansions the island could boast of, this was by far more charming.

Maggie James came to his side, and intercepting Lane's glance, she said, "Not exactly a palace, but it's home. You'll have to excuse the run-down look of it. My brother and I just moved in last November."

"It's lovely. Built 1910, 1915, wasn't it?"

"Why, yes," Maggie answered, giving him a surprised look. "How did you know?"

"I'm an architect," he replied. "I don't see many of these old places anymore."

"This is a lifer's cottage. It used to be part of The

Caloosa Key Inn up the road. One of the original investors of the place was given the cottage to use until the day he died—which he did . . . in the back bedroom. Robbie swears he can hear the poor old fellow wheezing and moaning some nights.''

"What about you?"

She smiled broadly. "Not yet, thank God, but I don't really expect to. My brother has a *very* active imagination."

"I *have* heard him," Robbie said in a low, belligerent voice, and the look he turned on Lane and Maggie was almost murderous.

"Okay," Maggie conceded wisely. "All those bags in the car go in the garage. Why don't you two make quick work of the load and I'll fix lunch. After we cool down, we can see about getting your car fixed. All right?"

"Sounds great."

"See you in a few minutes."

She left them, her sandals making soft, crunching noises on the shelly path. Lane watched her walk away, liking the way her hips moved with unconscious grace, her long shapely legs and well-turned ankles. Briefly, he wondered if the woman was aware of her attractiveness.

No. Not a chance. Maggie Rose James was completely natural in every movement she made. Her speech was open and genuine, with no coquettish flirtation; her manner lacked the coy seductiveness and artificial teasing he expected from most females. Chicago was full of woman, all shapes and sizes, and he'd managed to date a good many of them. Yet as he watched the woman bound up the stairs and into the house, Lane found himself intrigued and attracted by this delicately beautiful island flower, more so than he could remember being for a long time. *I want to know you better, Maggie James. And I will,* Lane decided.

When he turned back toward the car, Robbie was nowhere in sight.

*   *   *

By the time he finished stacking everything neatly in the dilapidated garage, Lane felt as though his heart might burst right out of his chest. The load had not been a heavy one, yet his pulse had reverted back to its bass-drum pounding and there was an unpleasant ringing in his ears. Add to that the nausea, double vision, and vertigo and Lane was certain God had planned a heart attack for him on this tiny island situated in the middle of nowhere. He thought of all the excellent hospitals in the Chicago area and wondered why God had decided to play such a cruel joke.

He leaned against the station wagon's hood and took several deep breaths, concentrating on clearing his mind. Gradually, whatever was doing its best to incapacitate him passed and his vision cleared. He still felt unwell, totally drained, but at least he wasn't in any immediate danger of passing out. His pride stung a little to have to admit it, but Maggie James had no doubt been right. He was probably suffering a bit from heatstroke, although it galled Lane to think a silly tourist ailment could lay him low.

On feet that felt as though lead weights had been slipped into each shoe, Lane went up the steps and into the house. The screen door squealed in protest, then banged shut behind him.

"Miss James—Maggie!" he called, and was eternally grateful his voice was not a mere whisper.

"I'm in the kitchen," the woman's musical voice responded from somewhere to his left. "Go on through the house and make yourself comfortable on the back porch. I'll be out in a minute."

Lane was dimly aware of a wide center hall with rooms off to the left and right, pine flooring, and ceiling fans. Another time he might have enjoyed the wide view of the Gulf of Mexico stretched before him like a huge painting, but, exhausted, his only interest lay in collapsing into one of the nearby chaise longues, a wooden contraption left over from the 1950's.

It felt incredibly good to sit down, and Lane wondered

if he'd ever be able to rise again. Resting his head against the backrest, he closed his eyes, lifting his face to the faint, salty breeze fanning his cheeks.

In a few minutes Lane heard movement behind him, and he opened his eyes to find Maggie coming out the double doors, a tray in hand. "Lunch will be ready in a minute. I thought you might like iced tea in the meantime."

She lowered the tray so he could reach one of the glasses, but something in his face must have alerted her all was not well. The smile froze on her lips. "Good grief, you look terrible!" she exclaimed, setting the tray down quickly on one side of the table.

Lane offered her a weak smile. "I'm all right. I think I just need to rest a bit."

"Don't be ridiculous!" Maggie responded brusquely. Her fingers reached out to feel his forehead. Her touch was cool, and Lane wished he had the strength to lift his own hand and capture hers. "Of all the pigheaded fools . . ." She seemed angry and made a little sound of disgust.

"I really will be all right . . ." Lane wasn't sure just who he was trying to convince more, Maggie or himself.

"Oh, be quiet! And lie still!" she commanded. "I'll be right back."

Realizing it was pointless to deny how he felt any longer, Lane nodded meekly and closed his eyes.

It seemed a long time later that he was aware of a cool towel pressed against his forehead. He heard his name being called urgently and he wanted to open his eyes and tell whoever it was to go away, but he couldn't summon up the strength. He just wanted to rest a moment, to be left alone, which didn't seem like such an enormous request. Drifting toward unconsciousness, he felt his body being shaken, but he ignored that, too, and pretty soon it went away.

TWO

When Lane Stafford passed out on the back porch of Banyan House, Maggie James was never more unnerved in her life. It was one thing to pass a few pleasantries over lunch with an attractive stranger, quite another to have that same stranger unconscious in your own home. She knew almost nothing about him except his name. What if he died! What if—

Stop it! she scolded herself sharply. Now was definitely not the time to panic. She'd seen heatstroke often enough to recognize the symptoms; it wasn't something she couldn't handle. Still, Maggie would feel better if Doc Holbrook examined the man, just to be sure it wasn't anything more serious. Who knew what Lane Stafford's medical history was like?

She made a quick call to Doc, relieved when he indicated he could be at her home in five minutes. In the meantime, she knew what to do. She must have sounded a bit panicky because he rang off with a pep talk of encouragement, reminding her what a sensible young lady she'd always been and how he had faith in her ability to handle the situation.

The minutes seemed to crawl by as she waited for him, crouched down beside the stranger's still form. He moaned a little as she placed cool towels behind his neck and across his forehead but did not open his eyes. Swallowing back the embarrassment of such intimacy, Maggie tugged Lane's shirt out of the waistband of his trousers, baring his chest to place another chilly cloth across its lightly furred expanse. Until Doc came, there was little else she could do.

For the first time, Maggie allowed her eyes to rove over the man beside her. His face was striking. Relaxed in sleep, his features seemed almost boyish, but he had a high, intelligent forehead, sculpted cheekbones, a firm chin, and a finely molded nose saved from classic beauty by a slight hump at the bridge, as though it had once been broken and then allowed to set improperly. Beneath the towel, his hair was thick, a deep chestnut shade, stylishly cut to feather away from his forehead but with a tendency to curl of its own accord along his neck. Although closed now, Maggie remembered his eyes had been a warm, liquid brown, and that when he smiled they seemed to twinkle as tiny laugh lines appeared at the corners. Those eyes had been the primary reason she had turned the car around and come back for him in spite of Robbie's objections, a risky thing for her to do, even on an island as crime-free as Caloosa Key. But in that brief moment as she had passed him by, she had glimpsed in them an open, honest appeal promising trust and friendship. Instinctively she had known there was no meanness in Lane Stafford, although how she could have known this she would be at a complete loss to explain. Now Maggie noticed that his lashes were that same sable brown, long and thick as her own, tipped with gold, as though an artist had trimmed them each with liquid sunlight.

With a curious sort of detachment, Maggie continued to scan Lane's face. It occurred to her she had once dreamed of making such a man her own, but that had been a long time ago, when she had still harbored hope of a life for herself away from Caloosa Key. Before she had come back from college to help her mother and become what Doc referred to as "a sensible young lady."

God, how she hated that description! It made her sound boring and predictable, which, when she thought about it, was probably—no, *exactly*—what she was.

Doc Holbrook came around the side of the house in the next moment, and Maggie breathed a sigh of relief. He was seventy-six years old, but still as spry as the day he and his wife had come across the bay to settle on Caloosa Key shortly after World War II. The only doctor on the island, he had treated everything from fish hooks embedded in tourist toes to an emergency appendectomy, his specialty during the season being the treatment of severe cases of sunburn and heatstroke. He had delivered Maggie and her brother, and been with both her parents when they died. In spite of his advanced years, Maggie trusted the old man completely.

"So," he said, drawing up a chair beside his patient and lifting one of Lane's eyelids. "What had you done to this poor young fellow, Maggie Rose."

"Nothing!" She explained the situation to the doctor. "He's not going to die, is he?"

"Not likely, but let's check his pockets for a wallet. Might be something else he's suffering from that we should know about."

They levered Lane sideways, removing his wallet from a back pocket. While Dr. Holbrook continued his examination, Maggie quickly sorted through the contents, feeling somewhat guilty about invading a stranger's privacy. She passed over credit cards, driver's license, a membership card to a Chicago health spa, voter's registration, and miscellaneous pictures of women, a few of whom bore a distinct family resemblance. No medic alert cards.

"Nothing out of the ordinary," she said at last.

"Didn't think so, but it never hurts to be sure. Looks like a classic heatstroke. You know what to do, so let's get started."

"Wait a minute! You can't leave him here!"

"Why not?" Doc asked, sounding truly puzzled.

"I don't know him!" Maggie offered a weak protest. "I can't put a stranger in my bed."

Doc snorted. "Oh, stop behaving like an eighty-year-old spinster. If it bothers you to have him in your bed, we'll put him in Robbie's."

"That's not what I mean," Maggie replied mulishly. "He's a stranger. We don't know what kind of person he is—"

"Right now he's a very sick person, and unless we get him cooled down fast, he's going to be even sicker."

"I just don't want to be responsible for him if something happens."

"Maggie Rose James, I have never known you to be uncharitable to a living soul. Whatever's got you so skittish about this fellow you just put aside right now and stop being so womanish. Now, get going."

"Womanish!" Maggie fumed, but realizing the battle was lost, she hurried to do as the doctor bade her.

In Robbie's room, she stripped the bed down to the mattress. Rooting through the linen closet she found an old rubberized pad left over from the days before her mother's death when Tyla James had been bedridden. This she placed under the bottom sheet. The top sheet, pictures of surfers on boogie boards in the midst of catching a big wave, she wadded into a ball, threw into the washbasin in the bathroom, and covered with cold water. For good measure, Maggie cracked two trays of ice cubes into the water, hoping to make it as chilly as possible.

Moving a grown man from a lounge chair into a bed proved to be no easy task. Lane Stafford was as limp as a sack full of potatoes and ten times as heavy. With Maggie at his head and Doc at his feet, the two of them pulled and struggled their way through the house. The distance between the porch and the bedroom had never seemed so far, and by the time they reached the doorway to Robbie's room, they were both panting with exhaustion.

With one last superhuman effort, they got their patient

to the bed. As they lifted Lane into it, his head lolled sideways, striking the nightstand with a loud thwack.

"Oh, God, I've probably given him a concussion on top of everything else," Maggie groaned, but Doc was so out of breath he couldn't reply.

Without another word between them, they began divesting Lane of his clothes. Maggie eased his arms out of his shirt, and by some unspoken agreement between them, for which she was extremely grateful, Doc was the one to inch Lane's pants down his hips, leaving him bare except for white undershorts.

The sight of Lane Stafford's muscular, nearly naked body brought color flooding to Maggie's cheeks, and with a mumbled, "I'll get the sheet," she nearly ran from the room.

Watching her go, Doc chuckled. "Well, young man," he commented to his unconscious patient, "you do seem to have an effect on our little Maggie Rose."

The treatment for heatstroke was a simple and effective one. Returning with the cold, wet sheet in a basin, Maggie and Doc Holbrook draped it over Lane Stafford, molding it to his body. The idea was to reduce the body temperature quickly, then give the patient cold sponge baths until consciousness returned, after which the process could be repeated until the patient's temperature had been sufficiently lowered. Heatstroke victims usually recovered quickly, and, barring complications, Lane should be up and around by the next day with nothing more than a slight headache.

"Well, that should do it," Doc said. "I'll call you tonight to see how he's doing. If he hasn't regained consciousness by morning, we may have to move him over to the mainland, but I don't think it will be necessary. Don't look so distressed. You know what to do. You're a sensible woman."

She winced inwardly at that description. Why did it always manage to sound like such an insult?

After Doc departed, Maggie sat beside Lane's bed, watching the slight rise and fall of his chest beneath the clinging sheet with all the nervous anticipation of a mouse pinned beneath a cat's paw. He had not stirred once since losing consciousness, which hardly made him a threatening figure. If anything, his position was appealingly vulnerable. Yet while she told herself this thrumming anxiety was foolish and misplaced, Maggie had to resist the temptation to leap up and run out of the room.

She didn't want this man in her house. She was afraid of him. Perhaps not physically, but emotionally. Maggie had known him such a short time, spoken to him so little; it seemed impossible to form an attraction for someone based upon such a meager beginning. Still, there had been a moment in the car when their eyes met, his filling with interest and a kind of amused surprise, as if to say, "Well, what's this, then?" She had felt her pulse jump with sudden awareness of him, felt herself smothering in his nearness, and known he was experiencing the same reaction. It was more than a physical attraction, and even while it filled her with a strange pleasure, Maggie had been frightened of that moment and drawn away from it.

Lane Stafford had seemed nice and funny and good-looking, and he scared Maggie James to death.

There were two things Maggie didn't want or need in her life right now—excitement or men.

She was finally over Tom Hadley. That quick, foolish infatuation had died a swift death once the pain of betrayal had passed.

Looking back on the incident now, nearly six months later, she chided herself for behaving like such a love-struck fool. She wished she could blame it on the chaotic mess her life had become the past year, but knew she couldn't. Maggie's parents had warned her often enough that she tended to be too impulsive and naive, too trusting by far. Having nearly brought about her ruin, she was grimly determined not to fall victim to those distasteful tendencies again.

She felt almost a sense of gratitude to the two women who had so abruptly brought her crashing back to reality.

Her pride stung; her self-esteem had been ripped to shreds, but there had been a lesson to be learned, and Maggie hoped she was a quick study. Belated wisdom at the age of twenty-two was better than no wisdom at all.

It was laughable now, to think that while she could barely remember what Tom Hadley looked like, she would never forget the lesson he had taught her.

Off-islanders who were rich, sophisticated, and charming did not become enamored with uncomplicated women who chose to shutter themselves away on a small island like Caloosa Key. At least, not for long.

Love was tricky. Even more so if you gave your heart to someone so ill-suited, so completely opposite from everything you were. . . .

Lane Stafford uttered a whispery moan, startling Maggie out of her reverie. Her eyes wandered appreciatively over his still form. This off-islander was no college student like Tom, but a man fully grown. Tall, well proportioned, even the concealing sheet could not hide the contours of broad, powerful shoulders tapering into a slim waist and flat belly, the long, well-muscled legs. Maggie's stomach fluttered with nervousness at the direction her thoughts took her and she was grateful no one was there to witness her sudden blush of discomfort.

Oh, yes. This man was dangerous. He aroused a plethora of emotions in her. Lane Stafford was quintessentially male, and he made her feel decidedly womanly. The sooner she had him back on his feet and out of her life, the better off she'd be.

"Get well soon, Mr. Stafford," Maggie murmured into the stillness of the room. "For both our sakes."

The afternoon passed quickly. Lane Stafford did not regain consciousness, although he began to mumble in his sleep and occasionally flinched when Maggie draped a freshly cooled sheet over him. His temperature no longer seemed to be out of control; he was still quite warm, but not dangerously so.

Chiding herself for a fanciful fool, Maggie conquered her fear of touching him and began sponging Lane's body with ice water. Such intimate contact brought her heart into her throat, but she swallowed around it, forcing herself to remain detached from the feel of corded muscles beneath her fingertips. Still, she would have preferred not to be alone with Lane, unconscious or not.

She wished Robbie had not pulled a disappearing act. Even the presence of her younger brother would have brought some small measure of comfort.

Except for the sound of Lane's harsh but steady breathing, the house was unbearably quiet. Maggie lifted her patient's arm, running a cold cloth down his shoulder, along his forearm, over the back of one well-shaped hand. His fingers were long and slim, the nails clean and unbroken. With slow, gentle care, she ran her cloth-covered hand along each of them, taking absurd pleasure in the feel of each bumpy knuckle, each blunt tip. Along the side of Lane's index finger was a jagged scar. It was obviously an old injury, but Maggie stroked it as carefully as if it were a fresh cut, idly wondering what had caused it.

"My father warned me to be careful, but I didn't listen." Lane's voice broke the stillness, as though he had somehow heard Maggie's silent inquiry.

She turned her head slowly toward him, knowing she should release his hand . . . but the message never reached her fingers.

His gaze was soft and confused at first, then sharpening as understanding of his situation dawned. A tiny smile tugged at the corner of his mouth for the briefest of moments, and something in his expressive brown eyes brought her heart to a stumbling halt. The tip of Maggie's tongue slid between her teeth to moisten her lips, a betrayal of nervousness, and she saw Lane's gaze drop to their wet fullness with curious intimacy. The tightness in her chest became viselike.

"And . . . what happened?" she asked in a whisper.

"My hand slipped and the fishing knife laid my finger

bare to the bone. Sixteen stitches and a ruined vacation. My sisters swore I did it on purpose so I could get out of cleaning the fish we'd caught.''

His tone was almost conversational, but Maggie wished he would stop scanning her face with such intense speculation. Her state of mind was becoming increasingly miserable.

Her beleaguered brain finally communicated the knowledge that her hand still held his, and she made a quick, fretful attempt to release it. Instead, Maggie found her fingers caught and held, the cloth falling free from her nerveless grip.

"No—don't," Lane commanded softly as she attempted to pull free.

"Mr. Stafford—"

"Lane."

"Lane, please," Maggie pleaded, making a weak effort to pull herself together.

"In a moment, I promise, I'll give them all back to you. I won't hurt you. How could I? I strongly suspect you saved my life."

"It's just a mild case of heatstroke," Maggie said, her cheeks flooding with embarrassment. "Our doctor examined you. You'll be fine by morning."

"*1812 Overture,*" Lane muttered.

"I beg your pardon."

"The Chicago Symphony is playing the *1812 Overture* in my head. Heavy on percussion."

"Oh." She winced visibly. "My fault. When Doc and I were lifting you into bed, I'm afraid I conked your head pretty hard on the nightstand. Sorry."

"Forgiven. But if you hear moaning tonight, it's not your ghost, it'll be me." Catching her look of genuine distress, Lane chuckled and said, "Hey, just teasing. I owe you a great deal."

Maggie shifted uncomfortably, wishing there were some way to recapture her hand without seeming childishly intimidated by his touch. "Really, I didn't do that much. Nothing more than any other islander would have done."

"But *you're* the one who picked me up, took me in." His eyes met hers steadily. "Are you always such a Good Samaritan, Maggie Rose James?"

"All the time. I'm the island rescue squad," she returned smartly, and was mortified to hear her voice come out in a trembling squeak instead of the light flippancy she'd been striving for. Good grief! He must think he had her completely rattled. How could Practical Maggie Rose have deserted her so?

His lips stretched into a smile of gentle understanding. "Poor Maggie Rose. I'm not trying to frighten you."

"You don't!"

"Then why are you looking like you've just walked into a lion's den?"

"How am I supposed to feel?" she argued reasonably. "I don't even know you."

"We can change that," he replied, lifting her hand to his lips.

Never breaking eye contact, Lane kissed the tip of each one of her stiff, cold fingers, running his warm tongue along the surface until they gradually relaxed. His touch upon her skin created a sensual tingling, and she emitted a little gasp of pure delight as shivery pleasure danced up her spine. With practiced care, he opened her hand until her palm was exposed. Lazily he placed nibbling kisses upon it, watching her quietly as he traced a hot, wandering pattern with his tongue. Beneath the artistry of his mouth, Maggie's courage was fast deserting her as she felt herself assaulted by the most unusual sensations.

"Please don't . . . do that," she said weakly, and even she was aware of how feeble the objection sounded.

"Why not?"

"Because . . . I don't . . . like it."

She felt his smile stretch against her palm, and when he spoke, his voice came low and husky. "Are you sure about that, Maggie Rose?"

"Yes," she lied.

"Absolutely sure?" His lips began an exquisite journey to the inside of her wrist.

"Yes!" The thought snapped into her brain that unless she put a stop to this madness soon, she might very well end up being tumbled in her brother's bed by a man she'd known less than twenty-four hours. "Stop that!" she yelped, and this time she pulled away with enough force that Lane could not prevent her from recapturing her hand. As though burned, Maggie absently rubbed her wrist. The look she sent Lane smoldered with resentment.

A laugh rumbled deep within Lane's chest, and he placed one arm behind his head, eyeing her with wry speculation. "What an interesting first date we're going to have."

"We are definitely *not* going out on a date," she responded primly.

"Then how will I ever thank you for all you've done?"

"You can send me a card."

"Much too cheap."

"Flowers."

"Too common."

"A box of chocolates, then."

"Too fattening."

Maggie's blue eyes narrowed. "Are you always this infuriating?"

"Probably. It comes from being spoiled all my life by four older sisters."

"Give me their address. I'll write and tell them what a monster they created."

Lane laughed again. "They won't believe you. They all think I'm the catch of the century. Some young lady is going to be extremely lucky to get me. Their words, not mine."

"Of all the vain, insufferable . . ."

The rest of Maggie's dissertation on Lane Stafford's shortcomings was derailed by the sudden appearance of Robbie. Behind him trailed a long-haired dog of indeterminable heritage who promptly collapsed at the youth's feet, head on paws, and, unbelievably, there was a skunk clinging precariously to the front of the boy's T-shirt.

The youngster blinked in surprise to find someone in his bed, and his eyes flew to Maggie for an explanation. "What's going on?"

"Where have you been?" she demanded. After verbally sparring with Lane, Maggie had little patience left.

"Out at the Indian mound with Tony. I told you this morning." His head jerked toward Lane. "I thought he'd be gone by now."

"The heat got to him. Doc suggested he rest up here until tomorrow."

"Sorry to commandeer your bed like this, Rob," Lane said.

The boy shrugged his shoulders as if it was of little importance to him, but Lane glimpsed the displeasure in his eyes, the way his glance kept darting back to his sister. The kid was no dummy. He could sense his sister's nervousness, the fact she was definitely out of sorts, and his sharp little mind was already latching on to Lane's presence as the reason for it. He was too young to be able to veil his thoughts tactfully, and one look he gave Lane was particularly savage.

Ah, the protective younger brother, Lane suspected. He'd experienced a few of those same feelings himself at Robbie's age when his sister Frances had started dating a man he'd considered totally unacceptable. The man had become his sister's husband, and that fourteen-year union had been blessed with two cute kids, a big house in one of Chicago's most elite suburbs, twin Mercedeses in the garage, and, most importantly, love and respect. Oh well, a fellow couldn't be right about everything.

He wanted to tell Robbie to relax. That whatever did or didn't happen between himself and Maggie wouldn't be governed by interference from anyone. But he didn't. Lane hadn't listened to advice sixteen years ago and he doubted kids had changed much since then.

What Lane couldn't know was Maggie was not the only one who vividly remembered last Christmas and Tom Hadley. Robbie still didn't understand the whole story, but he had seen a man hurt his sister, make her cry at night when she thought no one could hear. That man had been an off-islander, too, and Robbie wasn't about to let another stranger make Maggie sad again. In spite of his sister's bossy assumption that she was the head of the household, he was still the man of the family now that his parents were gone. Their lives were settling down. Maggie's happiness was important to him, a responsibility he did not take lightly, for all his young years.

The boy eyed the newcomer skeptically. He seemed friendly enough, but so had Tom Hadley. Maggie was sweet and trusting, and couldn't be counted on to use her head where men were concerned. He, on the other hand, wasn't about to be fooled by a handsome face or clever come-on. If he had to do something to protect Maggie, to keep this intruder from getting any more interested in his sister than he already was, he would. What that something might be, he wasn't sure, but with the typical confidence and conviction of youth, Robbie was certain he could think of a plan.

The sheet covering Lane's body had slipped to his waist, and Robbie's gaze latched onto the sight of the man's bare chest. "Where are your clothes?"

Lane grinned. "You'll have to ask your sister. She's the one who took them off me."

"I most certainly did not!" Maggie retorted hotly. A betraying blush crept up her neck, staining her cheeks a rosy pink. Her eyes refused to meet his. "I think it's time you rested, Mr. Stafford. I'll get a dry sheet and then we'll leave you alone." With quick efficiency, she began gathering up cloth and basin. "Robbie, I told you I don't like Beau in the house, so take him outside, please."

"Okay," the boy agreed reluctantly, but after his sister

left the room, he continued to regard Lane with sullen dislike. The skunk, which had heretofore been nesting quietly in the boy's hands, began a climbing expedition up Robbie's T-shirt and around his neck.

"Beau's the skunk?" Lane asked.

"Nope. This is Stinker. Beau's this guy." He reached down and swatted the dog affectionately on the rump. The animal responded with a tail-wagging frenzy.

"Your sister would rather have a skunk in the house than a dog?"

"Beau's not housebroken. He was on the way to the pound, but I talked one of our neighbors into giving him to me. I've almost got him trained, but sometimes he forgets. He ruined Maggie's kitchen rug, so now the house is off limits."

"Poor Beau. Sisters can be pretty picky about household matters, can't they?"

"Yeah." For the first time, the boy smiled. Like his sister, he had a generous, mobile mouth, but as soon as he realized his response was less than hostile, Robbie reverted back to a sulky pout. "Stop it, Stinker!" he commanded to the skunk, which was trying to burrow underneath the collar of his shirt.

"I take it you like animals," Lane said, trying to draw the boy out.

"I guess. Maggie says I have a rap-rapport with 'em."

"You have others?"

In spite of himself, Robbie's eyes lit with interest for his favorite topic. "A few. I'm setting up a lean-to behind the garage to hold them all. We've only lived here a few months, so it needs a lot of work. Maggie says the house has to come first."

"Maybe when I'm up and around, I'll help you. I'm pretty handy with a hammer and nails."

The boy cast him an assessing look and some of the fire left his eyes. "Maybe. I'm pretty particular about how I want it, though."

"We'd follow your specifications, of course," Lane replied in his most businesslike tone.

"Maybe," Robbie hedged again. "How long are you going to be here?"

"If by here, you mean in this house, I should be out by morning. Would that please you?"

"Yeah." The boy lifted the tail of his shirt, popped the skunk underneath, then pulled the edges tight so the animal was forced to root around for an opening. Evidently Stinker was not a very adventuresome skunk because the lump promptly settled down in the fullness of Robbie's T-shirt and went to sleep. "Do you like my sister?" the boy asked suddenly.

"Very much." The answer drew the frown of displeasure Lane expected, and he had to duck his head momentarily to keep a straight face.

"She's a terrible cook."

"Really? Well, you don't look too thin."

"And she snores," Robbie volunteered further. "Like this."

He did a noisy imitation and Lane thought, *Kid, Maggie would kill you if she could hear this.*

"Sometimes it's so loud I think the whole house is gonna fall down."

"This house looks pretty sturdy."

The boy looked extremely disappointed by Lane's reaction, then his eyes lit up with inspiration. "And . . . she likes Barry Manilow! Gross, huh?"

Lane managed to look totally aghast. "Now, that *is* serious."

Pleased, Robbie said, "Well, I'd better go. Maggie can be real mean if you don't do what she says."

"I guess you'd better," Lane agreed in mock-seriousness.

With the banished Beau hot on his heels, the boy bolted out of the room. Only then did Lane give in to a fit of delighted laughter.

THREE

The next morning Lane woke to find himself nose-to-nose with a gray, hairy creature with sharp black eyes surrounded by an ebony Zorro mask of fur. Blinking several times to bring his eyes into focus, Lane was surprised to find the raccoon still there, observing him quietly from the far side of the pillow.

"Jesus! Where did you come from?" Lane asked the beast softly. He lifted his head as far away from the furry creature as possible.

"Roscoe! Get down from there," Robbie's voice ordered, and the animal obligingly hopped off the bed and skittered out of the room.

Lane couldn't help a sigh of relief. Dogs were one thing, but skunks and raccoons were quite another. Waking up to find a wild animal trying to engage you in a staring contest was not his idea of a great way to greet the morning.

Pulling himself up in bed, his back against the headboard, Lane yawned and said, "Good morning."

Robbie James stood in his underwear in front of a tall mahogany dresser, his cornsilk hair tousled from sleep. He offered Lane a sheepish smile. "Morning. Sorry about Roscoe waking you. I just came in to get some clothes. I didn't know he followed me in here."

Lane tucked the sheet along his waist. He wasn't sure the kid hadn't planted the raccoon on his pillow deliberately, but he wasn't about to make an accusation. Pleasantly he commented, "You seem to have a rather odd assortment of pets."

"Not really. I mean, it's not like I have a gorilla or anything. Besides, I want to be a vet someday so it's important to get familiar with all kinds of animals." He stepped into a pair of ragged shorts that had been patched many times. "How do you feel?"

"Good, thanks."

He realized suddenly that he really did feel better. Yesterday's nightmare might never have happened. He had a bit of a sunburn, and a few insect bites itched annoyingly. A headache was beating a dull, warning throb behind his eyes, but other than that, there seemed to be no harm done. Maggie James was an excellent nurse.

Thinking of that attractive young lady, Lane asked, "Where's your sister?"

"Fixing breakfast. You missed dinner last night because you were asleep. She said you needed the rest but that you'd probably be pretty hungry this morning."

"I am. Do you know where my clothes are? I can't very well show up at the breakfast table in my shorts."

"Over on that chair," Robbie said, indicating a tidy pile of clothing. "Maggie washed them for you."

He hated to think what a go-round in the washer would have done to his silk shirt, but a complaint would have seemed ungrateful. "Your sister's an angel," he commented instead.

It was obvious the remark didn't sit well with Robbie, but surprisingly, he smiled. "Yeah, she's okay. I'll bet your clothes are better than new."

There was an odd, mischievous light in the boy's eyes that made Lane instantly suspicious. But before he could question the youngster further, Robbie gathered up his sneakers and padded out of the room.

* * *

Breakfast was a difficult meal to get on the table at one time. Planning was everything. Maggie was a good cook, but her meals tended to be simple, hearty fare; therefore, breakfast should have been a snap.

It was turning out to be anything but that.

Toast had been made too early and was already growing cold. An entire slab of bacon had been burned and a second now sizzled in a pan on the stove. Her specialty, scrambled eggs with bits of ham and cheese sprinkled throughout, was solidifying in another pan, in definite danger of cooking too soon and taking their place beside the chilly toast. She doubted Lane Stafford would mind. Having eaten nothing yesterday, he was sure to be ravenous. Still, she wished everything would come together in one triumphant moment of culinary excellence. Instead, Maggie couldn't seem to concentrate on anything this morning, and breakfast was sure to be a disaster.

She hated to think it mattered one way or the other to her. But it did. Since yesterday morning, nothing had been as it should be.

Oh, it was just too ridiculous that her mind should continually dwell upon Lane Stafford and yesterday's diverting—all right, delicious!—flirtation. The man had been feverish, for heaven's sake! He probably didn't even remember nibbling upon her hand and arm. While she, *she* couldn't get those moments out of her mind. . . .

She had dreamed of him last night. Wild, erotic fantasies that brought a blush to her cheeks even now just to think of them. Surely no decent woman had ever entertained such sensual, forbidden thoughts about a man who was virtually a stranger. So vivid were they that Maggie had startled herself from sleep, a fine sheen of perspiration cooling her skin, her breath coming in quick, harsh gasps, and a peculiar ache of unfulfilled longing throbbing within her breasts. It was mortifying to think she had so little control over her own body.

By the time morning came, she had cudgeled her senses into some practicality. All right, she *was* attracted to him.

But it was silly to place too much importance on such a small thing, Sensible Maggie argued. Natural to be flattered by Lane Stafford's skilled interest, but men like him and Tom Hadley knew the power of their own attractiveness. To them she was no more than a wide-eyed country bumpkin badly in need of an education. Trifling with an unschooled woman's affections could be an amusing way to pass time on Caloosa Key. She must never, *never* forget that.

And yet the thought of seeing Lane again this morning left her nervous and excited and downright scared.

You really are *an idiot, Maggie James,* she scolded herself.

Robbie had finished setting the table and came to stand beside her. He looked into the pan as though gazing upon a two-headed calf at a carnival sideshow. "You know I like my eggs soft. Those are gross."

Maggie flipped the eggs over with a quick flick of the wrist. They had browned a bit too much on the bottom but were still edible. So much for a perfect meal. "There's a study out that says runny eggs are not good for you."

"Says who?"

"Phil Donahue, Oprah, the Surgeon General—I don't remember. But this is how we're eating them today."

"But I—"

Maggie waved the spatula threateningly in her brother's direction. "One more word out of you and you can fix your own eggs."

Since Robbie's cooking ability was negligible, he conceded defeat. "Okay, okay," he grumbled. "Boy, you sure are acting weird." With an attitude of utter disgust, he plunked down at the kitchen table that sat in the middle of the room.

"Good morning," a cheerful male voice said from the doorway.

She didn't want to look at him right away, not without first schooling her features into some semblance of order. Instead, she busied herself with removing the eggs to a platter. "Good morning. How do you feel?"

"Hungry."

"Good," she said, turning in his direction at last. "I hope you . . ." Maggie's voice faded as her jaw dropped, her mouth forming a little O of surprise. "Good Lord, what happened to your clothes!"

Lane smiled at her. "I was hoping you could tell me. I've heard of clothes shrinking in the wash, but this is ridiculous."

Arms out, he did a turn for her benefit, displaying articles of clothing which could only be called—demented. They were the same blue shirt and navy slacks he had worn yesterday, beautifully clean now, but one might never have recognized them. The legs of the pants were missing; what remained was an uneven pair of homemade Bermuda shorts revealing Lane's well-shaped, muscular thighs to their best advantage. The shirt, once a lovely example of fine tailoring, had been—*hacked* was the only word Maggie could think of—into a clownish imitation of an athletic T-shirt. The entire bottom half was gone, leaving Lane's taut midriff exposed. The sleeves had been scissored away, as had the collar. The only thing holding the pitiful garment together were two buttons on the shirtfront.

Yet oddly enough, in spite of the havoc wreaked upon his belongings, Lane did not seem unduly upset or concerned.

"What could have happened?" Maggie asked disbelievingly. "When I folded them and put them on that chair this morning they were fine."

"Yes. Well . . ." Lane sighed and offered a hopeful smile. "Moths, maybe?"

There was a sudden increase of activity from Robbie's corner of the room as he busied himself with unfolding his napkin, inspecting his juice glass, and fingering the silverware. "Can we eat now?"

With dawning comprehension, Maggie swung in his direction. "Robbie, did you do this?"

"Do what?" the boy asked in a theatrical display of innocence brilliant enough to win an Oscar.

Unfortunately for him, Maggie wasn't buying it. "Answer me right now. Did you do this?"

The boy's eyes met hers slowly. "Yes. But it's not what you think!"

"Don't tell me what I think!" his sister shot back angrily. Maggie was horribly embarrassed by her brother's behavior and she couldn't imagine what had possessed him to act in such a willful, belligerent manner. He could be a prankster, but he'd never done anything so malicious before. She was furious with him and determined to mete out punishment. "I want an explanation, and it had better be a good one."

"Could we eat first?"

"No. You'll be extremely lucky if I ever allow you to eat again. Start explaining."

Realizing there was no way around his sister's wrath, Robbie swallowed. "Well . . . I—"

"I think I know what happened," Lane cut in.

"You do?" brother and sister chorused as they turned to look at him. Robbie's features were dismally expectant. Maggie gazed at Lane in surprised puzzlement.

"Of course," Lane responded good-naturedly. "Poor Beau. We all know how he's trying to shape up with Rob's help here, but he can't be expected to make an about-face overnight. Somehow he got hold of my clothes and had an accident on them. . . . Could I trouble you for a cup of coffee?"

Lifting the pot off the counter, Maggie poured the aromatic brew into a mug and handed it to Lane. In a voice dripping with skepticism, she said, "And I suppose he also got my scissors out of my sewing basket so he could destroy the evidence."

Before answering, Lane lifted the steaming cup to his lips, blew on it a moment, then took a small sip. Over the rim of the mug, his eyes met Robbie's, and although Maggie couldn't be sure, she thought some silent pact had been forged between them.

"He'd have to be one hell of a dog to do that. Mmm

. . . this is good. Well. this is where Rob comes in.
Seeing what Beau had done, and knowing the conse-
quences, he cut away the, shall we say, offending area.
Thinking my suitcase would be here, too, he probably
figured I wouldn't put on the same clothes I'd worn yesterday. Later he could slip the clothes in my case, and by
the time I discovered what had happened, I'd be miles
away. Isn't that right, Rob?''

"Yeah! That's exactly what happened," the boy replied
enthusiastically.

Easy, kid, don't blow it now, Lane warned silently.
"It's understandable. I'd have done the same thing when
I was his age."

. "That's the most ridiculous thing I've ever heard. Anyone
who'd believe that story should have their head examined."

"I believe it," Lane said matter-of-factly.

"So do I," Robbie piped in. Then added, "I mean,
that's what happened, Mag. Honest."

Maggie favored him with a scorching look, and the boy
paled and took a quick swallow of orange juice. He was
so patently guilty that she might have been amused by his
discomfort if she hadn't been so angry with him. Letting
him off the hook was too easy, and she couldn't imagine
why Lane Stafford would champion his cause. After all,
he was the one who had been victimized. She cringed to
think what it would cost to replace the damaged garments.

"Excuse me," Lane interrupted her thoughts, "but I
believe your bacon is starting to burn."

"Damn!" Maggie swore softly under her breath. Not
this batch, too! Was nothing going to be simple this
morning?

They ate breakfast quietly. Robbie obviously saw the
wisdom of keeping his mouth closed. Maggie was still too
upset with him to do more than glower in his direction,
and Lane was too busy eating everything in sight to bother
making polite conversation. He seemed blissfully unaware
of the tension between brother and sister as he happily

munched overdone eggs and bacon and cold toast as though it were a banquet fit for a king.

"Are you finished?" Maggie asked her brother in a severe tone, noting he had even managed to gulp down the unwanted eggs.

"Yes, ma'am."

"Then you may apologize to our guest for your behavior and leave the table. I want you to spend the rest of the day in your room thinking about the harm you did. Your allowance will be suspended for two weeks—"

"Two weeks!"

"—and I don't want to see Beau in here again until you can do something about his . . . problem. Is that clear?"

Grimacing, the boy nodded.

"Go on," Maggie prodded.

In typical kid fashion, Robbie threw his sister and Lane a resentful look, as though they were somehow to blame for his present predicament. "I'm sorry I cut up your clothes," he mumbled, then left the table in a rush. A few moments later they heard the door to his bedroom slam shut.

"I'm really sorry about what happened," Maggie said. "Of course I'll replace them."

"Don't worry about it," Lane said, swallowing a last bit of toast and washing it down with a sip of coffee. "After yesterday's marathon walk, they were pretty well shot anyway. Actually . . ." He plucked the front of his shirt away from his chest. "It's considerably cooler for me. Just what the doctor ordered."

Maggie couldn't help it. She wanted to maintain an air of irate regret over what had happened, but with Robbie no longer present, she couldn't contain her laughter any longer. Resting her face in her hands, she covered her mouth with three fingers to keep her giggling low. The last thing she wanted was for Robbie to hear and think she found the situation funny. Even if she did. Thank God

Lane was taking all this so well. He let her laugh, regarding her with mock affrontery.

"I hope you're not laughing at my outfit. This is the latest rage in Paris, you know."

"Oh . . . please . . . stop!" Maggie gasped between fits of hiccuping giggles.

Lane grinned, thinking how musical Maggie's laughter was, how open. It sprang from deep within her, like a bubbling brook trying to force its way past surface stone. She had a natural, genuine charm that only reinforced what he had decided yesterday. *I want to know her better.*

Gradually her amusement subsided, and she wiped tears of laughter out of her eyes with the edge of her napkin. "I'm sorry. It really was a dreadful thing for Robbie to do. I can't imagine what's gotten into him. He's usually a very sweet kid."

"Let's just chalk it up to brotherly love."

Maggie's brow lifted. "Love? What's that got to do with it?"

"It's just the two of you here, isn't it?"

"Yes. So?"

"Obviously the boy is greatly attached to you. He's just trying to look out for Big Sister."

"What does that have to do with cutting your clothes into pieces?"

"Look at it from his point of view," Lane responded with a half smile. "Yesterday he interrupted something he didn't like. Maybe he wasn't exactly sure what that something was, but he still regarded it as a threat to his family unit. What he did was just a way of protecting that unit. Perhaps not well planned, but I'd have to give him points for inventiveness."

"Protection?" Maggie scoffed. "He's the one who'll need protection if he ever pulls a stunt like that again. Besides, I can take care of myself."

"That's good to know, because I don't think my wardrobe can take too much more." Her arm rested on the table, and Lane's hand closed over it lightly. "And since

I plan on seeing more of his sister, it might behoove me to make my peace with the young knight.''

His touch was warm, sending a quiver of delight through her, but determined not to be caught at a disadvantage again, Maggie refused to look at him. She didn't want to read anything into his expression that wasn't really there. Instead, she rose from the table and began clearing away the dishes. He did not try to stop her. "Would you like more coffee?" she asked in an even voice.

"That would be nice."

He held out the empty mug, and she refilled it. He passed her plates and glasses from the table as she piled them in the sink, yet not once did she allow their hands to come in contact. Maggie knew she was being supersensitive, but she still felt better when he wasn't touching her in any way. Neither of them spoke for a few minutes as she ran water over the dirty dishes, redeposited place mats in a drawer, and sponged crumbs off the oak table. She could feel Lane's eyes upon her, probably filled with amusement, she thought dismally, but she lacked the courage to lift her head and find out.

"Maggie—"

Whatever Lane Stafford had to say, Maggie was absolutely positive that she wouldn't want to hear it. She interrupted quickly by asking, "So. How long are you going to be on Caloosa Key?"

"I'm not sure. A week, two at the most."

"Is this a vacation?"

"Not exactly. Although I do plan to take a few days off for myself."

"Then you're here on business."

"Yes. A friend of mine bought some property on the island and he wants me to have a look at it. He's interested in building a resort out here."

"I guess we can't stop progress," she said, glad to see Lane was willing to keep the conversation impersonal. "I've always thought the north tip of the island was a good spot. Where did your friend buy?"

Lane glanced down at his cup, wondering if there was any way around the truth. The facts were bound to set Maggie against him, the last thing he wanted to do right now. He could hedge a bit, prolong the hurt, but Lane discovered he didn't want to do that. Not with Maggie. The woman was sweet and trusting, and she deserved the truth. If he lied, he sensed she'd never believe him again.

He met her gaze directly. "The Caloosa Key Inn."

"Oh," she murmured, and without realizing it, she sat down hard in one of the kitchen chairs.

"My friend's name is Jerry Carlisle. I understand your mother sold the property to him last year."

She lifted her head sharply. "Then yesterday you knew who I . . ."

"Jerry told me. I should have said something when you introduced yourself, but I wasn't sure how you'd react. I didn't want to be pounding the pavement again. Later, of course, it never came up."

"I wouldn't have made you get out of the car," Maggie said, her voice holding a thread of annoyance.

"I couldn't be sure. Jerry seemed to think you were pretty unhappy about losing the place."

Maggie offered him a smile, yet it was oddly sad and twisted. "Mr. Carlisle's right. But Mother had her reasons, whether I agree with them or not. Your friend and I never met. My attorney tells me it was all handled through an agent. But Mr. Carlisle seems respectable. I checked up on him at the library—there've been quite a few articles written about him, you know—and he's in *Who's Who in Corporate America.*"

Lane grinned, thinking of his old college roommate, a man whose only care in life had been girls and beer, pictured alongside Lee Iaccoca. Thank God Maggie hadn't known Jerry then, before he'd inherited all his father's millions and become an upstanding citizen. He was relieved she was handling this so well, and wondered why he'd ever worried in the first place.

"We've all been wondering why there's been such a

long wait. I was beginning to worry the inn was going to turn to dust before anyone showed up to look at it.''

"Jerry's been pretty tied up the last six months with other projects," Lane commented over the rim of his cup. "I don't think he expected control over the property to come so soon."

"It's probably better this way. Tempers were a little high immediately after the story came out."

"So I've heard," Lane replied with a frown. "But why? Surely it was nobody's business but your own what your mother did with the land."

Maggie offered him an arch smile. "You don't understand island mentality. Caloosa Key is small, and whatever *anyone* does affects nearly all of us one way or another. To oldtimers, the inn has been like community property. It represents the old ways, something a lot of people want to see preserved. There was even talk of collecting enough money to make your Mr. Carlisle a counteroffer."

"I doubt he'd have taken it. Jerry's got pretty big plans for that land."

"That's what I figured," Maggie replied regretfully. "God knows, I didn't want to see the place go to a total stranger, either, but I couldn't see any sense in the town council making fools of themselves by offering some ridiculous price for the place. I think I've finally convinced everyone he'll do right by us."

"I haven't seen the property yet, but I understand from Jerry that the inn's in pretty bad shape."

"Not all that bad," Maggie replied defensively. "You can't expect a place to be closed up for a long time and not have some damage. Robbie and I lived in the manager's apartment, but the rest of the place was too big to keep open."

"I understand," Lane said sympathetically. "I wasn't finding fault. That's where I'll be staying, by the way, once I pick up the key from the real estate office. We'll be neighbors." Catching her grimace, he grinned. "Don't fret. We'll get along fine. Once I've had a chance to walk the property, I'll be drawing up some rough sketches to take back to Jerry, so I'll be out of your hair in no time. Then, when the inn's demolished and the land's cleared, I'll have to come back every so often to see that the specs are being met. . . . What's the matter?" he asked, noting the way Maggie's eyes had widened. "Does the idea of seeing me so often upset you that much?"

"What did you say?" she demanded in a hoarse whisper. Flesh bronzed a honey gold had suddenly gone pasty white. "The inn's not being torn down."

"Of course it is."

"No, it's not!"

Lane regarded Maggie uncertainly. "It's my understanding from Jerry that the inn has no part in his plan for the property," he said carefully. "The land the inn sits on, however, is ideally suited for a resort."

"I don't care how ideal the land is. Mr. Carlisle bought the property with the intention of renovating the inn."

"I thought you said you never met Jerry."

"I didn't. I told you—it was handled through his agent, a Mr. Peters. But that was the agreement."

"Maggie . . . Maggie . . ." Lane shook his head in exasperation. "Please tell me your mother got that in writing."

"Of course she did," Maggie protested quickly, but Lane could see the fear flare in her eyes and knew the woman was sure of no such thing. "Mother wasn't an idiot. She would have demanded certain stipulations. That's one of the reasons we were deeded the lifer's cottage."

"Did an attorney handle the sale for your mother's side?"

"I don't know."

"Then you'd better check," he advised glumly. "Because *my* instructions were to plan a resort suitable for a pretty fancy crowd. And they don't include resurrecting an old ghost that should have been laid to rest years ago."

"It's not a ghost!" Maggie snapped. "It's historic!" She stood up so suddenly that her chair rocked back precariously on two legs and only Lane's quick grab prevented it from crashing to the floor. With as much scorn in her voice as she could muster, Maggie said, "You've got no right to be so judgmental. You haven't even seen the place."

His own temper starting to flare, he responded, "Which will not matter one bit if your mother gave Jerry Carlisle the legal right to tear it down."

"She didn't!"

"Find out. She wasn't an attorney."

"And neither are you!" she shot back. She was livid with anger, knowing she was taking her anxiety out on the wrong person, but unable to stop herself. "You're just a . . . an opportunist, looking for a way to make some big bucks off of little Caloosa Key. Don't you think we've seen your kind before? You're worse than the carpetbaggers who tried to steal Tara away from Scarlett!"

The corners of Lane's mouth twitched at that, and he folded his arms across his chest. "Take it easy, Scarlett. I'm not the villain here."

Stamping her foot in vexation, Maggie spluttered, "Don't you dare laugh at me, you insufferable, sex-crazed maniac!"

To her increasing frustration, Lane continued to regard her calmly. One brow lifted in irritation and his deep-chocolate eyes glittered dangerously, but when he spoke, his voice was annoyingly unperturbed. "Sex-crazed? I wasn't aware we'd digressed into personality attacks. I would also like to remind you that I am not the owner of the inn. Jerry Carlisle is. I might have some influence with him as to its fate, but that's the extent of my involvement. So, before you continue to flay me with that clever little tongue of yours, I'd remember that."

"You knew who I was from the start, and you've been deceiving me ever since," she accused. "You just wanted to have some fun with a small-town hick while you were here. Put you out of the car? Huh! I wish I'd run you over!" She turned away from him quickly to face the sink, her fists balled upon the rim.

The inn was no longer the issue here, and they both knew it. She heard his chair scrape back, and in a moment he was beside her. When Maggie refused to look at him, Lane reached out a hand and brought her chin around. He was not overly surprised to see the shimmer of tears in the turquoise vulnerability of her gaze. "Maggie, you and I deserve a better beginning than this. I know you're hurt and scared, but I'm not someone you have to be afraid of. Let me help you."

She flashed him a malevolent look. "You don't want to help me. You just want—" She broke off as color flooded her features.

Lane favored her with a rueful smile. "I won't deny that the thought of you in my bed has its appeal. But I swear to God, I think you're the first woman I've ever wanted for a friend as much as for a lover."

She wanted to believe him. She could read the sincerity in his eyes that nagged at her sense of fair play, and Maggie wondered what those words had cost him. He didn't seem the sort of man to say such things lightly, but she'd been the victim of honeyed words before. How could she think with him standing so close? She needed time, when his touch wasn't playing such havoc with her nervous system.

"I think what I need now," she said slowly, "is to be by myself. I'd really appreciate it if you would go, Lane."

He released her instantly, so quickly Maggie couldn't be sure whether her words had hurt or angered him. She searched his face for some sign, but his attractively chiseled features had become blank and impersonal. Her own eyes pleaded with him for understanding. *Don't give up on me*, they begged. *I'm so new at this!*

Without another word or a backward glance, Lane left the kitchen. The front screen door played its squeal of protest, then shut with a firm click, and Maggie knew he was gone.

FOUR

The walk to town was short, thank God, and not particularly taxing. The heat seemed less oppressive today. Or maybe Robbie James really had done Lane a favor by tailoring his wardrobe to fit the climate.

Caloosa Key far exceeded Lane's expectations. He had anticipated a depressing little backwater community of ramshackle buildings, or worse, a theme-park assortment of ''cutesy'' structures, color-coordinated and designed to please the eye of rich tourists—clean, attractive, and functional, but totally devoid of any sense of individuality. Instead, the small town had a great deal of character and charm.

The buildings were a pleasant hodge-podge collection: Florida Cracker storefronts of treated lumber and concrete with a stucco overlay, solid-looking offices which utilized native coquina shell, and airy shops with plenty of windows. The town encompassed no more than half a square mile, but it appeared fairly self-sufficient.

There were few residents strolling the streets, and, considering his present appearance, this was definitely a blessing. Whether this was in deference to the heat or simply because there were not many year-round islanders, Lane did not know. The people he did pass regarded him with typical small-town inquisitiveness for any stranger in their midst. Lane waved and said hello to several of them and did his best to pretend he didn't look like a first-class idiot.

Ernie's Gas and Service was open, and as Lane approached it, the man hosing down the drive nodded a greeting. If he thought Lane's clothing was a bit unorthodox, he didn't say so.

"Good morning. I wonder if you carry spare hoses? My car quit on me yesterday—"

"You'd be the young fellow Maggie Rose picked up."

"That's right," Lane acknowledged with some surprise. "How did you know?"

"Doc Holbrook said you'd probably be by. We don't get many strangers here this time of year. Come on into the bay. I'm sure we've got something to do the trick. Mercedes, wasn't it?"

He nodded, and followed obediently in the man's wake.

"How you feeling? Heard you fainted dead away at Maggie Rose's feet."

Amazed and a little irritated by the swiftness of the island grapevine, Lane replied, "I'm fine now, thank you, and it wasn't quite like that."

"Well, what way was it, then?" the man asked bluntly.

It was more of the same the rest of the morning. By the time he had gotten the Mercedes fixed, with him and Ernie rumbling out to the car in a battered Chevy pickup, Lane felt like a bass drum was being beaten at the back of his skull. The questions never ceased. And Ernie wasn't the only one.

The woman behind the desk at the real estate office laughed openly at his attire, then, as he filled out the necessary form to pick up the full set of keys to the inn, grilled him nonstop about his "relationship" with Maggie James. Her questions were only slightly more tactful than Ernie's had been, but she seemed determined to read something into Lane's brief replies.

At the small market where Lane purchased a few groceries, he felt as though a sign had been pinned upon his back, Lane Stafford, Heatstroke Victim. There were whispers and stares, and one elderly woman was brave enough to come forward to offer a sunburn remedy.

Back at the Mercedes, Lane was ready to make a quick getaway out of town when he spotted the real estate agent scampering toward him in high heels, her hand waving frantically. Damnation! What now?

"Oh, Mr. Stafford. I'm so glad I caught you," she panted. "Mr. Carlisle's on the phone. He's been trying to reach you at the inn. I told him you'd been dreadfully sick, but seemed better now."

"Thank you, Mrs. Brewster. Would you tell Mr. Carlisle I'll call him back once I get settled in at the inn?"

"I really think you ought to speak to him straightaway, Mr. Stafford. He wanted to hold because he wasn't planning to be in the office much longer."

In spite of the pounding behind his eyes and temple, Lane actually managed to smile at the old bat. "Very well, Mrs. Brewster."

Back in the office, she ran around the desk quickly and moved the telephone to face outward. "Line two," she said expectantly, and Lane could almost see the woman's ears stand straight up in anticipation.

"I wonder if you might have an extension where I could speak privately?" Lane asked mildly.

Disappointment settled in Mrs. Brewster's features, but she was too slow to think of a suitable reason to refuse. "Of course," she said, indicating a second office at the back of the building. She hurried ahead of him to flip on the light switch, and, with a smile of thanks, Lane shut the door firmly in the woman's face. Levering himself upon the desktop, he picked up the phone receiver and punched the flashing button. "Hello, Jerry."

"Staff!" Jerry Carlisle exclaimed, reverting to the nickname he'd bestowed upon his friend in college. "What's this I hear about you fainting in some woman's arms?"

"I didn't faint," Lane ground out. "I passed out.

There's a difference. And if one more person asks me that, I'm not going to be responsible for what I do. It's a good thing you're two thousand miles away and not right here beside me."

"What's the problem? I thought you'd be glad to have a working vacation."

"Vacation!" Lane growled. "Sending me here was like consigning me to Dante's Inferno, you jerk. Did you know Florida's going through a heat wave right now? It's a hundred and ten degrees in the shade here, Jerry. *In the shade*. I almost had my brains broiled in my skull yesterday."

"But, you're okay now . . ."

"I don't know. I'll have to check with some of the town citizens."

"What?"

"This island is worse than Petyon Place. The people here know your business before you do. And they're not shy about asking questions to find out what they *don't* know."

"Small towns tend to be close-knit, Staff."

"These people think that once you get on the island, they own you. Do you know the witch who answered this phone had the nerve to imply I might have slept with the woman who picked me up yesterday?"

"Well, did you?"

"Goddammit, Jerry!" Lane exploded. "The next time I see you, I'm going to deck you. Of course I didn't. The lady probably saved my life. That would have been a hell of a way to thank her, now wouldn't it?"

"Don't get mad," Jerry chuckled. "It wouldn't have been exactly out of character for you."

"The lady found me about as appealing as a lump of cold oatmeal. She couldn't wait to get me out of her house."

"I don't believe you, buddy."

"Okay. So maybe she can be brought around. If I can survive her kid brother. The boy's a cross between Norman Bates and Marlin Perkins. He runs around with wild animals climbing all over him. They let skunks in their house, Jerry. And raccoons. Big ones. Mean, with big yellow teeth. You should see what I'm standing in right now. The kid took scissors to my clothes and tried to make paper dolls out of them. You owe me a new suit, Jer.''

''Whatever,'' Jerry agreed with a laugh. ''Do you feel better now that you've gotten a few things off your chest?''

''No. I'm not finished.''

''Okay.''

''What's the deal with the property you bought here? I was under the impression you were going to clear the land and start from scratch.''

''I am.''

''Well, that's not the impression Maggie James has. She thinks her mother had deed restrictions put in the contract to guarantee the old inn on the property gets restored. I told her you had other ideas, and now she's loaded for bear. And since you're not around, she almost settled for *my* hide.''

''That wasn't the agreement at all. Peters handled the matter. Perhaps her mother misunderstood. He's one of those legal eagles who like to baffle people with all that lawyer lingo. Surely she didn't think I'd shell out that kind of money just to restore that old relic?''

Lane sighed and glanced up at the ceiling. ''I'm afraid she did, Jer. And believe me, Maggie James is not the type to let it rest.''

''Then do what you can to *make* her that type,'' Jerry said firmly, and for the first time in their conversation, he sounded like his father. ''In the meantime, I'll have the boys in legal go over the contract with a fine-toothed comb. I want a full-facility resort on that spot by the end of next year, Staff.''

''I'm an architect, Jer, not a miracle worker. And not

one of your henchman, either. The girl's not going to budge on this."

"Legally, she may have to. But I don't want some sour-grapes islander turning the rest of the community against us. We're going to need their support and cooperation. All I'm asking you to do is bring me back some of those great designs of yours, and maybe, in the meantime, bring Miss James around to my way of thinking."

"It'll never happen," Lane remarked ruefully. "She's not going to listen to a word I say."

"Why not? I've seen that old Stafford charm melt butter."

"You know the woman who picked me up? The one who threw me out of her house this morning?"

"Yeah."

"*That* was Maggie Rose James."

"Oh." There was a hum of silence on the other end as Jerry digested that fact. "Well, I know you. You'll think of something."

He wasn't prepared for The Caloosa Key Inn. Coming upon it suddenly after following a shell drive similar to the one leading to Banyon House, Lane did not expect much. The sign proclaiming its existence was shabby and sun-bleached, and after four years of gentle neglect, the inn was bound to be in poor condition. But Lane's first sight of it nearly took his breath away.

He could understand why Maggie James had been so adamantly opposed to the demolition of the building. It was an incredible piece of architecture, and much older than he had been led to believe. Lane suspected it had been built around 1870, no later than 1880. It embodied the best of late-Georgian design in its six white Ionic pillars across the front, forming a two-story portico, broad porch, and a simple, hipped roof that carried to a high center deck. It culminated in a third-floor cupola perched upon the top of the building like the crowning ornament of a multitiered wedding cake. It was ridiculously ornate and old-fashioned, but there was no denying that the inn had a certain weather-beaten appeal. Tyla James must have agonized a long time over the decision to turn it loose.

Upon closer inspection, Lane confirmed his fear that it was in poor shape inside and out. Peeling paint and faded wallpaper. Rotted wood. A slender balustrade in a diamond pattern ran the length of the veranda, but it was dangerously unsteady, with so many sections missing or jaggedly broken that it resembled a barroom brawler's bridgework. The roof was so worn in some places Lane marveled it hadn't caved in.

But there were many elaborate, lovely touches, too. Nine-foot marble mantels over cavernous fireplaces. French doors boasting leaded glass, chandelier medallions made of intricately carved wood in the plum pattern of the Empire period. And surprisingly, the walls seemed sturdy, with no stress cracks along its stucco surface, no signs of settling or moisture.

After making certain it could support his weight, Lane climbed the stairs to the cupola. The Gulf of Mexico was a sparkling turquoise-blue from up here, and, shading his eyes against the sun, Lane watched a pelican nose-dive into its glassy depths, bob to the surface with a fish clamped firmly in its pouchy bill, then swallow it whole.

From this vantage point Lane could see a small cottage nestled amongst a stand of gumbo-limbo trees. It was newer, making no attempt to mimic the architectural beauty of the inn. Probably the manager's quarters. The place where the James family had spent years trying to stay ahead of the demands made by this old monster.

Thinking of Maggie, Lane's eyes searched the distance to his right. He thought he could just glimpse the roof of Banyon House over the tops of trees, and there seemed to be a winding path through the undergrowth connecting the two properties. Neighbors, he'd told her. Well, it didn't seem likely she'd stop by for any neighborly visits after this morning.

Lane wondered if she had taken his advice and shown

an attorney her copy of the deed. He hoped so. And in spite of his friendship with Jerry, he hoped she was right; that somehow this great old place might be saved from the bulldozer. It needed a lot of work. No, truthfully, it needed an *army* of workers to return it to its former beauty. But Lane suspected the effort would be well worth it. The gulf breeze ruffling his hair, Lane's sharp eyes surveyed the property once more. Jerry was pretty shrewd. The land was beautifully situated and easily adaptable to his plans. His friend was a fair and honest businessman, but he wasn't likely to let one woman's sentimental attachment to an old inn keep him from developing the resort he wanted.

Well, it wasn't *his* property, and, therefore, it wasn't *his* problem, Lane told himself as he ran his hand along the unsteady railing. He was here to do a job, and from the looks of it, a pretty simple one, really, and after a bite of lunch he'd get started. In spite of Jerry's encouragement, he had no intention of courting Maggie James's approval. If there were no deed restrictions to prevent the inn's destruction, she'd have to live with her mother's mistake. Too bad about the old place. But as much as Lane relished the idea of getting to know Maggie better, he wasn't about to get in the middle of a property dispute between the woman and one of his best friends.

Almost unwillingly, his eyes traveled back across the treetops. What was she doing right now? Lane wondered. Did she think of him at all? Or had he been a minor irritation quickly forgotten? His breathing picked up a swifter rhythm, and Lane emitted a muffled groan. Lord, that she might have put him from her mind already, when *he* couldn't seem to stop thinking of her.

What a wonderful mixed-up personality she had. A shy spinster who quaked like an Aspen leaf at a man's touch, then a magnificent Valkyrie, spitting at him like a cat whose tail he'd trounced upon. Even as she hurled her most poisonous dart his way, it had been all Lane could do to keep from jumping up from the table and kissing her senseless.

He didn't understand it. She wasn't his type at all. The women Lane dated were confident, career-oriented lovelies who didn't need lessons in anything. *Least* of all how to behave around a man. He had no patience for shy, inexperienced females who couldn't meet him halfway—in bed or out of it. And yet the sight of her in pedal pushers and ponytail stirred him ten times more than all the low-cut evening gowns and seductive perfumes worn by the women Lane usually preferred. Maggie put him in touch with feelings he never expected to have and didn't really want to acknowledge.

What are you doing to me, Maggie James? What is it about you that intrigues me so?

Lane shrugged those disturbing questions away. He could admit to himself that he was almost afraid to know the answers.

The phone wouldn't ring. Expecting the attorney's call this morning, Maggie had stayed near the telephone for nearly two hours, reduced to watching it the last fifteen minutes just to see if she could *will* it to ring. She couldn't.

As much as she hated to admit it, Lane was right. She needed legal advice. Maggie couldn't see anything wrong with the way the deed was worded, but a second opinion couldn't hurt.

Shortly after Lane Stafford had walked out of Banyon House yesterday morning, Maggie took the small runabout across the bay to Fort Myers. Armed with every scrap of paperwork she could locate, she paid a quick visit to the attorney who had handled her mother's estate. Maggie explained the situation over coffee and the man agreed to scrutinize the documents. She hoped he could offer an immediate answer, but, unfortunately, he did not. With a promise to call her as soon as he reviewed the records, the man sent Maggie back to Caloosa Key.

neighbor, but she seriously doubted if Lane Stafford would help her. They'd hardly parted on the best of terms. And did she really want him to see her at such a ridiculous disadvantage?

Robbie had to be nearby. Surely he'd hear her. Standing up, Maggie climbed to the highest point, hoping to catch sight of him. He often combed the wild undergrowth surrounding the house, looking for birds and small animals. It was still early. He could have taken his windsurfer to the gulf before it became too hot.

Cupping her hands around her mouth, Maggie called her brother's name until her throat began to feel scratchy. There was no response. She checked her watch. Nine-thirty. Robbie always managed to show up at mealtimes, as though his system ran on an invisible inner clock. He'd be back at the house by noon, but that was two and a half hours away. Could she wait that long for rescue?

Yes. If she had to. And if the roof got too hot, she'd just have to jump and chance a broken bone.

She completed the job she intended to do; there was no sense in leaving the roof the way it was as long as she was trapped up here. Reflecting the increasingly hot sun, the tin began to grow warm, but not unbearably so. Sitting with her knees drawn close to her chest so that the hem of her shorts absorbed the heated metal, Maggie prepared to wait, grateful now that her attorney had yet to telephone. At least she was spared the frustration of hearing the phone ring and knowing she was unable to get to it.

By a quarter to eleven she was bored and irritated by her predicament and irrationally angry with Robbie for not being around when she needed him. Patience had never been one of Maggie's strongest virtues, and the warmer the roof grew, the angrier she got—at Robbie, at Beau and Roscoe, but, most of all, at herself. She should have made sure the animals were out of harm's way, or waited to fix the roof when Robbie was there to help her—

"Well, what have we here?" A voice broke into Maggie's self-recriminations and she stood up.

The last person she wanted to have see her in this sorry spot was Lane Stafford, but there he was, standing in the backyard with his hands on his hips, gazing up at her with a smug smile plastered across his handsome features. Today he would never be taken for a city dweller. He looked relaxed and fit in a pair of army-style shorts with deep pockets and a pale-blue T-shirt with BERMUDA emblazoned across his chest. The breeze had sifted his nutmeg hair attractively, and except for the fact he was not deeply tanned, he might easily have been mistaken for an islander.

Maggie was relieved to be rescued, but why oh why did it have to be him?

"Let me guess," Lane called up at her. "You can't get any privacy in the house with all those creatures and your brother running around, so you like to escape up to the roof."

With the ladder lying on its side only a few feet from Lane, her situation was quite obvious. Maggie found her irritation growing to realize the man couldn't resist teasing her. She glared down at him. "I don't suppose I could expect you to be decent about this and not make fun."

She couldn't.

He struck his forehead as though suddenly inspired. "No, that's not it. You've decided to take hang-gliding lessons and you went up there to see if you could stand heights."

"Stafford—"

"Birdwatching?" he ventured.

She gave him a look that could freeze boiling water. "Very funny. Now, are you going to help me down or not?"

"First tell me how you managed such a delightfully absurd predicament."

"It's a long, stupid story, which I'm sure you'd find immensely entertaining. But since you're the last person in the world I want to talk to, I'm not going to tell you. Just help me down."

Lane shrugged and crossed his arms over his chest. "Suit yourself. But if I'm really the last person in the world you want to talk to, I don't see why I should do you any favors."

"What!" Maggie yelped. She came as close to the edge of the roof as she dared. "Look here, I demand you put that ladder back up here this instant!" She stamped one sneakered foot for emphasis, and the tin echoed hollowly.

"You're really not in a position to demand much of anything," Lane replied mildly. "I came over here this morning to talk to you about the inn—"

"I don't have anything further to say to you on that subject!"

"Well, I do. And until I have your promise to listen to me, you can stay up there."

"You cruel, miserable . . . worm! It's hot up here."

"Likely to get hotter."

"Fine. Don't help me. I'll jump."

"Uh-uh. You'd have done it by now if you were going to. I'll be nearby if you change your mind and decide to be civil." He began to move out of her line of vision, heading toward the back porch.

"Stafford, you jerk! Come back here!"

"Nope."

She heard him move up the steps and knew the moment he lowered himself into one of the creaking deck chairs. Furious, Maggie sat down on the roof once more, almost directly overhead of where Lane sat.

Imagine the nerve of the man! He was inhuman. "Creep!" she shouted aloud. After she'd been nice enough to "—save your miserable hide, and that's the way you repay me!" she bellowed down through the tin. "Ungrateful wretch!" she added for his benefit. Once she got down from here, she'd give him more than heatstroke!

For ten minutes she seethed with impotent fury, hurling every invective she could think of in Lane's direction. Through it all he remained placidly silent. Maggie might have suspected he had gone away and left her, but just

when she began to fear he had, she would hear the wooden
chair groan as he shifted his weight. She ought to go ahead
and jump as she'd threatened. It would serve him right if
she leaped off the roof and broke her neck. She'd haunt
him for the rest of his worthless life. A glance at her
watch told her it was only ten after eleven. Still an hour
before Robbie might—*might*—show up for lunch. The tin
was hot now, getting hotter. She could feel the unpleasant
warmth of it through the cotton seat of her shorts. Not hot
enough to burn yet, but soon.

Ten minutes more and Maggie's temper began to cool
even as the tin began to burn. She supposed Lane had a
right to be uncooperative, considering her lack of enthusiasm over his sudden appearance. But he *had* made fun,
and, embarrassed, she'd responded by being less ... n
friendly. However she looked at it, it was obvious he h
no intention of helping her until she could be agreeable.
And if being *that* got her off this damned roof . . .

"Mr. Stafford?" she called tentatively.

No answer.

Maggie made her way to the roof's edge, positioning
herself so her head hung upside down over the side. The
heat was uncomfortable upon her bare midriff, and she
used the crook of her arm to swipe hair out of her eyes
so she could see underneath the porch overhang. Lane was
still there, gazing up at her with an unperturbed, smug
smile.

"Lane . . ."

"Yes."

"Please help me get down from here," she asked in
her most contrite tone of voice. "Please."

"I don't want you to beg for my help. I want your
promise to listen to what I've come here to say."

Maggie levered herself forward with one hand so that
her eyes met his squarely. "You're not being very nice."

Lane's brown eyes twinkled with merriment. "The day
before yesterday we made a deal. I'd unload your car and
you'd help me get the Mercedes fixed. Instead, I was

turned out into the streets in an outfit only an inmate from an insane asylum would be seen in. I've had my brains nearly baked, been face-to-face with wild animals, been the victim of a jealous twelve-year-old, and been gossiped about by an entire town of nosy rustics.'' His brow hiked incredulously. "And you want *nice?*''

"Aren't you overdramatizing just a bit?" Maggie asked, and was rewarded with a look of scornful determination. This man was not going to budge. In spite of herself, she had to laugh. "Okay, you win. I don't promise to agree with whatever it is you have to say, but I'll listen.''

Lane winked up at her. "Sensible girl.''

He pushed himself out of the chair immediately, and in no time the ladder was back in place. Lane stood at the bottom, bracing it with outstretched arms, smiling up at her with that damned annoying grin of his. "Okay, Rapunsel, come on down.''

Flashing him a malevolent look, Maggie began to back down the rungs.

A moment later she nearly jumped out of her skin when his cool hands wrapped around the bare, warm flesh of her upper thighs. She turned her head quickly to find Lane had come halfway up the ladder. Only a few inches separated them, and Maggie's cool blue gaze swung to meet his accusingly. His expression was intimately sensual, his lips softening into a lazy smile.

"What do you think you're doing?" she demanded crossly.

"Making sure you get down safely.'' His tone was pure innocence, but his hands began a caressing exploration down the tanned contours of her thighs, around her knees, stroking ever so slowly the back of her calves.

"I'm perfectly capable of getting down from here without any help from you.'' She wished her heart would stop fluttering so crazily.

Lane's eyes sparkled wickedly. "Are you sure? You look a little unsteady to me.''

Anxious to escape his touch, Maggie continued her

descent, thinking Lane would follow suit. He didn't. Instead, she found herself almost level with him, stuck two rungs from the bottom with no place to go and little room to maneuver. Lane Stafford seemed disinclined to cooperate, and she could feel his breath stirring at the back of her hair, his eyes on her, no doubt highly amused by her discomfort.

Annoyed and nervous, Maggie took a deep, fortifying breath, then executed a tricky turn that brought her face-to-face with her tormentor, a movement she immediately regretted. There was no escaping Lane's nearness now, his body pressed close to hers as he made no attempt to avoid the natural reclining position of the ladder. She could feel the wooden rungs along her backside and bit her bottom lip in frustration. Short of propelling herself outward and toppling them both from the ladder, there was nothing she could do to improve her position.

"Maggie, my dear. You never cease to amaze me," Lane said with a dry chuckle.

She tossed her head in what she hoped would be interpreted as defiance but what she feared was taken for nervousness. "And why is that?"

"Just when I'm wondering how I can get you into my arms, you accommodate me by moving right into them."

She flushed scarlet with embarrassment and anger. "You presume a great deal," she said shortly, and turned her head to one side. She couldn't look at him. His chestnut gaze could mesmerize, and even through the irritation she felt toward him, Maggie could sense her body responding to the electrifying nearness of his. *I'll just ignore him and he'll go away,* she reasoned desperately. *I'll just ignore him and he'll go . . .*

His lips were suddenly at her throat, finding the pulse leaping wildly there. "Mmm . . . you taste good, Maggie Rose," he whispered huskily. "Like a sun-warmed peach. So ripe and soft . . ." He drew back slightly, one hand gently turning her chin so their eyes met. "Do you know your pulse is racing a mile a minute?" he asked softly.

"Are you just scared, Maggie? Or is it me?" His gaze searched hers, and Maggie felt scorched by the look of warm intimacy. "I want it to be me."

Whatever answer he saw in her wide blue eyes, his lips were suddenly upon hers. His touch jolted Maggie into screaming awareness, and she stiffened. But even as she turned loose of her death-grip on the ladder and brought her hands up to push Lane away, the protest was dying in her throat. He took her wrists gently, guiding them over her head and out of harm's way so she lay stretched and vulnerable beneath him. Lane's mouth moved fiercely over hers with insistent pressure. Her lips parted slightly, and Lane needed no further invitation. With teasing lightness his tongue traced the soft curve of her lips, over the satiny smoothness of her teeth, finally settling upon a leisurely exploration of the sweet, dark cavern of her mouth.

A shock wave went through Maggie. *No one* had ever kissed her like this before. Not even Tom, who for all his pretense of love, had never invaded her senses the way Lane Stafford dared. She felt weak and confused, totally out of control. She wished he would stop, give her a moment to think, to sort through the myriad of shattering sensations assaulting her body. But even as she wished it, Maggie was suddenly returning his kiss, her lips clinging passionately to his, her body stretching to make contact. . . .

Lane sensed her acceptance and was pleased. Had she been any other woman of his acquaintance, he might have pressed this sudden advantage. It was only a short distance to her bedroom, and he'd enjoyed many an afternoon tryst under less promising beginnings. It was not his nature to refuse an opportunity, and certainly the game was one he knew and played well.

Yet he went no further than this delightful joining of their lips, quelling the quick throb of desire heating his loins. Not yet, his inner voice warned. Too soon. It might all be a wonderful game, but suddenly the rules didn't seem to suit Maggie James.

He was the one to pull back, lifting his head to give her a look both teasing and regretful. "Maggie, Maggie, as much as I'd like to pursue this, even *I* lack the sexual prowess to do much on this damned ladder."

He read the disappointment in her eyes, that lovely aquamarine gaze that was a true window to her feelings. Then the look was gone, shuttered carefully away.

Angry, but refusing to acknowledge it, she pushed against him until Lane was forced to step backward off the ladder and put one foot on the ground. She took quick advantage of the distance between them, leaving him without another glance. A few moments later the screen door banged shut behind her.

Lane followed at a slower pace, first returning the ladder and Maggie's supplies to the garage, allowing time for the girl's anger to cool. He knew his actions had bewildered her.

Hell, they hadn't been exactly clear to him, either.

FIVE

By the time Lane entered the cottage, Maggie was composed: not overly friendly, but at least no pots and pans were hurled his way. However, his attempts at conversation were unsuccessful, her responses monosyllabic. She seemed perversely determined to discourage any semblance of polite discussion.

The strain between them lessened somewhat when Robbie put in an appearance at noon. He was only a little less hostile than Maggie, but Lane was determined to win over at least *one* member of the James clan. Using his best powers of persuasion, he wrangled an invitation for lunch from the boy, ignoring Maggie's scowl of grudging acceptance of his company.

Over paper plates laden with tuna sandwiches and a tossed salad sprinkled with a homemade basil-and-wine dressing, Lane gradually laid waste to Robbie's resistance. The boy tried hard to withhold his friendship and Lane did not try to rush him. They discussed everything from windsurfing to animals to whether or not tunafish should be embellished with chopped onion and pickles, as Maggie had prepared it, wisely deciding it should indeed. By the time Robbie slammed out of the house again to meet up with his friends, the fragile beginnings of a friendship had been formed.

Maggie's attitude was less antagonistic. She had even favored Lane with a smile or two over lunch. The man had an undeniable charm, she had to admit. She was pleased to see Robbie open up to him. With no male influence in the boy's life, she'd been worried lately that her brother was becoming too insulated from the rest of the world.

Her attorney had yet to call. Not once had Lane brought up the subject of the inn, but she knew it was only a matter of time. With Robbie no longer around to act as a buffer between them, and feeling edgy about what Lane might want to discuss, Maggie picked up her gardening basket and left the house. He was so insufferably cool, a persistent man. If whatever Lane had to say to her was important, he wouldn't leave without eventually broaching the subject.

A week ago Maggie had planted a small garden at the side of the house. For all its sandy soil, the island was blessed with a long growing season. In the past, she'd successfully raised tomatoes, squash, eggplant, and peppers. She had the same high hopes for this crop, although the dry spell they'd been having would mean increased watering and a bit more care.

As she bent to evict the first weedy invaders from the neat rows of seedlings, she was aware when Lane came out of the house to join her. He watched her wordlessly for a few minutes, then sat back on his heels at the end of one row, his fingers scooping up a clump of soil and idly letting it sieve through his fingers.

"Need any help?"

"No, thank you."

The silence spun out between them. Maggie concentrated on repacking earth around eroded areas where her watering had created small craters.

"I've never known anyone who actually kept a garden."

"You're kidding," Maggie remarked with some surprise. "Even Detroit has dirt."

"Chicago."

"Oh. Sorry. Well, even Chicago must have its share of growing things."

"Flowers." His eyes traveled over the stakes at the end of each row that held seed packets inverted over the tips. "Never vegetables."

Mashing earth down around a tiny squash plant, Maggie looked at him askance. "Didn't your mother ever grow tomatoes on a windowsill?"

Lane laughed at the image of his dainty, society-minded mother up to her elbows in potting soil. "My mother wouldn't know the difference between tomatoes and turnips. We kids were city born and bred. The only time we got out to the country for any length of time was three weeks in the summer when my dad insisted we escape to The Great Outdoors. He claimed it was important we get back to our roots. My sisters and I loved it, but my mother sulked the entire time."

"What a pity. *My* mother thought every woman should know how to grow her own food."

She smiled with sudden remembrance, and Lane thought how serenely beautiful Maggie was, the afternoon sun casting shadows upon the sharp contours of her features, her pale hair sifting back and forth over one shoulder like translucent sunshine.

"When we had the inn, we kept fresh home-grown fruit in all the guest rooms. The people loved it. Mom made terrific sea-grape and strangler fig jelly."

"About the inn . . ."

"I have a few jars left. You'll have to try some."

"Maggie . . ."

"I don't really want to talk about the inn. You have your opinion and I have mine."

"You promised to listen," Lane reminded her.

Maggie rocked back on her heels, and, with a reluctant sigh, she met his determined gaze. "Okay. I guess I did.

But now I know you're Carlisle's man, so whatever you say won't make me change my mind about the place."

"Fair enough," Lane said with a tight smile. "Have you taken my advice about having someone look at your copy of the deed?"

"Yes. In fact, I'm expecting a call any minute from my lawyer who's reviewing it."

"Good."

She gave him a direct, challenging look. "You might as well tell your boss that even if the news is bad, I'm prepared to fight if I have to. That inn is not going to be torn down, regardless of what trickery your friend may have used to have it his way."

Lane stood suddenly, wiping dirt off his hands. When he spoke, his voice was calm but implacable. "Look, let's get something straight. I'm not Jerry's flunky, and I've got no stake in what happens here. In spite of what you may think, Jerry's not a trickster, just a very determined businessman. He sees a golden opportunity in that land and he's pretty well set on how he wants to use it. He's got a lot of money to see his wishes get carried out. A lot, Maggie. And nothing I've seen here leads me to believe you're in a financial position to survive a long court battle."

Maggie's hand angled upward defiantly. "So what are you saying?" she demanded tartly. "That I should just give up because I can't fight big business?"

"No."

She stood, pulling her gardening gloves off her hands with sharp little movements of annoyance. Lane could feel the heat of her anger across the distance separating them, and when she faced him at last, hands on hips, the look she sent him was stubbornly suspicious. "Then what do you suggest?"

He could have shaken her until her teeth rattled. Common sense told him he should leave and forget about the idea that had been brewing within him since yesterday afternoon. She wasn't going to be receptive. Not at all.

"Well?" Maggie said, offering him a false smile of encouragement. "What's your brilliant solution to this problem?"

Her scornful tone stretched Lane's irritation to the limits and he stalked down the garden row to face her. He loomed over her, so close Maggie blinked in surprise and took a tentative step backward. The man was clearly out of patience.

"Damn it! I'm getting a little tired of being painted the villain in this picture, and it occurs to me that maybe you don't deserve what little help I can offer. Now, are you going to listen to me or not?"

She had never seen him angry before, and Maggie flushed guiltily. Lane was right. She'd been uncooperative and churlish, and the whole situation really wasn't his fault at all. She didn't trust him to betray his friend's interest in the property, and hopefully she wouldn't need his advice if there proved to be nothing wrong with the deed. But the least she could do was listen to what he had to say. A promise was a promise.

"You have my full attention," she said softly, and this time there was no sarcasm peppering her words.

Lane nodded curtly. "Good." He heaved a disgusted sigh and raked one hand through his hair. "Ah, hell. This isn't the way I wanted this to come out." He took a deep breath, as though what he was about to say required fortification. "First, there's a good chance the deed will prove useless to you. I know Jerry. He's shrewd, and what he wants, he usually gets. I've never known him to cheat anyone, but if his lawyer, this Peters fellow, was told to get that property, then it's quite possible he did it by any legal means he could. Even if it meant baffling your mother into thinking Jerry had other plans for the property. It probably wasn't difficult. Your mother was concerned about the future of you and your brother, probably not in the best frame of mind to negotiate. If she was anything like you, she'd be a little naive and overly trusting about such matters."

Maggie opened her mouth to protest that humiliatingly accurate description, but Lane silenced her with one upraised hand. "Don't get your back up. That wasn't an insult. People do this sort of thing all the time. Most human beings tend to believe a person can be taken at his word, and you're no different. The courts are full of people suing each other because they broke their promises. Unfortunately, unless you've got a pretty strong case, you lose.

"Anyway, for the sake of argument, let's say Jerry's now got your property to do with exactly as he wishes. What he wishes is a resort and he's picked a good spot for it. I've walked the property. It's perfect for the low-key, high-class place Jerry has in mind. I'm not going to have any trouble at all putting three or four designs in front of Jerry that will give him what he wants. The inn doesn't present a problem. It's in bad shape. A wrecking crew could have it down in one day."

"This doesn't sound—"

"I'm not finished yet. Be quiet." She gave him a sullen look, but acquiesced. "Architecturally, the inn is interesting but not unique, although the cupola adds a nice touch. Structurally, the roof is shot and so is most of the flooring, but the walls look solid and all the bric-a-brac can be replaced easily enough. I guess what I'm leading up to here is not the importance of the inn itself, but what it represents. I had expected a building constructed in the early nineteen hundreds. Instead, it's a hell of a lot older than that, and probably one of the few remaining examples of its era still standing in the state. Florida weather takes a pretty heavy toll on coastal structures. It's a miracle it hasn't been knocked into a pile of matchsticks by some previous hurricane. What I'm saying *is*, while your old place might not stack up very well to some of the antebellum mansions along, say, the Natchez Trace, for Florida it's a genuine treasure. There can't be more than a handful of homes like it in the entire state. In terms of historic value, there's almost an obligation to restore it."

Maggie looked considerably relieved. "Then you're saying Carlisle will *have* to refurbish it if the State of Florida declares it—"

"No. It's still private property. Jerry can do with it as he pleases."

"Then, what?" she asked in consternation.

Drawing a deep breath, Lane met her eyes directly. "I'm saying *if*, and it'a a very big if, Jerry can be persuaded to save it, restore it as a historic landmark, he could still have his resort built around it. By incorporating the inn into his plans, making it a focal point of interest, the inn can be saved and Jerry would be happy."

"Why should he bother?" Maggie asked, assuming the role of devil's advocate. "Surely it would be cheaper to tear the place down."

"It would be. And he may yet. He'd have to be persuaded to do otherwise. As I said before, I have a bit of professional and personal influence with Jerry. I'm willing to see what I can do to change his mind."

She looked at him sharply. "You're willing to do that . . . for me? Why? I haven't been exactly . . . pleasant to you."

He favored her with a cutting glance of dismissal, annoyance mixed with disapproval. "I'm not keeping score, Maggie."

Color stained her cheeks. "I'm sorry. I guess I'm not used to having men do nice things for me. At least, not without having an ulterior motive in mind."

Lane's hand lifted to her face, and with a whispery touch, he stroked away a smudge of garden dirt from Maggie's cheek. His smile was one of dry amusement. "I don't doubt that for a moment, sweetheart. And it would be a mistake to peg me as a candidate for sainthood."

"Then, why?"

His shoulders lifted in nonchalance, and, despite Lane's penchant for making direct eye contact, he seemed suddenly intrigued by the horizon. "Let's just say I have a professional interest in seeing the place restored. Architects don't spend all their time tearing down old buildings so they can throw up monolithic office complexes, you know. We can appreciate the craftsmanship that went into building great places like the inn.''

Maggie felt a sting of disappointment at his answer, and sensed there might be more to his explanation than that, but, like Lane, she was unwilling to explore further.

"So what can I do to help?" she asked, her tone its most businesslike.

"Not much right now," he responded, following her lead. "If your mother's lawyer calls to say you're in the clear with the deed, then we've done all this plotting for nothing. If the news is bad—then we get busy."

The news *was* bad. With solemn regret, the attorney told Maggie he could find nothing illegal in the deed which might hold up in court. Carlisle's lawyer had carefully structured the document to avoid future problems. When Maggie inquired about her chances should she take the case to court, the attorney strongly counseled against such action.

In a haze of disconsolate remorse, Maggie spent the remainder of the day wracking her brain for possible solutions to the problem.

No answer came to her.

None except Lane Stafford's unexpected offer to help.

The sun sizzled into the gulf, a huge wavering red ball of heat that tinted the sky a deep pink and lavender. Caloosa Key sunsets were spectacular. In season, a crush of people ventured to the water's edge to witness God's artistry. They strolled the beach in early evening, gathering pretty shells, bird-watching, lazily walking arm in arm with someone they loved.

Maggie was suddenly glad it was off season. She didn't feel like voicing a friendly hello to strangers she might pass, and tonight the beach was deserted. Not even the locals were out, perhaps because the unrelenting heat wave made the twilight still uncomfortably warm.

She had left Robbie at the cottage, lounging in front of the television. He would not question her disappearance as Maggie often walked the beach in early evening, enjoying the peaceful, lulling sound of the gulf lapping against the sand, the comic posturing of birds feeding at water's edge, the delightful discoveries she often made in the tepid pools left behind by low tide.

Tonight she indulged in none of these pleasures. She wandered aimlessly along the gulf's foamy fringe, her thoughts as unsettled as the sand shifting beneath her feet. The numbing shock of the attorney's disclosure had worn off, but no solution had taken its place. She felt a frustrated helplessness in her position—and anger, too. Her mother had not been unintelligent. Even in the height of her illness her mind had remained exceptionally keen and alert. Then, *how* could she have been so easily misled? The picture of her mother Lane had painted earlier—a sick woman, scared and confused—did not fit Maggie's image of Tyla James.

The sharp edges of a broken conch shell dug into the ball of her foot, and, with a muttered oath, Maggie kicked it aside. Little good it did to rehash her mother's decision, she reminded herself harshly. The problem now was to change the outcome and somehow save that which was legally lost to them. But how?

Perhaps subconscious thought led her, but Maggie glanced around and was surprised to find she had come to the beachfront boundary of the inn. Through the low, twisted sea-grape thickets and choking strangler figs, she could see it, its pale-yellow facade looking forlorn and abandoned amongst the lush tropical setting. For the first time ever, Maggie gazed at her former home with an unprejudiced eye, trying to picture the structure as Jerry Carlisle might view it.

She could admit to herself the inn was in poor condition. There was no denying the deterioration, the decay eating away at the heart of the building. The structure was old and tired and useless. If it had been an animal, someone would have had the decency to put it out of its misery, and Maggie wondered briefly if this was what her mother saw when she looked at it. Had Tyla James known what needed to be done and set the wheels in motion?

Knowing she had no legal right to be there, Maggie nevertheless wound her way along the beach path to the gazebo. Like the inn, it was in poor shape, but, sitting on a low dune and surrounded by fragrant oleander, it offered a lovely view of the Gulf of Mexico and a gentle breeze. Many a moonlight tryst had been kept here by various guests of the inn, a fact well known by Maggie's parents, though seldom commented upon.

In the summer of her fourteenth year, Maggie had sneaked out of the apartment one night to see for herself just what attraction the place might have. But two hours of being eaten alive by mosquitos and crouching in the bushes until her calf muscles cramped unbearably had yielded little more than the sight of a few stolen kisses and an inept fumbling at zippers and buttons. To her horror, the numbness in her legs made her careless, causing Maggie to stumble a bit, and, at the unexpected sound, two would-be lovers had flown like scalded cats. It had been a big disappointment, heightened by the fact that the next day Maggie had been consigned to a washing detail of every window in the inn, followed by a subtle lecture by her mother about the importance of guests' privacy.

Poised on the threshold of the gazebo, the memory brought a faint smile to Maggie's lips, then, just as quickly, she was jolted back to reality by the sight before her. It had been months since she'd been inside the open-air structure, and the elements had been especially cruel here. The pine-board flooring had once been swept twice a day. Now a fine layer of white beach sand covered it; in some corner it had drifted into tiny dunes. The wooden deck chairs and comfortable chaises were weathered and shaky-looking; Maggie couldn't remember what had happened to the colorful cushions they'd once had. Weaver spiders had formed cobwebs in every crevice left untouched by the salt breeze, and perhaps, worst of all, several sea birds had discovered the easy accessibility of the rafters for building nests. Their droppings were everywhere.

The slow destruction of this delightful refuge would have been unthinkable in her parents' time, and only accentuated the wretched turmoil within her. With an anguished groan, Maggie brushed away the sand from one of the sturdier-looking chairs and sank into it. Lifting her knees to her chest, she folded her arms across them, then let her head rest upon the pillow they provided.

What *was* she to do?

Lane Stafford's suggestion of a historic site seemed hollow hope in view of the situation. He was an expert in his field, but if the neglect of the inn was one-tenth as severe as in this small structure, why would Jerry Carlisle bother? From a financial standpoint, it had to be much easier, even more sensible, to tear the place down and build from scratch. He was a businessman, not a philanthropist.

With all her heart Maggie wanted to believe Lane's opinion that the inn was salvageable as a historic site, but she wasn't sure she should. Had he been truthful with her, or was he merely telling her something she wanted badly to hear? He'd made it quite obvious he was attracted to her. Was he the type of man to use the inn as bait to further his own interest? Maggie didn't think so, but with her limited experience, how could she be sure?

With the tip of her nose, Maggie rubbed away a few grains of sand clinging to the back of her hand. How awful it was to be so sexually immature, she thought bleakly. Men like Tom and Lane Stafford seemed to know instinctively just what buttons to push, while she was left floundering to figure everything out all by herself! They never seemed unsure or scared or frustrated by their emotions, while *she* never seemed to be in full control of her feelings at all. It was a little like being a helpless passenger on a wild roller-coaster ride, she decided, and Maggie just hoped to heaven she wasn't the only female to ever feel this way.

Maggie had to admit she liked Lane Stafford. She even grudgingly conceded she was attracted to him. But what was the point? He would be here for such a short time, to do a job that could only cause her heartache. In spite of his overtures toward friendship, did he really care about what happened to one broken-down excuse of an inn? Logic told her his motives could not be so pure, and yet . . .

She sat a long time in the gazebo, her head nestled in her arms. The gentle stillness of the island surrounded her, unbroken except for the occasional scuttle of a lizard amongst the leaves and the sudden splash of a pelican as it arrowed into the water for its supper. She should go. It would be dark soon, and although she could find her way back home easily enough, she wouldn't relish tripping over a fallen palm or tromping upon an unsuspecting crab.

Maggie sighed despairingly. The island quiet had not helped her tonight. There were no answers to her questions here. Perhaps there were none to be found anywhere.

Some sixth sense warned her she was no longer alone, and without lifting her head, Maggie turned to look toward the gazebo's entranceway. Lane Stafford was there, his features indistinct against the fading light, yet something in the way he stood suggested a quiet seriousness.

"I'm sorry," Maggie offered softly. "I know I'm trespassing . . ." She let the words trail away. To her horror, they sounded weak and emotional. The last thing she wanted to do in front of this man was cry.

"So the deed's no use to you." It was a statement, not a question.

She nodded almost imperceptibly. "I don't know what to do."

Her voice was so dazedly wooden that Lane's gut wrenched with pity for her. He had expected as much, yet to witness the confirmation of it in Maggie's eyes, their startling blueness gone as flat and vacant as a becalmed sea, left him feeling bereft, as if that miserable inn had been his very own.

Experiencing a confusing mixture of sympathy and need, Lane went to her. He was inordinately pleased to see that his touch released some inner control within Maggie. She uncoiled from her position with an odd naturalness and slid into the welcoming circle of his arms. He pulled her close, and she turned her face inward; he could feel her breath stirring the hairs exposed at the neckline of his shirt, warm and soft as a butterfly's wing. The top of Maggie's head rested beneath his chin, and he dipped his nose into the satiny mass of her hair, luxuriating in its softness, the clean scent of it mingled with just the slightest hint of salt air. Desire splintered through him, but he bludgeoned it under control. She was hurting now. He would not add to her pain and confusion. Still, he was not quite noble enough to loosen his hold a bit or keep his lips from unconsciously planting nibbling kisses along her hairline.

It seemed to Maggie that all the misery and uncertainty left her body the moment she stepped into Lane's embrace. A week ago he had been a stranger to her. Circumstances being what they were, he was actually in the employ of a man who must now be considered her enemy, yet she felt heartened and strangely secure in his grasp. There was something infinitely soothing about his hand roaming along the length of her back, gently stroking, kneading the tension out of her muscles. Maggie reveled in the warmth emanating from him; the feel of his breath at the top of her hair, the tingling anticipation she felt as his lips touched her lightly.

Lane made no further comment, and she was grateful to him for that. Perhaps he guessed that her emotions were raw and painfully close to the surface. The least sympathetic word could bring a flood of unwelcome tears, and Maggie was thankful she might be spared that final indignity.

They remained in each other's arms a long time,

scarcely moving. The darkness began to shutter away their surroundings, and only then did Lane pull away from her. Below him, Maggie's face was a pale oval, her features stolen by the night, but with practiced skill his hands found each side of her head, his thumbs stroking the downy softness of her cheeks.

"Come back to the apartment with me. Between the two of us we'll figure out what our next step should be. All right?"

She nodded mutely, and Lane led her out into the open air. There was not much moonlight and their surroundings were simply varying degrees of total darkness. After only a few steps, Lane stopped short. "Damn," he swore softly.

"What's the matter?"

"If this were Chicago, there'd be streetlamps. I can't see a blessed thing. And I'm not real sure which direction the apartment is."

In spite of her melancholy mood, Maggie couldn't resist a laugh. "City slicker," she teased, capturing his hand in hers. "Stick with me. I can find the way back with my eyes closed."

"I'm afraid instant is all I can offer," Lane called from the kitchen.

"That's fine," Maggie replied absently, settling into one of the overstuffed chairs that had been her father's favorite. It seemed odd to be back in the apartment this way, a guest in her own home. Lane had removed the protective sheeting from a few pieces, and everything was so achingly familiar that Maggie's heart tightened convulsively in her chest. She glanced down at the arm of the chair, where a small pink stain marred the pattern. She remembered well how that accident had happened. Robbie coming from the kitchen, a cup of cherry Kool-Aid clutched precariously in his four-year-old hands. Dad had tried to fend him off, but in Robbie's efforts to reach his father, some of the drink had splashed out of the cup.

Their mother had scrubbed and scrubbed at the spot to no avail—

Maggie shut her mind to the memory and looked quickly away. It was dangerous to dredge up the past, especially here where so much of her life had been spent. No good could come of it. She had to start viewing this place with a realistic eye, impersonally.

"I remembered you took sugar," Lane commented as he placed a tray upon the coffee table between them. His eyes caught hers and he frowned. "You all right?"

Maggie offered up a weak smile. "Sure."

He observed her pale features silently for a moment or two, then added, "Would you rather we go to your place to talk?"

The knife-edged accuracy of his perception surprised her, and Maggie felt warm gratitude for the man's consideration seep into her. "No, really. Here is fine," she said quickly, and made a short, unsatisfactory attempt at a brilliant smile. Having failed miserably, she occupied herself with the coffee.

She heard Lane's muttered grumble about "stubborn women," and for a few minutes they each kept to their own thoughts. Maggie could feel Lane's eyes upon her, warm and speculative, but she was too much of a coward to meet him look for look. At the gazebo, the diminishing light made it easy to accept his presence, but here in the lamplight, Lane seemed real and overpowering—and totally in command. She felt uncomfortable to be alone with him on his turf, and wished she *had* taken his suggestion they return to her home, where Robbie would be slouched in the living room and *she* would be the one to set the tone.

Maggie wondered why he didn't speak, then cursed herself for her own lack of conversation. It was bitterly annoying to realize that around this man she was consistently tongue-tied and awkward.

"What did the lawyer say?" he asked finally, and even

though Lane spoke softly, Maggie still jumped at the sound of his voice.

"What you said he'd say. There's nothing to keep your friend from tearing down the inn."

"Tell me everything," Lane urged, and while she recounted all that had been told to her, he watched her face with silent intent.

The pinch of anxiety was evident in her pale features, and he was moved by it. Yet at the same time, Lane was drawn by her beauty, the way the lamplight did magical things to the silver highlights in her hair, the play of shadow along her collarbone. A few grains of beach sand clung to the inside of one knee, twinkling in the light, and it took every once of control Lane could muster to keep from levering himself out of the chair opposite Maggie and brushing the grains away with his lips. Coherent thought threatened to desert him as he watched the subtle lift of her breasts, imagined trailing his fingers over the silken texture of her skin. He clamped down ruthlessly on his wandering mind and concentrated on what Maggie was saying.

He asked her questions and made a few comments, lightly probing with a skill designed to put Maggie at ease. He knew she was upset and nervous, and Lane was pleased to see her respond to the quiet nuances in his voice, like the gentle calming of a spirited racehorse. Gradually Maggie relaxed and the tension left her. He could see it in the way her slim shoulders slumped tiredly, the soft vulnerability smudging her features.

"So what *am* I to do?" she asked simply. "Did you mean what you said about having the inn declared a historic landmark?"

Lane's beautifully shaped eyes glinted softly. "I never say anything I don't mean. But it's not going to be easy. Here are my thoughts on what our next step should be . . ."

They spent the next two hours creating a plan of action. If Jerry Carlisle could be made to listen, just *listen* to a proposal then Lane felt it was imperative that they gather as much credible information as they could as to why the inn should be saved, and, more importantly, if the restoration could be accurately done yet still be cost-effective. There were two big drawbacks to any kind of preservation. It was often cheaper to replace a structure than to rebuild, and adapting old relics to fit modern needs could be expensive and time-consuming. On the positive side, Lane told her, in recent years the government had offered developers large tax credits for investments in historic sites and dangled federal grants before their noses as additional inducement. It was unlikely Jerry Carlisle needed that kind of funding, but it couldn't hurt to add incentive.

Regrettably, the architectural firm Lane worked for had little experience in historic preservation. Restoration was a highly specialized field, and in the next few days Lane promised to pay a visit to a Florida firm he'd heard good things about.

While he worked on cost estimates and approvals, Lane suggested Maggie research as much of the inn's history as she could. It was critical to know what was original to the structure and what remodeling had taken place at a later day. Patiently, he drew up a long list of crucial data he would need and offered suggestions as to where she might locate such information. He explained the importance of every item on the list and what it could tell them about the inn. Given the building's age, he doubted they could unearth an original floor plan or blueprint, but he was hopeful they could pinpoint the exact date of construction, the name of the architect, and the materials originally used. It was a tall order, but Maggie was eager to get started.

Folding the list in half, Lane extended it across the coffee table to Maggie. "This should keep you occupied for the next few days. We can get started first thing in the morning."

Maggie folded the paper into a small square and slipped it into the pocket of her shorts. "You don't think we're jumping the gun a bit?" she asked. "I mean, suppose

Jerry Carlisle just rejects the idea outright and won't even listen? We'll have collected everything for nothing.''

"Oh, ye of little faith," Lane chastised good-naturedly. "You don't know how persuasive I can be. I can't guarantee success, but I'll definitely have a chance to get my point across. And when I do, I want to be fully prepared. Jerry's like a shark. If he spots a weakness, he'll go in for the kill. We're only going to get one chance, you know.''

"I know. But I wouldn't even have that if it weren't for you." Her eyes dropped and she shifted uncomfortably in her chair. "I'm very grateful to you, Lane.''

A long silence fell between them; then at last Lane made a low sound of incredulity. "Sweetheart," he said softly, "of all the things I want from you, gratitude is the *last* on my list." When she remained silent, staring down at her hands in her lap, Maggie heard him draw a deep breath, then let it slowly out again. "But hell, I guess it's a start. Right?''

With a swiftness she didn't expect, Lane's hand reached out and he pulled her out of the chair. "Come on. Enough plotting and planning for one night. We're both tired and we have a lot of things to do tomorrow. I'll walk you back. Didn't I see a path connecting this place and Banyon House?''

"Yes. But that's not necessary. I know the way.''

Lane favored her with a good-natured grin. "Don't worry. I promise not to get us lost. I'll even drop a trail of breadcrumbs if you like.''

"It's not that . . .''

"Then what?" he encouraged, then laughed as comprehension dawned. His smile was wide and devilishly wicked. "Relax, sweetheart. If I was going to ravish you, I would have done it by now, and it would have been in the middle of a big, comfortable bed like the one in that bedroom over there." He reached out to push a strand of silver hair back over her shoulder. His brown gaze lit upon her bared flesh for just an instant. "I'm not in the habit of tumbling women in the bushes like some sex-starved teenager.''

''I didn't think you were!'' Maggie snapped hotly, chagrined to feel the heat rise to her cheeks.

He looked skeptical and swallowed a chuckle, and she could have slapped him for the way his eyes brimmed with amusement. ''No? Then let's go.''

The path between the two properties was narrow and meandering. The moonlight was bright enough now so that the trail was easily discernible; years ago someone had sprinkled a fine layer of crushed oyster shells upon it to improve visibility. The vegetation crept across it in some places, but there was still no way a person could get lost as long as they avoided side trips into the undergrowth.

Maggie opened her mouth to protest Lane's company once more, then closed it. He probably wouldn't listen to her anyway. He captured her hand again, and Maggie noted his grip was warm and dry—and inescapable. The path wasn't wide enough to allow them to walk two abreast, so she was forced to fall in slightly behind him as Lane pulled her along.

It had turned out to be a lovely night—cool, and breezy enough to keep the mosquitos from settling on their exposed skin too often. After the hot days they'd been having, the breeze was a welcome change, and as she followed in Lane's wake, Maggie began to enjoy her surroundings. She lifted her face skyward, counting stars and listening to the soft monotone chirp of crickets, the throaty mating call of tree frogs. She drew in deep draughts of night air, savoring the fragrant perfume of the deadly oleander and wild orchids, the astringent tang of key limes from the abandoned groves that had been planted in the 1920's.

Once a brown marsh rabbit darted across their path and Lane pulled up so short that Maggie bumped into his back. He glanced over his shoulder at her, his face ghostly in the moonlight but clearly visible. ''Are there alligators in this area?'' he asked sharply.

Maggie lifted her shoulders. "I don't know. It's not like the Stars' Homes of Hollywood Tour, you know. We don't get a map telling us where all the gators live."

"You're a big help."

It was Maggie's turn to grin. "Don't worry. Most of them are small and stay closer inland where there's brackish water."

"Do *they* know that's where they're supposed to be?"

"I guess. Besides, they wouldn't be interested in us. They're too busy feeding."

"Oh, great," Lane muttered.

She couldn't help herself. The man was so patently out of his element, Maggie had to laugh. Her hero!

Lane's brows quirked into a frown at the sound of her uncontrolled mirth. "What's so funny?"

"Don't get mad at *me*," she giggled. "You're the one who insisted on playing Pathfinder."

"A gentleman doesn't leave a lady to find her way home alone."

"I could have been home five minutes ago if you'd let me be. Instead, I have to be dragged along after you like some caveman's conquest while a mosquito makes dinner out of the back of my neck."

He swung to face her. "Are you always so unappreciative of a man's offer to help? Or just mine?"

Maggie ignored the question, preferring instead to resurrect their previous argument. "I don't need your help to find my way home. I've lived on this island all my life and I could walk this path blindfolded. It isn't Chicago."

Lane slapped at a mosquito that had zeroed in on his arm. "It sure as hell isn't," he remarked with amused exasperation. "In Chicago it's . . . civilized. We have the symphony and art galleries and Lake Michigan—"

"—and gang wars and muggings and police sirens to lull you to sleep at night instead of the sounds of nature." With a sharp gesture, she placed her hands upon her hips. "I saw *The Godfather*. I know what the place is like."

"That was New York," Lane corrected with patient humor.

"Oh." She took a moment to recover, then thrust her chin out triumphantly. "What about the St. Valentine's Day Massacre?"

"That was sixty years ago!"

"Are you saying crime doesn't exist in Chicago?" she asked with smug sweetness.

"At least there they just shoot you. They don't try to make a meal out of you." He shook his head. "*This* place—it's primeval. I keep expecting two guys from *Deliverance* to pop up out of the bushes. And what the hell is that noise?"

"What noise?"

"Like someone cracking peanuts."

Maggie listened silently for a moment. The sound was so familiar to her that she hadn't been aware of it until Lane brought it to her attention. "Oh, that. Those are night herons. They feed on mangrove crabs that live in the trees. The birds make that noise when they crunch the crab's shell."

Lane pulled a face. "Jesus. This place really is survival of the fittest, isn't it?"

"What did you expect? *Fantasy Island*?" Maggie asked with a laugh.

"Why in God's name Jerry would want to build a resort on this place is beyond me." He recaptured her hand. "Come on. I've had enough nature for one night."

Tripping to keep up with Lane's swiftly retreating form, Maggie called after him. "Why don't you try to convince Mr. Carlisle of the error of his ways?"

"I just might do that," Lane threw back over his shoulder.

They reached Banyon House, stopping on the front porch steps. Lights were still on, but the house was quiet and Maggie suspected she'd find Robbie sound asleep in front of the television. She wasn't sure whether Lane intended to come inside, but he seemed disinclined and she didn't know if his hesitancy was a relief or a disappointment.

She turned toward Lane uncertainly, feeling suddenly awkward and shy, like a schoolgirl being dropped off from her first date. Cursing the resurfacing of those two traits, two of her worst, she nevertheless managed a brief smile. "Here we are." She stated the obvious, then chastised herself for such a blatant lack of originality. "In spite of all the teasing, I really do appreciate the escort home," she offered politely.

"I'll bet," he replied softly. "If you're ever in Chicago, I'll make you walk *me* home. See how you like it."

She laughed lightly, but the sound died in her throat as he closed the short distance between them to capture her lips. It was a brief, steady pressure, quickly withdrawn before Maggie had time to respond. Still, she felt oddly bereft when the contact ended.

"Sleep well, Maggie Rose," Lane whispered. "I'll be in touch."

She nodded mutely, her fingers pressed to the spot where his lips had touched hers. For a long moment he gazed down at her, as though debating his next move, and then he was drifting back into the shadows away from her, and the moment was gone.

"Lane," she called softly.

"Yes."

"The path's that way." Her hand waved to the right, and even in the darkness, she felt his self-deprecating grimace reach her.

"Oh. Thanks."

SIX

Maggie was excited.

She'd been worried that reconstructing the inn's full history would prove to be an impossible task, producing sketchy results at best. But thanks to an excellent Records department in Lee County, Maggie collected enough data to fill a large notebook with hard evidence that the inn was a bona fide monument to Florida's past certainly worth of preservation.

With Robbie's help she unpacked her parents' private papers, discovering an abstract of title, several building permits, guest registers dating back to 1915, and two books on local history that mentioned the inn frequently and in lavish detail.

At the island library she unearthed yet another book, this time an autobiography written by one of the original islanders, who described several visits to the inn before it had opened to the public and was still privately owned. At Lane's suggestion, she visited several old-timers on the island, questioning them thoroughly about the previous owners and any incidents they might remember involving the property. With the exception of Ada Ryan, who didn't like anyone and had moved to Caloosa Key sixty years ago to have complete privacy, they were an informative, cooperative lot. What they couldn't furnish in the realm of cold, hard facts, they more than made up for in colorful anecdotes and gossipy tidbits that fleshed out the inn's history.

Encouraged by her luck, and growing more jubilant with each piece of the puzzle she uncovered, Maggie spent one full day in Fort Myers. At Lee County Courthouse, she paged through endless tax rolls, photocopied remodeling plans and permits in the Department of Inspection, and researched deeds in the County Recorder's office. She talked with heads of every preservation society in the area and paid a visit to all the historical museums she could find listed. After hours spent hunched over countless volumes, her shoulders ached and she was having difficulty convincing her eyes to focus. By the time she returned to Caloosa Key she was hot and bone-weary, but she had in her possession nearly everything Lane had requested, and one or two surprises he wouldn't expect.

Lane.

She'd hardly had time to think of him. He had not called her. She wasn't sure whether that fact could be taken as a good omen or bad, and she wondered how he'd managed with the Site Specialist in Tallahassee. So much would depend on their recommendation. What if they turned down the application? What if Jerry Carlisle could not be convinced? That was still a very real possibility.

Maggie shoved aside the unwelcome thought that Carlisle might reject the idea of saving the inn without weighing the possibilities. All their hard work would surely not be in vain. She could not imagine Lane Stafford investing so much time and energy in a harebrained scheme that might never be given a chance. And a chance was all they needed. Stafford was Carlisle's friend and business associate, obviously someone the millionaire trusted. Lane would make him see the benefit. He had to. He just had to.

*　　*　　*

On the third morning after she and Lane Stafford constructed a plan to save the inn, Maggie slept in, rousing just before eleven o'clock. She had stayed up late the previous night to mark passages in the books she had collected, interesting bits and pieces about the inn's construction she thought Lane should read. When she finally fell into bed, she was sure she would fall asleep instantly. Instead, she tossed and turned restlessly for over an hour before exhaustion overtook her and she drifted off.

She did not sleep soundly.

For the past several nights her dreams had been peppered with endless erotic scenarios, all of them involving Lane Stafford and various stages of undress. Whether it was the nature of her dreams or the warmth of her bedroom that awoke Maggie she could not be sure, but as she kicked away the confining sheet, she wondered how much longer she'd be plagued by these ridiculous fantasies. Since Lane entered her life, every night had been the same—shameless, wanton images of the two of them locked together in passionate embraces, cavorting naked on the beach, in broad daylight yet!, touching each other in places too intimate to be considered remotely acceptable. Maggie wished the vivid pictures would stop. It was both irritating and embarrassing to realize that while she might have a semblance of control over her actions during her waking hours, her subconscious mind was determined to frolic while she slept.

Feeling far from refreshed, Maggie levered herself out of bed and slipped a thin housecoat over her nightgown. The bedroom was too warm, the overhead paddle fan doing no more than circulating hot air. She couldn't smell the salt tang of the gulf, which meant no breeze was stirring. Another day without rain, Maggie predicted, and made a mental reminder to herself to water the garden. She'd neglected it the past two days and the vegetables were sure to be parched.

She heard the soft clatter of dishes coming from the kitchen and wondered if Robbie had managed a decent breakfast on his own. Probably not, and now he'd be searching the cupboards for something to snack on. The boy was always hungry.

She padded on bare feet into the kitchen, raking a hand through her tangled hair and hoping against hope that Robbie had been thoughtful enough to fix a pot of coffee for her. She pulled up short in the doorway when she came face-to-face with Lane Stafford rummaging through the refrigerator. Instinct brought her hand clutching at the neck of her gown, and she wondered if her surprise at finding him here registered on her features.

It did.

Lane gave her a wide grin, his sharp sable gaze focusing on her with annoying familiarity and interest. The sight of him locked her breath in her throat. His well-muscled legs were encased in a pair of faded cut-offs, his chest covered by a colorful Hawaiian print shirt that couldn't conceal the taut play of flesh across his shoulders. To Maggie he looked incredibly sexy and masculine, and she was humiliatingly aware of her own poor appearance—her features still puffy and sleep-filled, the torn lace at the collar of her gown, the wild haystack of her hair swinging free about her face. She wanted to crawl back into bed and never come out. At the very least, could she politely excuse herself now that Lane had noticed her presence in the doorway?

"Good morning," he greeted brightly. "Did you sleep well?"

"No." The memory of her dreams, and their very present subject matter, clutched at her. Maggie could feel the heat rise to her cheeks. She frowned and shook her head, trying to banish cobwebs. "What are you doing here?"

"I came over this morning to talk to you, but since you were still asleep, Rob and I decided to work on a few cages for his menagerie. It was getting a little warm in the garage so I came in here to get a couple of sodas." She watched silently while Lane cracked ice into plastic glasses, refilled the trays, and returned them to the freezer. "He's a good kid. I think we're coming to an understanding of sorts."

"That's wonderful."

He threw her a wry smile and Maggie felt her insides twist.

"You're a slow start in the morning. I knew you would be."

The look she gave him was acid-sweet. "You're not, I suppose?"

"Nope. I hit the ground running. Comes from growing up the youngest. Last one up got the least amount of time in the bathroom." He fished a coffee cup out of the dish drainer. "You need a cup of coffee. Robbie fixed a pot that will grow hair on your chest, but it's drinkable." He poured a cup, spooned in a generous helping of sugar, and held it out to her. When Maggie hesitated, he said, "Look, stop standing in the doorway like a rabbit that's about to be flattened by a speeding car. If it's propriety you're worried about, I promise I won't tell a soul I've seen you in your pajamas. And I'm not going to turn into a lusting maniac at the sight of a little lace and nylon. I've seen plenty of women in their nightclothes."

"I'll bet you have," Maggie shot back sarcastically.

Lane laughed. "I *meant* my mother and four sisters. Will you relax?"

His smile was so warm and friendly, his charm so infectious, that Maggie felt some of the hot jumpiness inside her melt away. She took the coffee from his outstretched hand and sat down at the kitchen table, offering him a smile of thanks over the rim of her cup.

Liar! Lane admonished himself harshly. He *was* in danger of turning into a lust-crazed maniac. After an absence of only two days, the sight of Maggie sent his gut into a backflip. It was all Lane could do to keep from reaching out for her, sliding her hand away from its death-grip on the neck of her gown, and planting gentle kisses along every area of exposed flesh. Dear God, Maggie Rose

James was driving him mad! Tantalizing him no matter what she wore, no matter the time of day. The absurd pleasure he took in just being near her was beginning to grate on him, a familiar torture Lane neither understood nor accepted.

He watched her silently as she sipped coffee, glad that she seemed disinclined to meet his eyes. He wasn't at all sure he could keep the desire he felt for her out of his face. A silence erupted between them, not wholly unpleasant, but Lane knew he should say something, *anything*, to put Maggie at ease. He couldn't do it. Words refused to form as his eyes settled upon the tempting sight of her body, the soft, pink glow of her flesh thinly protected by a few scraps of material. He had never found her more appealing, all sleep-mussed and vulnerable. Beneath a veil of blue nylon he imagined he could see the pale outline of her nipples, envisioned brushing his fingers across the tender swell of her breasts until they responded to his touch with a life of their own.

Desire, hot and potent, threatened to sap all reason, and, giving a sudden push away from the kitchen counter, Lane snatched up the two soda glasses. Clearing his throat, he said, "On second thought, why don't I give you some time to wake up? Rob and I will be finished in about an hour. We can have lunch, and then you and I can sit down and compare notes. Okay?" He did not wait for her response. Using one hip, he pushed the screen door open and disappeared from sight.

Speechless, Maggie frowned after him, wondering what she'd said or done to upset him. One minute the man seemed delighted to see her, the next he couldn't get out of her sight fast enough. Sighing, she rested her face in the palm of one hand. Oh, it was too early to try to figure out that man. Every day she knew Lane Stafford, he became harder to second-guess.

"What do you think?" Lane asked as he held up a newly completed rabbit hutch for Robbie's inspection.

The boy's eyes lit with excitement for just a moment, then settled into mild appreciation. "It's nice," he commented without enthusiasm.

"Nice?" Lane repeated. A frown puckered his brow as he witnessed Robbie's attempt to subdue his interest. The kid was sure hard-headed. He gave the boy a leveling glare. "Listen, pal. This is one heck of a home for a rabbit I've created here. Sort of a penthutch."

Robbie laughed.

He couldn't help himself. He'd tried very hard to keep the barriers erected. All morning he'd done his best to show Lane Stafford he wasn't interested in being his friend. It just wasn't working. After three hours of the man's jokes and stories and word games, Robbie knew he was lost. He enjoyed hearing about exotic places Lane had been to, the tales of growing up in a house with four older sisters. He was smart and funny and he built great hutches. The simple fact of the matter was—Robbie liked the guy. Having Lane Stafford around was like suddenly having a big brother.

Lane watched the boy closely, and he could almost *feel* Maggie's brother shed the last of his restraint. "That's more like it," he said with a thread of laughter in his voice.

They labored in amiable silence over the last hutch together. Lane stretched baling wire over the frame of the cage while Robbie pounded nails. As the boy took aim with the hammer, Lane snatched his hand away. "Hold it. Can I trust you with that thing? I like all my fingers."

"I won't miss. I'm good with a hammer."

"And scissors, too, if I remember correctly."

The boy flushed scarlet. "I'm sorry I did that. Really."

"Does that mean I don't have to worry about you ventilating any more of my clothing?" Lane teased.

Robbie nodded. "I just wanted you to go away. I didn't want you to make Maggie sad."

"I don't want to make Maggie sad, Rob. I like your sister. A lot."

"That's what Tom Hadley said last Christmas."

"Who's Tom Hadley?"

"An off-islander Maggie met at her shop. He got real friendly with her. And then one day he was just gone. He didn't call her anymore." His mouth took on a sullen pout.

"Maybe Maggie didn't want him to call. Did you ever consider that?" Lane asked gently.

"Then how come she cried? Lots of times I'd hear her in the middle of the night. And she missed him, I could tell."

Lane sighed. How did you explain love to a twelve-year-old boy who hadn't discovered girls yet? And just how important *had* this Hadley fellow been in Maggie's life, he wondered with a faint twinge of jealousy. "There are times in a relationship between a man and a woman when they just don't see eye to eye, Rob. Sometimes things don't work out the way we plan."

"Are 'things' working out for *you* and Maggie?"

"Definitely not the way I planned," Lane admitted. "But I'm willing to work at it."

"Maggie likes you."

"That's good to know."

"I guess I like you, too."

"Now there's high praise."

"Just don't make Maggie sad. Okay?" The boy's eyes were anxious.

Lane heard the stress in Robbie's voice. His worry for his sister was a sweet, loving thing to witness in one so young, and Lane wondered just how deeply brother and sister had been affected by Tom Hadley's perfidy.

After surveying the newly built hutches and offering up the appropriate number of ooh's and aah's for their handiwork, Maggie fed the two hungry carpenters a hearty lunch of BLT's and homemade potato salad. Watching the two of them, it was obvious Lane had won the battle for Robbie's friendship. She observed the byplay between them with mixed emotions. The boy was in awe of Lane Stafford, practically hanging on to every word the man spoke. He was sure to be crushed when Lane left Caloosa Key for good and returned to Chicago. She wished there were some way to protect her brother from becoming too enamored with the man.

Ever perceptive, Lane caught her eye and winked, coupling the action with a smile of encouragement. Maggie felt her heart turn over and wondered glumly if it was really her brother who needed protecting.

After coercing a promise of more help from Lane for the following afternoon, Robbie banged out of the house and onto his bike to meet up with friends.

Maggie began removing lunch dishes while Lane wedged leftover potato salad into a plastic container. "You're good with kids," Maggie told him.

He gave her a crooked smile, as though slightly embarrassed. "Yeah, I guess I am."

"You sound surprised."

"I am, a little," he replied with a shrug. "I never thought of myself as much of a family man, but this morning out in the garage . . . It was kind of nice, you know . . . ?" He broke off with a laugh. "Maybe Rob just took pity on me, I don't know."

Maggie wagged a spoon in his direction. "Don't forget that this is the same kid who tried to scissor his way through your wardrobe."

"Believe it or not, he apologized for that little stunt. I was so surprised I almost pounded a nail through my thumb."

Maggie slid dishes into the soapy water. "Lord, there's hope for the boy yet."

"He also gave me permission—in a roundabout way— to take you out."

She went deathly still. "I'm sorry. He's such a kid sometimes. . . ."

"Don't be. Actually, it was nice to have the seal of approval put on our relationship."

"What relationship?" Maggie shot him a sharp look over her shoulder, then instantly wished she'd just ignored his statement.

He licked potato salad off the serving spoon and gave her a look that was secretive, but full of-promise. "The relationship you and I are going to have—if I have anything to say about it. Which I do."

"So do-I," she warned, and went back to washing dishes. "I wouldn't count my chickens before they're hatched if I were you."

Lane made no comment to that, and the noise she made sloshing dishwater covered the sound of his approach behind her. Before Maggie could react, Lane brought his arms around her, forming an effective trap. She jumped in surprise and turned her head to glare at him, but the clever man had maneuvered himself so the scathing look was wasted. "What do you think you're doing?" she demanded.

"Careful. You'll get soapsuds everywhere." He nudged aside the silver webbing of her hair to trail a series of nibbling kisses along the side of Maggie's neck. She gasped, but made no move to stop him. "Need help with the dishes? I'm very . . . experienced."

It was a long moment or two before Maggie could find her voice. "I'm managing fine by myself, thank you."

"Sure you don't want my services?" Lane purred with a playful huskiness, then nipped at the soft shell of her ear.

Over a shiver of delight Maggie, returned briskly, "Quite sure." She lifted the soapy sponge from the sink, aiming where she was certain Lane's face would be, and was delighted to hear his sputtering oath as the soggy missive found its target. "You *could* sponge off the table for me if you're so determined to be helpful," she said sweetly.

"My pleasure," Lane choked out, and his arms fell away.

Gradually Maggie's heart settled back into a normal rhythm.

"You haven't asked me how my visit to Tallahassee went."

Wiping her hands on a dish towel, Maggie lifted one shoulder. "I guess I was afraid to hear the outcome."

"You shouldn't be. It went very well. I think there's a good chance the board will approve an application if we can convince Jerry it's worth the effort."

"Honestly?"

He nodded encouragement. "Honestly. I spent most of yesterday with a firm here in Florida that specializes in historic preservation. After I've determined the structural integrity of the inn, we'll be able to work up cost estimates. One problem we might have is getting the material we need shipped out here. But I'm working on that. Now, what have *you* got to show me?"

With all the pride of a first-time parent, Maggie trotted out her collection of photographs, books, and documents for Lane's perusal. He showed obvious surprise at how much information she'd been able to garner, and complimented her on her tenacity. She sat quietly while he leafed slowly through the material, feeling ridiculously pleased when he offered her an occasional smile or appreciative comment.

When he finished studying the material spread before him, Lane leaned back in his chair and favored her with a broad grin. "This is good. Once we get everything in date order, we'll have almost the entire history of that place at our fingertips. You'd make a great Sherlock Holmes, Maggie James."

"Ha!" she laughed with smug satisfaction. "Better. Even Holmes would have had a hard time laying his hands on this!" From behind her back Maggie produced a scrolled parchment, wagging it back and forth in the air like a victorious relay runner waving his baton. "Ta-dah!"

Lane knew what it was instantly and shot forward in his seat to capture it. "My God, the original floor plans!"

"Yep."

With an almost loving reverence he spread the ancient document upon the table. "Fantastic," he murmured.

"It's a little water-damaged in this corner. See. And you'd need a microscope to decipher some of the wording, but I think it's the genuine article."

"Where did you get it?"

"Our own library. Mrs. Harrison was helping me go through some books when she remembered coming across a box of old blueprints in one of the storage rooms; a lot of things had been used for the bicentennial display. We had to sift through a bunch of miscellaneous junk before we found it, and at first I was afraid to pick it up for fear it would disintegrate in my hands. Actually, it looks pretty sturdy, considering."

"That's because it's printed on sheepskin. Common practice back then." He squinted down at the far right corner. "My God, look at this. It's the original architect's signature. Dated, too."

Maggie leaned forward until their noses were almost touching. "Williamson Allen Stewart," she read. "Eighteen sixty-nine. Do you recognize the name?"

"No. We'll have to find out more about him if we can." He raised his head and gave her a penetrating look. "Maggie, do you know what this means?"

"More work at the library?"

"It means, we have a very good chance of being able to re-create the exact same structure standing on that property over *one hundred years ago!* This is terrific!"

He reached out with both hands and captured her face, drawing her toward him to give her a swift kiss. It happened so quickly that Maggie had no time to react, and just as quickly, it was over. Maggie smiled at him, trying hard not to give the kiss too much importance. Lane was excited and he was just expressing that excitement, Maggie told herself sternly. *Make your heart settle down, girl.*

More than a little flustered, she tried to turn her attention back to the matter at hand. "You think Carlisle will go for the idea, don't you?" she asked on a shaky breath.

"I think he'd be a fool *not* to," Lane reassured her. He reached out to stroke one finger across Maggie's downy cheek. "You let me worry about Jerry. Okay?"

She nodded agreement, but could not meet the sudden intensity of his gaze. "When will you discuss it with him?"

"We have a meeting scheduled for the eleventh."

A little over a week away. She told herself his leaving was inevitable. Lane had been a part of her world for such a short time, what possible difference could his absence make in her life? Yet the answer to that question was not one Maggie cared to evaluate too deeply.

Lane watched the shadow touch her face and wondered if Maggie was as aware of time slipping away from them as he was. The thought of leaving seemed suddenly unthinkable.

He pushed away from the table, a sudden movement. "Enough homework for now," he proclaimed brightly. "Do you realize that I'm supposed to be on a vacation of sorts? Here I am surrounded by water and I haven't been swimming yet. What do you say we check out the ocean?"

"Gulf," she corrected.

"Same thing."

"Not to Floridians it's not," she laughed, then added in a teasing voice, "Can you swim?"

Lane looked offended. "My dear, if I were any more adept in the water, I'd grow gills. And even if I wasn't, I'd lie. This may be my only chance."

"Only chance for what?"

He rubbed his palms together and gave her his most menacing look. "To see that lovely body of yours in a skimpy bikini."

A smile playing on her lips, Maggie replied, "Boy, are *you* in for a big disappointment."

* * *

He wasn't, although Maggie seemed to have done her best to dampen his interest.

They met on the beach in front of Banyon House, the only bathers in sight. Lane had gone back to the inn apartment to change into boxer trunks that molded to his admirable physique with a sexiness that brought Maggie's heart to a standstill. Watching him approach was pure pleasure; he was so lean and fit, it was almost a sin to cover a body like that with clothes, Maggie mused, then scolded herself sharply for such licentious wanderings.

As he drew closer, she saw him frown at her attire. The head-to-toe coverup she wore was obviously not what the man expected or wanted to see. Maggie concealed a secret grin of amusement.

"You're not going to swim in that, are you?" Lane demanded to know.

"Of course not. When you're out of the water the sun can be pretty brutal, although I guess I don't need to tell you that. Anyway, I'm not going to burn just so you can get an eyeful."

"Spoilsport!"

When Lane turned away from her to spread his towel on the sand, Maggie shrugged out of her robe and ran down to the water. She heard Lane's shout behind her, but ignored it and dove in.

The gulf was salty but cool, with no breeze to ruffle its glasslike surface. It felt so good against the heat of Maggie's skin. She'd had little time lately to indulge herself with a swim, and she realized suddenly how much she'd missed it. Touching sandy bottom, Maggie pushed upward, parting the water with a small splash and flinging her hair out of her eyes.

She turned, squinting against the harsh glare of the sun to find her companion. Lane was waist-deep, coming toward her with the slow, steady stride of someone caught in unfamiliar territory and not liking it one bit.

"Come on," Maggie called. "I thought you said you could swim."

"I can."

"Then prove it."

"In a minute. Let me get used to the water first."

"It's not cold. Honestly, Lane, sometimes you're such a Yankee."

He shook his fist playfully in her direction. "When I catch up to you, I'm going to paddle your little Rebel butt for that remark."

"Have to catch me first," Maggie taunted.

"I will."

"Big talk for a grown man who can't swim."

She was sure he couldn't, at least not nearly well enough to keep up with her. He seemed uncomfortable and disinclined to venture out over his head. Maggie was disappointed; she'd hoped to swim with someone who'd offer a bit of a challenge to her own ability in the water. Still, there was a small part of her that found this sudden superiority over Lane a heady thrill and couldn't resist flaunting it. It was delightful to have the upper hand for a change.

The mood between them was light and frisky. "Come on, Poseidon," Maggie urged with playful exasperation. "You can still touch out here. I promise to hold you up if you start to go under."

Lane threw her a menacing look, but did not budge.

With sudden mischievousness Maggie would never have suspected herself capable of, she untied the halter top of her modest two-piece suit and waved it over her head. "Look!" she called. "You wanted to see my suit. Here it is. Why don't you swim out here for a closer peek?"

Lane's eyes widened in surprise and he went still. "Maggie James, what the hell do you think you're doing?"

The shock in his voice evoked a watery giggle from her. She'd never have been so brazen, so daring if she thought he had the remotest chance of reaching her, but it was embarrassingly obvious that she could swim circles around the poor man. And while her behavior was a surprise to Maggie, she took a small, strange pleasure in seeing Lane so astonished. Nice to see *him* set back on his heels for a change.

She tossed an insolent look in Lane's direction, then slid beneath the water, striking out away from him. She resurfaced twenty feet from her original spot, gulped air, and continued to swim, cutting through the water with powerful, economical strokes that had carried her through twenty years of island living. Exhilarated and confident, she never once looked back at Lane, but she smiled as her mind formed a picture of him watching her with quiet awe, maybe just the tiniest bit annoyed by her expertise in the water.

She supposed it wasn't really fair of her to tease him so, and certainly he was being a good sport about it. It wasn't his fault he was such a landlubber. He'd taken her jabs without complaint, but she didn't want to rely on Lane's good nature too much longer.

But about the time Maggie had made up her mind to stop swimming, pull her top back on and return meekly to Lane's side, she felt such a strong sudden pull upon her ankle that she sucked water and lost her hold on her suit top. She fumbled to get her feet under her, relieved to find the water was only shoulder-deep. Coughing up seawater and shaking her hair away from her face, Maggie made a quick, silent prayer that she hadn't had the misfortune to run into a small shark, then wished she had when she opened her eyes to find Lane Stafford planted firmly in front of her.

"Lose something?" he inquired mildly, dangling her suit top in one hand. He wasn't even breathing hard, and the grin on his face made Maggie's hand itch to slap.

"You can swim," she accused hotly.

"I told you I could."

"I thought—"

"I know what you thought, and this just serves you right for being such a tease."

Even grudgingly, she could admit to herself he was

right. She'd taunted him unforgivably and he'd reacted as any normal healthy male would.

"All right, I'm sorry," Maggie apologized quickly, then added with a sheepish grin, "Lord, you scared the devil out of me when you grabbed my ankle. I thought I'd stumbled onto a feeding shark."

"The danger's not over yet," he responded pleasantly, but there was a huskiness in his voice that made Maggie frown. The blood in her veins seemed to bubble nervously as she witnessed his eyes darken with desire.

"Lane . . ."

"What?"

"Give me my suit."

"Why? You're the one who was so anxious for me to see it that you were waving it around like a flag on the Fourth of July."

"That was before I knew you could swim."

"Ignorance is no excuse. Don't play games, little girl, if you're not prepared to lose."

Perverse of him not to make this easy for her. "You're a gentleman," she reminded patiently.

He gave her a severe look. "Who said such a thing?"

"You did. The other night when you walked me back from the inn."

As Lane shook his head, water danced down his neck. "Nope. That only applies to walking women home after dark. A gentleman who fails to take advantage of a . . . compromising situation such as this isn't a gentleman. He's a fool."

Disconcerted, she glanced down, wondering how much longer she could keep her breasts covered. Maggie had never considered them to be large, but now they seemed determined to bob up to the surface like two enormous coconuts heading for the Gulf Stream. She bit her lip in frustration, searching for a dignified way out of this ridiculous jam.

After a moment, Lane himself provided the solution, though Maggie did not find it much to her liking. "I'll tell you what," he sighed. "I'm not an unreasonable man. We'll make a deal—a trade. I'll give you back your top and you give me something of yours."

Maggie's eyebrows shot upward suspiciously. "Like what?"

"Well, let's see," Lane mused, as though the transaction required a great deal of serious consideration. Then with sudden inspiration: "I know! How about a kiss? Sort of a thank-you for me not taking advantage of the obvious."

"Think of something else."

Lane's mouth twisted into a wicked grin of pleasure. "I like *this* solution."

"No."

"Suit yourself." He shrugged indifferently and made no further move.

"I don't really need my top," she bluffed desperately. "My robe's on the beach."

His dark gaze sparkled and genuine amusement quirked his mouth. "Want to bet which one of us could reach it first?"

Ten minutes ago she might have played the odds. She was fast and she was good, but was it enough to beat Lane? Never much of a gambler, Maggie wasn't sure she could afford to take the chance. She could picture herself lunging out of the water, making a mad dash for the cottage, and the humiliating vision made her want to grind her teeth in frustration. The beach might be deserted, with no one to witness her folly, but that didn't make the idea any more palatable. If it hadn't been almost impossible for her to do so in four feet of water, Maggie would have stamped one foot in anger.

"You are a horrible man!" she blazed.

Lane seemed unperturbed by the accusation. Noting the sudden mulish tilt of her chin, he asked, "Are your kisses so valuable that you can't spare even *one?* I think it's a pretty small price to pay considering the pleasure I'm giving up." He let his eyes rove meaningfully over her body.

The water was crystal-clear and there wasn't much he couldn't see.

"All right," Maggie capitulated suddenly.

She didn't feel like arguing anymore. The embarrassment of her situation hadn't diminished and the sun was beginning to feel uncomfortable on the tops of her shoulders. Better to get it over with. One little kiss would hardly turn her into some sort of . . . of love slave. Lane was going to be sadly mistaken if he thought to elicit some sort of response from her against her will. She knew him well enough now to guess he wouldn't be happy with a sisterly peck, but if he persisted and got too fresh—well, Maggie had been taught the right places to strike a man to dampen his ardor.

Satisfied with her answer, Lane placed the suit upon her outstretched palm and Maggie turned away from him to slide her arms into it.

"Would you like me to tie it for you?" he offered, enjoying the sight of her gently curved bare back.

"No, thank you." she responded primly.

She faced him calmly, her color still high but her spirit determined not to receive Lane's punishment like a coward. After splashing cooling water along her burning cheeks, Maggie's gaze met his levelly and her chin jutted upward. "Okay," she acquiesced reluctantly. "But I'm warning you. No funny stuff."

Her threat was so appealingly childlike, Lane could scarcely resist the temptation to laugh aloud. And when she closed her eyes and offered up her lips like a sacrificial lamb, it was all he could do to contain his mirth. Not that he didn't want to kiss her—Lord, he couldn't wait.

From the moment she'd hit the water he'd been mesmerized by the sight of her, enchanted by her sleek, powerful movements as she sliced through the water. Lane had enjoyed one enticing glimpse of her body before she'd dived, and the sight of Maggie's supple curves were enough to set his blood to pounding. She seemed beautifully proportioned, with the smooth, muscled grace of an

Olympic swimmer. Watching her arms and legs scissor through the waves, Maggie seemed longer, leaner, more flawlessly built than any woman he'd ever met. The soft, pampered females he dated in Chicago seemed to pale in comparison.

He glanced down at her features, fighting the desire to take what she offered in spite of her resentment. Oh, yes, he wanted to kiss her. He wanted more than *that*. He wanted to lift Maggie out of the sea and into his arms, carry her across the short lawn leading to the cottage, and lay her upon her bed. Make love to her with the thrilling sweetness of newly discovered passion. But how was the joy of that discovery to be savored when Maggie would come to him with all the anticipation of a convict meeting his executioners? Where was the satisfaction in that?

Maggie still waited patiently for his touch, the dignified victim. With a sound that was part amusement, part regret, Lane brushed his lips to hers in a kiss the most inexperienced teenager would surely have labeled unexciting. He didn't even bother to gather Maggie into his arms, so unemotional was the contact.

Maggie's eyes flew open, their pale aquamarine depths registering surprise and confusion. A brotherly touch was certainly not what she'd steeled herself for, and her fluttering nerves sank like a stone, leaving her feeling weak and oddly dissatisfied.

Lane was turning away from her, and Maggie latched on to his arm with suddenness that sent a splash of water over them. "Lane . . ."

"What?"

"Would you please tell me what that was supposed to be?"

He looked genuinely surprised by her reaction. "A kiss. You kept your part of the bargain."

"But . . ."

He splashed toward shore, eating up the distance in long, easy strides that sent a small wake veeing out behind him. Maggie hurried after him, more confused than ever and experiencing a sudden irrational anger toward the man. How dare he lead her on to expect something and then calmly snatch it away!

SEVEN

She caught up to him when they were both thigh-deep in water, recapturing his arm to make him turn and face her. "You are the most exasperating man. I don't understand you at all."

Lane cocked an eyebrow at her. "I beg your pardon?"

Maggie stared. "Did I miss something here? I thought you just spent the last few minutes twisting my arm to get me to kiss you. Then when I agree, you're not interested."

"I thought you didn't want to kiss me."

"I didn't!"

"But now you do."

"I don't!"

"Then what's the problem?"

Maggie looked chagrined. "I'm not sure. You're confusing me."

As Lane shrugged, droplets of saltwater trickled down his chest. Maggie's eyes were drawn to the erratic pattern they wove as the beads skipped through the short sable hairs matting his upper torso. "Look, Maggie, it's pretty simple, as I see it," he said with a sigh. "I've been doing a lot of flirting with you since I came here, some of which has been met with reluctance or even open hostility. I'm mature enough to accept that there are times when my many charms just don't do anything for a woman.'' As though this ill-devised spurt of honesty didn't set well, he amended, ''Most of the time it does, mind you, but not always. Anyway, if it just doesn't click for you, I'll be damned if I'm going to keep trying to get blood out of a stone.''

''What's that supposed to mean?'' Maggie snapped.

''It means, when I want to kiss a woman, I want someone who's going to be receptive to me. Willing to take a chance on what I have to offer. I don't want to waste my time thawing out some frozen little ice princess.''

Maggie's eyes widened at his blunt words as the barb found a home. ''I am *not* an ice princess!'' she protested hotly. ''I like kissing as much as the next person.''

Lane gave her a skeptical look. ''Really? Well, you couldn't prove it by me. The Christians met the lions with more enthusiasm than you've just shown.''

Furious now, her pride stinging, Maggie lashed out. ''Why, you overbearing, egotistical—''

''What's the matter? Does the truth hurt?''

''Oh!''

Her hand stretched to make contact with his face, but Lane was prepared and captured her wrist easily. Jerking her body close to his, he gave her a fierce, taunting look. ''Not that way, little ice princess. Prove to me what a woman you can be.''

''You're the vilest human being—'' Maggie spat.

Lane wouldn't let up and he wouldn't let go. Maggie's breath was coming quickly now, her breasts heaving against his chest. Her face was flushed with anger and the look she gave him was murderous. To Lane she had never looked more beautiful. ''So prove me wrong, Maggie Rose,'' Lane challenged mildly. ''Show me you can be more than just a sacrificial virgin.''

''I hate you!''

''Have you ever been a woman, Maggie? Or have you been tucked away on this godforsaken sandbar so long, you've had all the life drained out of you? I want—''

She stilled his vicious tongue in the only way she could, and, without realizing it, the only way he wanted her to. With a forcefulness that rammed his teeth against the inside of his lip, she mashed her lips to his. Her mouth twisted upon his angrily, forcing him to acknowledge her, her fury at Lane so great that she forgot to be appalled by her own aggressiveness. She tossed her pride aside and arched toward him determinedly. There was no skill involved in her assault, and certainly no love—only a savage, insane desire to see Lane proved wrong.

At last she pulled away from him, her lips bruised a deep red but the light of triumph in the smoky-blue depths of her eyes. "Is that enough response for you, Don Juan?" Maggie demanded to know, the defiance in her voice shaded with an annoying sliver of shakiness.

For a man who'd just been attacked by an angry hoyden bent on bestowing proof of her womanliness, Lane looked irritatingly unperturbed. His lips, as swollen as Maggie's own, nevertheless stretched into a wry smile. "It's a beginning, sweetheart. Now let me teach you how to enjoy it."

He reached for her, and she was too startled to fight him. Her limbs were still shaking with the delayed reaction of her anger and brazen action to do more than make a token resistance. Where her lips had crashed against his with brutal force, his took hers gently, a warm, sweet pressure that was pleasant but undemanding.

Maggie was certain she could remain unmoved by Lane's touch. After all, she wasn't a complete novice at this sort of thing; she'd been kissed before. Tom Hadley had schooled her well in the art of intimacy, and she wasn't about to lose her head.

He pulled her closer, and it was a shock to feel his bare flesh against her, the scratch of saltwater drying upon their skin, the hard ridges of his ribs, the short, coarse hair covering Lane's chest prickling the tops of her breasts, along her bared midriff. His free hand found her buttock and Maggie stiffened; for one crazy moment she feared he meant to strip the bathing suit bottom from her body. A bubble of panic surfaced, then burst as he seemed content to merely mold her form closer to his.

Giving her no time to summon control, his lips became more insistent, branding her mouth with a searing hunger that begged sustenance. The tingling pleasure she'd felt earlier melted into a pool of hot desire, turning her limbs to liquid. She tasted saltwater and the iron bite of blood, and a peculiar sweetness she couldn't identify and wasn't prepared for.

Startled, she jerked her head back to break the contact, scrambling to draw breath. "That's enough . . ." she gasped.

He didn't listen, of course. With practiced skill, his lips sought the column of her throat, nibbling at its soft warmth, tracing his tongue along its salty sweetness until she moaned with pleasure at such exquisite torture. He didn't stop there, damn him. Lower and lower his mouth went, lingering on the pulse pounding at the base of her neck, scattering kisses across the hard line of her collarbone, stroking the tops of her breasts with his nimble tongue.

When Lane pushed aside the thin material of her bathing suit to find the nipple of one breast, Maggie knew she was lost.

His lips skimmed across it playfully, and it hardened with embarrassing quickness. Useless to pretend sudden exposure to the cool breeze had brought it to life! With an eager tug, he nipped and suckled its satiny peak, sending shock waves careening throughout Maggie's body. Unable to resist Lane's expert handling, she uttered a gasp of guilty excitement, the movement swelling her breast within his mouth. Her response pleased him; she could feel his lips stretching into a smile against her flesh. Soon he would find a way to divest her of her suit entirely, clever man, and the thought was not altogether undesirable. She was throbbing with anticipation, weak with the erotic ache of unfulfilled lust and frustrating self-denial.

This was her dream lover turned into a beautiful reality; pointless to deny this was what she had wanted from the very beginning.

Lane's intuitiveness never ceased to amaze her. He seemed to sense the exact moment she came to terms with her own surrender. His lips stopped punishing her flesh and he straightened to regard her warmly. She was pleased to see Lane himself was not totally unaffected. His face was flushed and he looked almost as dazed as she felt.

"I want you, Maggie Rose," he murmured huskily. "For days I've wanted you . . ." He brought his hands up to capture each side of her face, and she was surprised to feel the slight trembling of his fingers. His warm brown eyes swept her features, full of frustrated longing. "No more games," he said, his voice softly textured with aching desire. "Tell me. What do *you* want, Maggie?"

Her teeth sank into her lower lip and her eyes dropped. Stating her innermost thoughts was not something Maggie did well or often. "I . . . I don't know what I want, Lane. I'm not very good at this."

"Maggie, look at me," Lane urged with sympathetic tenderness, and she did. "I'll never do anything to hurt you, sweetheart. You know that, don't you?"

"I think so," she sighed. "I guess I'm just scared."

He laughed, a low, throaty caress. "Sweetheart, believe it or not, so am I. I've never spent so much time trying to make a woman like me. My ego's taken one hell of a beating."

"I like you," Maggie reassured him with a shy smile.

Lane's brow tipped upward. "I was hoping for a bit more than *that*. And I think we've just established that there's more here than just a casual friendship. The question is, what should we do about it?"

"What would you *like* to do about it?" Maggie whispered, her cheeks stained crimson. She cleared her throat. "I mean, I'm a big girl. I'm not adverse to a . . . a . . ." She broke off, searching for the right word. "Affair" sounded too sophisticated, "night of passion" too melodramatic. "Fling" seemed awfully nonchalant, though that was probably closer to the truth. She settled for something less flamboyant. ". . . relationship." She was somewhat shocked by her own boldness. Prim and proper Maggie Rose James would never have approved, but the liquid warmth in Lane's eyes and his thumbs gently caressing the hollows of her cheeks had driven away all good reasons for cautiousness.

A regretful smile lingered at the corners of Lane's mouth. He knew what that admission had cost her and would never have anticipated her frightened candor could touch him so. "Maggie," he said wearily, "one day soon all the talk will be over and there we'll be, just the two of us. Right now," he grimaced, "we've got company."

Lane's hands slipped away from her and he tilted his head toward shore to indicate a lone figure hurrying toward them across the lawn.

Robbie.

Maggie jerked away from Lane quickly, struggling to put distance between them. Her efforts were almost comically inept against the dragging pull of the gulf as she churned sand and sea water.

Lane steadied her with a hand upon her elbow and leaned close to whisper in her ear, "Relax. The boy didn't see anything."

"You don't know that," she hissed back at him. "He's my little brother, for heaven's sake!"

Shaking his head slowly, Lane began to laugh, and Maggie threw him a scathing look. "Try to look like we've been swimming."

"We *have* been swimming."

"You know what I mean."

She waved at her brother and acted so heartily glad to see him that the boy would have to be the most thick-headed idiot not to suspect his sister was up to something. They met on the sand, Maggie chattering away like a guilty schoolgirl caught in the backseat of her boyfriend's car. Lane intercepted Robbie's look of suspicion. The boy was curious, but there was no malice in his face, thank God. As if to say he had no idea what had gotten into Maggie, Lane offered her brother a minute shrug.

Inwardly, he cursed the unfortunate timing of Robbie's appearance and was disappointed to witness the resurgency of Maggie's shy alterego. Once he'd broken through her resistance, he'd hoped the walls wouldn't be so easily reerected. Covertly, he watched her fiddle nervously with one of the string ties of her bikini bottom, wondering if she was already regretting her candidness of only a moment ago. Probably.

His gaze settled on the gentle curve of Maggie's hip where her fingers were plucking unconsciously at the knot there. The bottom of her modest bikini had slipped just a fraction, revealing a thin line of untanned flesh. He swallowed hard. It didn't pay to think of what lay beneath that tiny scrap of blue fabric, the creamy softness of her womanhood almost within his grasp.

Oh, Rob, my friend, why couldn't you have joined us just one hour later?

Yet in spite of the frustration Lane felt, there was an odd exhilaration within him as well. As though a door previously closed to him had suddenly swung wide of its own accord, revealing a hidden treasure far beyond his wildest imaginings. He felt the delirious gaiety of a child on Christmas morning, and, to his own dismay, no smug satisfaction at the thought of crumbling Maggie's hard resolve; no pampering of an inflated male ego on the verge of sexual conquest. Only a delightful rippling pleasure to know that soon, very soon, he would come to know this charmingly unique creature in the most intimate of ways.

The neck wouldn't come out right. No matter how many times Maggie reshaped the clay, it was either too long or too short. She restudied the photographs and sketches she had made of the blue heron with a critical eye, wishing she could imbue her sculpture with the same life and sense of grace she'd managed to capture on film. But an hour later Maggie had angrily pounded the clay into a hopeless muddle. It was no use. The heron refused to become a heron and insisted on resembling a flamingo.

Disgusted, Maggie spun away from her worktable and fished a pitcher of iced tea out of the archaic refrigerator. The shop was warm in spite of the sputtering hum of the air conditioner, a concession she usually reserved for tourist season.

Although vacationers liked to escape the Florida heat by browsing the island shops, it was unlikely that even the most adventurous visitor would be out today. Over the rim of her glass, Maggie peered out the front window. The streets were deserted, the few short blocks of Caloosa Key almost a ghost town. With the heat wave still punishing the state, most of the island's establishments had not bothered to open their doors.

So why had she insisted on spending the hottest part of the afternoon in her craft shop? Waiting for some nonexistent tourist to seek refuge in her tiny establishment? Wasting countless hours struggling to create a simple sculpture that stubbornly refused to shape? Why *had* she bothered?

Because, Maggie admitted bitterly to herself, *you are the world's biggest coward, that's why*. She was a spineless jellyfish who didn't have the nerve to face a man after she'd been foolish enough to confess an interest in him. Interest? Hah! That was a bit of an understatement. She'd practically *begged* him to take her to bed!

Her cheeks *still* burned to think of the brazen admission she'd made to Lane. Even if by some miracle he'd been too dense to understand her words, the man couldn't possibly have misinterpreted her response to that kiss. That horribly wonderful kiss that had seared away the last of her good sense and left her shaking with raw desire—more importantly, had left her vulnerably exposed to Lane's expert handling. She could still feel the warmth of his fingers tripping along the knobs of her spine, the sudden chill of his breath upon her hot flesh, the delicious, frightening sensuality of the short hairs pelting his upper thighs brushing lightly between her legs, touching the naked flesh there with a compelling urgency. . . .

The obvious contradiction of her own thoughts annoyed Maggie and she pressed the iced-tea glass to her cheeks, wishing the cool beads of moisture clinging to the outside of the vessel could somehow douse the heat within her.

Yesterday's folly had brought her absurd pleasure and Maggie still couldn't put the memory of Lane's touch from her mind.

The problem was, she was afraid to face him now. Afraid of what she'd read in his features, or worse, the hunger he might glimpse in hers. Lane was a sexually sophisticated man of the world. Behaving like an imbecile, wearing her heart on her sleeve in the most immature, schoolgirl fashion would surely prove fatal with a man like that.

The bell over the front door jangled and Maggie opened her eyes to see Robbie entering, closely followed by Lane, the last person on earth she wanted to see. They were both dressed casually in shorts and T-shirts, and it occurred to Maggie that Lane was looking more and more like a native islander. The unfortunate redness of his sunburn was fading into a warm brown, deepening his eyes to polished mahogany.

She looked away quickly before she had to meet those eyes, and unconsciously moved to put the worktable between them.

"Hi. How's it goin'?" Robbie greeted.

"Great," she replied brightly. Lane was studying the misshapen mass of clay upon the center of her sculpting table. Maggie caught his frown and amended, "Well, not great, really, but I'm making progress."

Ever observant, Robbie glanced around the shop at the various pieces displayed upon the shelves. "Doesn't look like you've sold much since the last time I was in here."

"I didn't expect to do a lot of business today."

She watched Lane wander about the room. He inspected

her work with leisurely interest, occasionally lifting a piece for a closer look.

"Then why did you bother to come in?" Robbie persisted.

"Because the season will be here before we know it, Robbie," she explained, trying to keep annoyance from coloring her voice. "I can't wait until the last minute to get things ready."

The boy frowned at that response. Tourist season was months away; it didn't make sense to open up the shop on one of the hottest days of the year. In Robbie's opinion, his sister was acting pretty goofy. But as touchy as she'd been lately, he refrained from telling her so.

"This is beautiful," Lane interjected from across the room, and Maggie glanced his way quickly. He held one of her more intricate pieces in his hands, a snowy egret amongst tall grass. "It almost looks alive."

"Thank you," she responded quietly. "I wasn't really that pleased with it. The legs didn't quite come out the way they should have."

Robbie looked sharply at his sister, absolutely sure now that Maggie was going soft in her head. She loved that piece! When she had finished it, she'd immediately proclaimed that stupid bird the best thing she'd ever done. So why was she trying to cut it down?

"On the contrary," Lane was saying. "The legs are just right. Long and graceful, but powerful enough to support the body." His hands roamed over the clay almost reverently, like a blind man committing each twist and turn to memory.

Maggie's breath quickened. She was struck by the oddest notion that Lane's warm, tender touch no longer brushed along the hard, cold lines of the sculpture, but along *her* flesh instead, his skilled fingers caressing not an inanimate work of art but *her* body with an unsettling sensuality. A tiny portion of her mind warned Maggie that such an idea was foolish and fanciful, a byproduct of an unattractive wantonness she should strive mightily to evict from herself. Unfortunately, her body wasn't getting the message. Her stomach quivered reflexively and she couldn't seem to find her voice.

"And look at the neck," Lane pressed in a silky tone. To Maggie, his voice seemed almost mesmerizing. "Slender but delicately arched. I like the way it curves gently, so that it seems to flow into the body in one long, smooth line. Lovely."

"I'm sure you've seen better," Maggie finally stammered out. "You're just . . . being kind."

"Not at all," Lane replied, setting the sculpture carefully back upon the shelf. He gave her a direct look, and their eyes met in a brief moment of communion. "I meant every word."

"But then, you're not really that familiar with the island wildlife, are you?" Maggie countered, smoothly emphatic. "Perhaps you've mistaken that piece for something else."

He smiled slightly, but continued to fix her with an unswerving stare that knifed through her composure. "I don't think so. At any rate, I know what I like."

Watching with more than a little confusion etched upon his young features, Robbie thought the man was sure making a big fuss over a simple lump of clay. He caught Maggie shifting uncomfortably on her stool and suspected his sister was embarrassed by such high praise.

There followed a silence so odd and tension-filled that even Robbie's youthful inexperience could not prevent him from misreading it. Time moved heavily, and he wondered if Lane and Maggie were even aware he was standing there, his features pinched with uncertainty. Losing patience with two adults who didn't seem to be able to converse in anything but riddles, Robbie cleared his throat loudly, and with boyish candor said, "If you like it that much, why don't you buy it? Everything in here is for sale, isn't it, Mag?"

His sister sputtered a quick denial, and for some reason, Lane found the idea amusing. He laughed heartily and shook his head. "Rob, there are some things you just can't put a price on."

That didn't make much sense, especially when the bird Lane was admiring had a little price tag openly attached to one foot, but Robbie wasn't about to mention that fact. Maybe the guy couldn't afford it or was just being nice, like his sister said. He'd learned a long time ago that adults did and said a lot of things they didn't really mean. He gave up trying to figure out either of them and subsided into sulky silence.

"Rob and I came into town to pick up a few things at the market. I thought *I* could fix lunch for a change. How soon before you'll be finished here?"

"Actually, I wasn't going to take a lunch break."

Lane frowned. "That's not good for creativity. You need to eat. Besides, I make a pretty mean chef's salad."

Maggie wet her lips nervously, but she was determined. "I'm *not* hungry. And I'm old enough to know if I need to eat," she said, her voice holding such a terse edge that Robbie glanced at her in surprise.

Lane didn't seem offended. But without ever taking his eyes off Maggie's face, he said in a soft, distant tone, "Rob, would you be a sport and go over to the market? Pick out some good-looking vegetables for our salad. I'll be along in a minute."

Robbie obeyed instantly, and Maggie watched him go with more than a little regret. The boy wasn't much protection, but at least his presence kept Lane at bay. With a mulish set to her jaw, she ignored the man she least wanted to be alone with and began cleaning her sculpting tools.

As soon as the door banged shut behind Robbie, Lane got right to the point. "Why are you avoiding me?"

"I'm not."

"Then close this place up for the day."

"That's very easy for you to say. Unfortunately, I have a living to make."

"And how many things have you sold today?"

She reddened, not willing to offer up a lie, especially not such a feeble one. "That's not the point," she hedged.

"Then kindly tell me what is."

His clipped, patient tone grated, and Maggie found refuge in anger. "I don't have to justify my actions to you. I can do as I damned well please."

"*Exactly* as you please. You don't owe me a thing. You also don't have to hide out in town just to keep from running into me."

His perceptiveness only increased her irritation, and with a sudden jerk, she whirled to face him. She knew her cheeks would seem like twin flags of color, but Maggie was determined to exhibit a little backbone at last. "I'm not hiding out. I have a legitimate business to run."

"Maggie, yesterday—"

"Yesterday was a mistake," she snapped. "I got carried away with the moment. I said things . . ." she could feel herself flushing a deeper crimson, ". . . I mean . . . I may have led you to believe . . ." She stopped, unsure how to proceed and hating herself for her uncertainty.

"Damn you, Maggie James," Lane growled sharply, and she blinked at him in surprise, dismayed at the glint of unexpected anger she glimpsed in the man's eyes. "Don't *ever* apologize for having a woman's feelings. Be scared if you want. Be confused. But don't resent the fact that you can *feel* something for another human being."

Maggie shook her head. "You don't understand."

"I understand a lot more than you think," he replied simply.

There was a long moment of silence. Lane wandered to the display shelf where the egret he'd previously admired sat. Although he didn't lift it, his fingers trailed over the clay slowly, with idle interest. Maggie suspected that Lane was struggling to bring his anger under control. He did not look at her, but continued to stare out the front window.

She waited.

"I was right about your work," he said, at last. "It's extraordinary. The strangest part is that you seem to be able to endow your art with a sense of freedom you won't allow yourself."

Maggie gasped. "How dare you! I don't appreciate your dime-store psychology—"

Lane's head swiveled and his eyes pierced hers. "And *I* resent being lumped into the same category with past lovers like Tom What's-his-name."

Lane couldn't have rendered Maggie more speechless if he had slapped her. She felt the color drain from her face.

One look at her stricken countenance and Lane's anger fled.

He would not have hurt Maggie for the world, yet he had managed to do just that by piercing her fragile defenses with the reminder of past folly. He cursed the quick cruelty of his tongue and wondered how this slight, naive creature could bring out the best *and* worst in him all at the same time. She was infuriating. Sweet. Stubborn. Her mistrust of men in general, and him in particular, annoyed Lane to distraction, yet the soft vulnerability of her mouth could set his heart to pounding like a green kid on his first date. She intrigued and excited him, and glancing at Maggie's pale features, her crystalline blue eyes filled with remembered pain, the tender contours of her full lips stretched into a twisting tightness, Lane suspected he was dangerously close to falling in love with her.

Uncomfortable with that thought, and ashamed of the hurt he had caused, he looked away. "I'm sorry," he said softly. "You're right. I have no business lecturing you."

"What do you know about Tom Hadley?" The thread of stunned surprise was in her voice.

It was more an accusation than a question. Lane weighed his response carefully, suddenly aware there was more than he'd expected. Watching the girl's face, Lane knew the broken relationship had been *very* serious, at least from Maggie's point of view, creating a devastating hurt within her. There was pain in the bright-blue depths of her eyes, but humiliation as well, so much more than the slight embarrassment talk of past loves could create. He wondered what monstrous discovery Maggie had made in her relationship with this Hadley fellow. What had he done to put such bleak disillusionment in her eyes? Lane's gut coiled with sudden hatred for a man he'd never met, and he wished he could go to Maggie, gather her close, and warm her with gentle kisses.

Instinct warned him such a move would be a serious mistake.

"I know very little," he said cautiously. "Robbie mentioned you had been involved with someone last Christmas."

She turned her face away from him, and Lane struggled against an unacknowledged pang of jealousy. Was Maggie still in love with the man? So much so she couldn't bear to discuss what had happened between them?

Sighing, he continued. "Look, Maggie, what happened between you and this guy is your own damned business. I don't know anything but a few *very* sketchy details. The only reason I brought him up was because I seem to be in danger of being tarred with the same brush. He and I may both be northerners and off-islanders, but that doesn't mean we're cut from the same cloth. It sounds to me like Hadley was only interested in a quick summer fling. I'm not, and it makes me angry as hell that you'd even consider me that superficial."

He watched her closely, wanting to see her expression. But she continued to keep her face averted, and what he could glimpse in her profile was stony and unreceptive. He was too miserable to be angry with her anymore. For every step forward he took in establishing a relationship with Maggie, the woman persisted in taking two steps backward.

It was an impossible situation, and Lane wondered why he should care if the attraction between them succeeded in dying a quick death. Easier, much easier to put Maggie Rose James behind him and return to a life in Chicago he was familiar with. The women there were generous, loving creatures who delighted in pleasing him as much as he enjoyed pleasuring them. Unsophisticated Maggie James could be out of his system in two weeks' time.

But every time he looked at her, Lane knew himself to be a liar, and the thought of never seeing her again left him feeling bleak and disconsolate. *Oh, Stafford*, Lane chided himself, *what have you gotten yourself into?*

"I'm not Tom Hadley," he repeated softly, determined to get through to her. "The sooner you realize that, the sooner you can put all that unpleasantness behind you. Just don't wait too long, Maggie Rose."

She told herself he was not to be trusted. After all, he was, by his own admission, a man used to getting his own way. An expert at honeyed words and stolen kisses. Lane knew how to cajole and fluster and . . . oh, damn him, he'd done just that!

Face it, Maggie berated herself. *You may not trust Lane, but you can't stop thinking about him.* With profound self-disgust, she accepted the knowledge that just envisioning his touch upon her flesh could set wildfire tripping through her veins. One of Lane's sudden smiles half took her breath away and could bedazzle her blind. The heat of his gaze conquered her easily as coherent thought fled.

She hadn't been one-tenth as unnerved by Tom Hadley, and she'd thought herself in *love* with him!

Maggie dropped the trowel she'd been using to evict weeds from her garden.

Oh, Lord. Was *that* what was wrong with her? Love? Surely not. She wouldn't be so foolish, so impractical, so . . . unMaggielike. Divided between a wave of blind fury at her own stupidity and a surge of exquisite hope, she told herself that she was jumping to all the wrong conclusions. Attraction was one thing. Love was quite another. Maggie knew the difference, and love was definitely *not* what she was feeling for Lane Stafford.

Round and round her thoughts went for the remainder of the day and well into the next. But no matter how she attempted to explain away the peculiar, unfamiliar emotions Lane Stafford made her feel, Maggie kept coming back to that simple, impossible explanation.

The realization brought no peace.

Robbie practically disowned her.

Neither of them had seen Lane since yesterday afternoon, and the boy was quick to place the blame for his friend's desertion at Maggie's door. Robbie's scowling, black looks did little to improve her flagging spirits, and she was relieved when he asked to spend the night at his friend Tony's house.

Maggie threw herself into an orgy of activity. She prepared a simple dinner for herself, watered the garden, and finally coerced the clay flamingo into a heron.

Lane did not put in an appearance.

Was he exacting a small punishment for her earlier behavior? Maggie wondered. Or perhaps giving her time to reconsider their relationship? She hoped the latter was the case, although she could not think of one thing she had done to deserve such thoughtfulness. She wouldn't have blamed Lane if he never bothered to darken her door again.

She ate dinner alone, envisioning the future before her. With the inn no longer her concern, that left only Robbie. Her brother was growing up. If he continued to show interest in a career in medicine, he would be gone before she knew it. Then what would she have left?

The shop was scraping by, but what had happened to her dreams of a meaningful career? A professional showing of her craft and recognition by her peers? Somewhere in her future there had once been plans for a husband and children, people to rejoice in her successes, commiserate with her during the low times. She was still young, but the island was small and most of the locals middle-aged and older. Who would she marry?

It was a bleak image to see herself in her mind's eye forty years from now. Aged and alone. Her talent dissolved into a few poorly produced sculptures lacking originality. Anxiously awaiting the next visit from Robbie and his family, who would no doubt lecture her incessantly on getting off the island more and taking precautions against the sun and eating balanced meals. It was a dismal prospect.

No. If she was to avoid that trap, Maggie realized she must take more control over her life. Obviously, part of the solution was to come to terms with the outside world and men like Lane Stafford. She could widen her circle of friends, be more receptive to change and new ideas. Take a chance once in a while.

Realistically, a relationship with Lane was a fool's dream of infatuation. Lane had been honest with her. His interest in her was the basic, instinctive need of all men. He offered no wedding ring; his heart was not committed. *Can you accept that kind of relationship?* Practical Maggie asked as she watched the late night news. The weatherman was particularly gleeful, predicting a chance of rain overnight, the first in almost a month. *Maybe. Maybe not. I just know I'm miserable when he's not in my life.*

The hall clock chimed eleven times. Maggie went to bed, lying in the darkness and listening to the wind sing through the Australian pines. Heat lightning flashed occasionally, illuminating the bedroom in an eerie silver light, and she could hear the water in the gulf churning, rippling into small waves. Outside, the clash of palm fronds rustled against her window. Perhaps the weatherman was right.

She tossed and turned. An hour dragged by, then the better part of another.

What if Lane decided not to waste any more time on her? Perhaps he had already written her off as too much trouble, discarded her hopes for the inn's restoration, and returned to Chicago. The thought didn't bear considering, but it could account for his absence. Fate had thrown them together briefly, but had she stubbornly managed to drive them apart?

EIGHT

Had she been asleep, Maggie might not have heard the soft rap upon the back door.

She padded through the house in pajamas and bare feet, curious as to who would pay a visit at such a late hour. It never occurred to her to ask who it might be before opening the door. Peeking through the peephole was a city precaution and had never been necessary on Caloosa Key. Still, she only opened the door six inches, and was surprised to discover Lane on the other side of the screen.

He was slightly out of breath, his dark hair rumpled by the wind. The moonlight concealed the true color of the shorts and T-shirt he wore, but Maggie couldn't fail to see the slight smile he offered. She tried to still the happiness flooding her body at the mere sight of him.

"Hi. Sorry to wake you," he said, "but a guy named Hunter Bradshaw just showed up at my door with a message for you that he insisted I deliver. He didn't know you had moved. I tried to tell him that if you were like any normal person you'd be asleep, but he just laughed and said to tell you, so here I am."

"Hunt's on the island?" Maggie exclaimed. "That's terrific! What's the message?"

"He said to tell you Babette's back. Whatever that means."

"Babette! I can't believe it! I'll be right out. Wait for me."

"Should I know—" Lane started to say, but the door closed upon his words.

In less than a minute Maggie yanked on a cotton shirt, slid into a pair of shorts, and pulled on sneakers over her bare feet. When she rejoined Lane on the porch, it was her turn to be slightly out of breath, but there was a sparkle of excitement in her eyes and her voice held a thrilled note of pleasure.

"Thanks for waiting. Come on. A city boy like you shouldn't miss this."

Before Lane could demand further explanation, Maggie was sprinting across the yard with athletic grace and an unnerving sense of direction. She found the path separating Banyon House and the inn easily and fled down it, Lane close on her heels.

"Where are we going, and why?" Lane called. He was concentrating on sticking close to the pale glow of Maggie's blouse ahead of him. The woman must have a cat's vision. Even in the moonlight, with occasional flashes of lightning, he was having difficulty seeing where he was going.

"You'll see," she responded enigmatically.

Her headlong flight eventually brought them to the beach. Lane was surprised to see the twin shafts of car headlights piercing the darkness and the hulking mass of a vehicle. Maggie had told him automobiles were prohibited on the beach, the fragile ecology of the dunes being closely guarded by island government. A man's figure cut across the light momentarily, and shadows leaped and danced. Lane caught the glint of golden hair and knew it would be this Bradshaw fellow Maggie seemed so glad to be hearing from. She continued to rush ahead, but Lane slowed his pace to a walk, not certain what to expect.

As he approached, he watched Maggie greet Bradshaw

effusively. She hugged him, and he responded by lifting her right off the ground. The man was tall, good-looking in a rugged sort of way, and seemed *very* familiar with Maggie. Lane felt his gut roll uneasily. Who was this guy and why hadn't he heard of him before?

"I was so afraid she was dead," Maggie whispered excitedly, and Lane wondered why she had lowered her voice. There couldn't be another living soul out on the beach this time of night.

"Figured you'd want to know," Bradshaw said. "When did you move out of the inn?"

Maggie offered a brief explanation of what had transpired in the last six months, then seemed suddenly aware of Lane's presence. "Oh, Lane, come here. I want you to meet a dear friend of mine."

"We've met," Lane said, giving Hunter Bradshaw a short nod.

The man smiled in acknowledgment. He had good eyes, open and friendly, with laugh lines radiating out from the corners. Even in the poor light, Lane could see he was deeply tanned, and where his eyes crinkled, the creases were white, as though he did a lot of smiling and those creases got little exposure to the sun. It spoke well for the man. He had a sun-bleached thatch of unruly hair that gleamed like newly minted gold. Lean and well muscled, he was probably a few years older than Lane, thirty-two at the most. He looked extremely fit, a man comfortable in the out-of-doors, obviously at home on an island. Lane found himself suddenly aware of the peeling redness of his own nose.

Hunter Bradshaw shook Lane's hand and displayed a damnedably perfect set of white teeth that only accentuated his excellent tan. "Sorry for the late-night visit, but I knew Maggie wouldn't want to miss this. You must think we're crazy."

"Well . . ." Lane hedged. He was beginning to wonder. He'd never seen Maggie so animated. Was it the presence of this man or the mysterious reappearance of

Babette, whoever the hell she was. "I wouldn't mind someone shedding a little light on what's going on here."

Bradshaw laughed softly. "Maggie, she's your baby. Why don't you introduce your friend here to Babette?"

Delighted to have the honors, Maggie came to Lane's side, curling her arm in his conspiratorially. "Try not to make too much noise. We don't want to upset her."

"Of course not," Lane agreed with only a trace of sarcasm.

She led him along the path made by the headlights, trudging through thick sand and broken shells. Veering to the left suddenly, out of the brightness and into the shadows, they stopped a short distance away from what appeared to be a large rock. "Lane," Maggie whispered, "this is Babette."

He had a momentary vision of some enormous practical joke being played at his expense. And then the rock moved suddenly, tossing sand into the air and emitting a low hiss of displeasure that made him step back in surprise.

In an awestruck voice Maggie said, "Isn't she beautiful?"

No. She wasn't.

On her best day, with all the fates of chance working determinedly in her favor, Babette would never be considered even remotely pretty. What she was, was prehistoric. A monster. A not-so-subtle reminder that even God could play a joke now and then and could create something that was . . . well—just plain ugly.

"She's a turtle," Lane observed simply.

Maggie emitted a low giggle. "Not bad, Yank."

He threw her a menacing look. "I've seen turtles before, you know. I even had one once."

He had. A cute but smelly little creature who had sported a daisy decal on its back and been foolhardy enough to attempt an exploration of the world outside its shallow bowl. His mother had told him the little fellow was lonely and had walked to the nearest lake to rejoin his friends. It was only years later that Lane's father had confessed to accidentally squashing it in the doorjamb when he'd gone into the bathroom.

No one was ever going to paint a flower on this fellow's back, Lane suspected as he circled the beast warily. Even the big turtles he'd captured on vacation at the lake were midgets compared to this monster.

"Will she bite?"

"No, she'll tear your leg off. Don't get too close."

He squinted into the shadows, fascinated and overwhelmed by the enormity of the thing. Its heavy-looking brown shell was covered with barnacles and green algae, like some subterranean inhabitant. Its yellow scaly skin looked like leather, and when it lurched its head in his direction, Lane shivered at the sight of its cold, lifeless stare. It seemed to be stuck in a shallow hole, the broad swoop of its flippers only succeeding in digging the creature in deeper. Yet it methodically continued to dig, as though unaware its great weight on land made it helpless. Babette easily weighed one thousand pounds.

"How do you know this is Babette?" he asked.

Maggie favored him with a black look, as though he had just accused a mother of not knowing her own child. "Of course it's Babette. Even if I didn't recognize that propeller scar on her back flipper, Hunt would have checked her tag." She pointed to a small metal clip attached to the right front appendage.

"Oh. Is she stuck?"

"No, she's laying her eggs. This is going to take a while. We might as well sit down and be comfortable." A few feet away lay the long trunk of a fallen coconut palm. Maggie lowered herself onto it and patted a spot beside her. "Have a seat."

He did so, keeping a wary eye upon the beast a few feet away from him. He didn't think turtles could move very fast on land, but he wasn't going to take any chances. In spite of her earlier warning, Maggie seemed relaxed in the gargantuan's presence.

The glare from the headlights flickered, and Lane was

dimly aware of Hunter Bradshaw crossing back and forth in front of them, absorbed in checking a hoisting boom mounted on the front of the vehicle, a Jeep of indeterminable age and condition.

"Would it be silly of me to ask how you happened to make Babette's acquaintance?"

"Did you know Babette's species goes back a hundred and seventy-five million years? Loggerheads—that's what Babette is—always return instinctively to the same place every year to lay their eggs. Babette's been coming to this spot on the beach in front of the inn since before my parents moved here. A honeymoon couple came upon her one night years ago. Scared them to death. Since that time she's been kind of an inn mascot. We'd be on the lookout for her every breeding season. You could always tell when she'd been here.". She indicated a long track in the sand leading from the water's edge to the place where the loggerhead was still steadily tossing sand. "Sometimes the babies would hatch in the middle of the night and we couldn't do anything to save them. Ghost crabs feed on them, birds pluck them off as they try to reach the water. The few that do make it are prey to fish. Out of a hundred babies, maybe one or two will reach deep water. Anyway, laying season is May, and when Babette didn't show up as usual, I thought maybe she'd been drowned."

"Drowned?" Lane asked in surprise. "Can turtles do that?"

"Happens all the time," Hunter Bradshaw said from behind them. He hunkered down in the sand beside them. "See those lights out there?" he asked, gesturing to the disembodied yellow glow from boats on the horizon. The glimmering specks of phosphorescence were the only thing to distinguish the inky blackness of the gulf waters. "Trawlers. Their nets kill about two hundred of these fellows a year. Loggerheads are bottom feeders and they get scooped up along with the shrimp and fish. Their brain's about the size of a grape, so they're too stupid to figure out how to swim out of harm's way, and they end up being dragged along until they drown. The boat crews call them 'incidental catch' and it makes them madder then hornets to find one in the nets.''

"Why?"

"Tears the hell out of them. If they do manage to bring one up alive, they'll kill it just for spite." He glanced over at Babette. "Yep. Figured she was a goner for sure this year.''

The beast hissed, as if to deny such foolish thinking, and even across the distance separating them, the reeking foulness of her breath was overpowering. Amazingly, Maggie and Bradshaw seemed oblivious to the smell.

"Where's Sandy tonight?" Maggie asked Hunter.

"Eric's down with the chicken pox, poor kid. Sandy's been going crazy the past two days, so I told her I'd make these last few sweeps of the beach alone." By way of explanation to Lane, Hunter added, "Sandy's my wife."

The man was married. Good. Hunter Bradshaw was difficult to dislike and Lane found himself suddenly feeling more friendly toward him. "You bring your wife out on nights like this? Pretty romantic."

Hunter smiled broadly and Maggie laughed outright. "My wife's got more credentials for this sort of work than I do. We're biologists working for a marine institute based in Fort Myers. They're funding a program to revitalize the turtle population here in Florida. Every season we record data on the specimens we find, collect the eggs, and incubate them back at the institute. Sort of gives the little beggers a fighting chance. Speaking of which," he said to Maggie with a nod toward the underbrush, "did you notice the peanut gallery watching?"

Three pairs of golden eyes gleamed in the shadowy bushes not more than twenty feet away. Lane grimaced, wondering what other monsters were lurking out there.

"Raccoons," Maggie answered the unspoken question. "Wretched little thieves love to steal warm turtle eggs."

"I've seen them snatch eggs right out from under the mother before they've had a chance to drop into the nest,"

Hunter added. "Well, not tonight, you little bandits. Maggie and I will make sure of that." He surged to his feet, heaving a broken conch shell into the darkness. There was a sudden skittering retreat, and the watchful eyes vanished. "They'll be back. They're brazen as hell. Glad to have your help tonight."

Maggie smiled agreement, then glanced uncertainly at Lane. "I thought you might find this interesting, but if you're bored or tired, you don't have to stay. I'll understand."

"No, I'd like to stay and help," he said, and surprisingly, he realized he meant it.

The three waited patiently for Babette to finish her chore, sharing coffee from a thermos Hunter had stashed in the Jeep and getting better acquainted. Maggie explained how Babette had come by that absurd name—christened for a fifth-grade classmate who she had disliked heartily and who had been horrified to have a turtle named after her. Hunter talked a great deal about his wife and son, his voice lowering slightly with the depth of his feelings for them, and Lane even volunteered the tale about his hapless pet who'd met an untimely death. They laughed together softly, took turns frightening away the more defiant raccoons, and, in general, enjoyed each other's company.

Except for Hunter Bradshaw's presence, it was a perfect night for romance, Lane thought. It was cool and breezy enough to frustrate the hungriest mosquito. The moon was high, shining on the silvered gulf waters like liquid mercury, and heat lightning strobed occasionally, adding a crackling tension to the night air. They were close enough to the inn's overgrown garden to smell the heavy sweetness of the oleanders planted there, so fragrant yet deadly. The sound of the small waves foaming against the sand was a gentle, lulling gurgle.

The faint whisper of leaves rustled against each other in the wind, but the island was quiet. The night creatures seemed to have found other business to attend to tonight.

Cloistered on the beach, with only the two narrow tunnels of light to offer illumination in such total darkness, Lane wondered if his two companions felt as isolated as he. They might well have been the last three people left on earth. The atmosphere seemed to hold a magical enchantment, and Lane looked at Maggie hard, wishing he were alone with her now, wanting nice Hunter Bradshaw to go away somewhere and take a long, long time coming back. He felt himself grow hard with longing and leaped up to hurl a coconut at one unfortunate raccoon before his private thoughts became public display.

Observing a loggerhead turtle dig a nest and lay eggs was a little like watching grass grow. The animal was slow and clumsy, and certainly there was no illusion of beauty in Babette's movements. Regardless, Lane found himself fascinated by the beast's efforts to continue her species and Hunter and Maggie's determination to assist her. He couldn't think of one person of his acquaintance who would find this work remotely interesting, and he was slightly amazed by his own enthusiasm. It must be the night air or the pull of the tides or the bewitching influence of island living, Lane surmised. He couldn't account for the heady delight he felt, the odd notion that in witnessing this slow ritual, he was privy to something mystical denied the common man. Wouldn't his friends laugh to hear him rhapsodizing over such an ugly creature as Babette, he thought suddenly, and a short, deprecating sound escaped him.

Beside him, Maggie turned to glance his way, offering a small smile. He could see the sea mist clinging to her heavy lashes like tiny diamonds; her eyes were warm, sparkling sapphires. A fog of wispy curls framed her face.

He looked at her a long moment, aware of Bradshaw not far away making puttering noises at the Jeep. Reaching out suddenly, he captured her neck in one hand and pulled her close for a swift kiss. "I'm glad you wanted to share this with me," he said softly.

Maggie blinked in surprise at the unexpectedness of his

touch, but he was pleased to note that she did not seem upset by it or inclined to move farther down the log. Maybe the night held a certain allurement for her, too.

Babette finished her task at last, covering the nest as neatly as was possible for a thousand-pound monster to do. When she heaved herself off the mound and began a slow, awkward crawl to the water, Maggie and Bradshaw went into action.

Handing Maggie a specially built container for the eggs, Hunter said, "You know what to do, Maggie girl," and motioned for Lane to follow.

Babette barely reached hard-packed sand before the two men caught up with her. The turtle didn't seem unduly concerned by their presence on either side of her, just grimly determined to continue on her way.

"Not so fast, darlin'," Hunter said, snagging one of the beast's front flippers. With an expertise and strength that impressed Lane, the biologist flipped the mammoth creature onto her back. Babette's yellow belly shell was a pale oval in the moonlight and her leathery appendages stroked the air frantically, trying to no avail to right herself. "Don't let her go anywhere," Hunter instructed Lane pointlessly. "I'll be right back."

While Lane stood an uneasy sentinel over the animal, Bradshaw positioned the Jeep close to the loggerhead, lowering the hydraulic hoisting boom attached at the front of the vehicle. He spread a large, heavy-duty net on the sand near the boom's tip.

"Now comes the hard part," he said with a grin. "Grab that other front flipper and let's see if we can scoot this old girl into the net. Stay away from her head. I'd hate to see you lose a finger and I'd have a hell of a time explaining it to my boss."

Lane followed Hunter's example. The flipper was as leathery-feeling as it had looked, and unpleasantly cold and clammy as well. Babette hissed angrily, and the stench of her breath was unbearable. Up close and personal, the beast was losing a lot of its mystery and appeal.

It wasn't an easy task. The two men pushed and pulled, grunted and groaned, trying to avoid those snapping jaws and keeping a tight hold on the creature's wildly ranging appendages. Babette seemed as disenchanted by the procedure as they, refusing to cooperate one bit. After what seemed an eternity, the turtle was positioned in the center of the net and the two men straightened with a groan of relief.

"Whew!" Hunter said, wiping sweat off his brow with the sleeve of his shirt. "I think Babette's put on a few pounds since last year."

"I realize this is for a noble cause," Lane remarked, "but are you sure you *enjoy* this sort of work?"

"Believe it or not, I do," Hunter replied with a laugh. "So does my wife, Sandy. You should see *her* haul loggerheads."

"No offense, but your wife must be an Amazon."

"She's smaller than Maggie. It just takes practice. Ask Maggie. She's flipped a few in her time."

"You're joking."

"No. Maggie can be a tough little cookie."

Lane glanced over at the woman who was on hands and knees in front of Babette's mound, industriously scooping sand from the nest. He frowned, thinking there was much about Maggie Rose James that remained a mystery to him. He said as much to Hunter.

"Well, I've always thought the right man would want to make the effort," Hunter said. "Lord knows, she's turned out pretty enough after those awful high school years. Hand me that corner of the net, will you?" Lane did, and the biologist clipped it onto the hoisting hook. "She didn't bounce back as fast as I thought she could after her mother's death, and this mess with the inn shook her up some, but she's a plucky kid. She'll make some man a great wife." When Lane made no response to that remark, he added, "She seems to like you quite a bit."

Lane couldn't possibly have missed Hunter's train of

thought. With a laugh of dismissal he said, "I'm not in the market for a wife."

Hunter chuckled at that answer. "Neither was I until I met Sandy. Women have a way of sneaking up on you and getting under your skin. It's the damnedest thing."

He pulled the last corner of the net onto the hoisting hook so the huge turtle was effectively snared. With a flick of a switch, the hydraulic mechanism hummed to life, creaking arthritically as it lifted the heavy animal off the ground so the biologist could get an accurate weight reading from the large scale attached to the boom. Thunder rumbled angrily, followed by a flash of genuine lightning over the horizon. "Hope the rain will hold off until we finish," Hunter said with a grimace.

"Anything more I can do to help?"

Hunter barely glanced up from the clipboard on which he was busily scratching data. "I've got quite a few measurements to record, samples to take, and I'll need to retag her. Not much you can do for me, thanks. Why don't you help Maggie collect those eggs?"

Lane nodded, trudged across the dunes, and dropped down on his knees across from Maggie, who was plundering the exposed nest as quickly as possible now that it seemed quite likely they were going to be drenched by rain any minute.

She smiled at him excitedly. "Sixty-eight so far, but I'd bet there are at least a hundred here. She's outdone herself this time."

Lane looked into the hole. The turtle's clutch didn't really resemble eggs at all, but were rather the same shape and size as Ping-Pong balls. They were still warm to the touch, and, following Maggie's lead, Lane gingerly helped place them in the heated container Hunter had provided.

"Not sorry you stayed?" Maggie questioned.

"Not a bit."

She glanced up quickly at the sky, where clouds were scudding across the face of the moon. "In about ten minutes we're going to get soaked."

"Looks that way."

"You're pretty hardy for a city boy," she teased.

"I have to admit, this isn't exactly the sort of entertainment I'm used to. You're probably the only woman I've ever met who would come out in the middle of the night to help a poor dumb creature who's as ugly as Babette."

"She's not ugly." Maggie offered an affronted objection. "She's . . . majestic."

"Right," Lane agreed, unable to keep amused sarcasm out of his voice. "Queen Babette."

With a bright laugh, Maggie sat back on her heels to look at him, her head cocked to one side. The wind was kicking up, whipping silken strands of hair across her face, and, with the back of one sandy hand, she nudged it out of her eyes. "You must think I'm pretty crazy."

Just looking at her brought Lane's heart slamming against his rib cage. He stopped what he was doing, his features suddenly serious. "I think you're a lot of things," he said softly, "but crazy isn't one of them."

They sat there for a full minute in utter silence, ignoring the sound of thunder and lightning, the wind plowing harshly through the trees to announce the coming storm.

Lane's eyes held hers; Maggie felt his gaze upon her like a physical touch, caressing her face, skimming across her breasts. Her heartbeat quickened and her stomach muscles fluttered nervously, a reaction Maggie forced herself to ignore. If she was ever to meet a man on his own terms, it had to be now, while she was still smarting from the brutal self-evaluation she'd indulged in earlier. There was no mistaking the look in Lane's eyes, the hungry need she saw written upon his features, and she forced herself to meet that look, refusing to withdraw her gaze in cowardly retreat.

Lord, please don't let me make a fool of myself, she prayed silently, and before her new-found courage could desert her, Maggie stated quietly, "You really aren't like Tom Hadley at all, are you?"

His eyes went wide with sudden understanding. He

knew what those few words could mean to their relationship. For a long moment Lane was silent, and Maggie had
to press her lips together hard to keep them from trembling
a betrayal of her nervousness.

"Good Christ, Maggie." His voice was low and hoarse.
"You're driving me mad."

"I'm sorry," she stammered.

"No," he murmured quick reassurance. "It's all right.
I'm the one who should apologize. Sometimes I push too
hard to get what I want. I went off the island yesterday
on business, and coming back I realized just how insulated
ur life here must have been. My God, Caloosa Key's
arely acknowledged the twentieth century! I can't expect
you to react the way other women . . ." He broke off,
realizing that what he was saying was perilously close to
coming out the wrong way. Better try again. "I mean,
growing up on an island this size is bound to make you
abnormal . . ." No. That *definitely* wasn't right. Jesus,
what the hell was wrong with him? If he kept this up, he
was going to kill every chance he had.

He looked so comically stricken Maggie had to laugh out
loud. "It's all right, Lane. I think I know what you're trying
to say. I'm just glad you think I'm worth the extra effort."

"Oh, there's no doubt in my mind about that, sweetheart," Lane reassured her with a relieved smile.

"Hey, you two!" Hunter called, breaking across their
thoughts. They both swung their heads to offer a guilty
look, and he gestured excitedly toward the rumbling sky.
"In case you haven't noticed, we're about to become victims of a deluge. Get a move on!" As if to add impetus
to his words, the first cold drops of rain started to splatter
upon them.

Moving with as much haste as their work would allow,
Lane and Maggie collected the last of Babette's brood,
one hundred and twelve in all.

"Last one," Lane said, holding his palm out to reveal
the final egg.

They smiled at each other, savoring a moment of shared

excitement for a job well done, but as Maggie started to lift it carefully, their hands touched and Lane brought his fingers up to surround Maggie's, egg and all.

She felt the heated electricity of his grasp. It seemed to burn right through her, and a little gasp of sound escaped her lips, equal parts of surprise and desire. She lifted her face, knowing what she would see in Lane's features, and yet no longer afraid of it. The wind was whipping madly now, raking Lane's dark locks into wild disarray, tossing minute particles of sand against their flesh. Rain plopped upon their skin in big, fat drops, a warning of greater things to come. Lane seemed oblivious to it all. His eyes held hers, seriously intent. "Maggie . . ." he murmured. "Stay with me." His fingers squeezed hers ever so slightly, a gentle communication of his desire. "Tonight."

Maggie swallowed hard. Then she nodded.

Further conversation became impossible. The rain began to fall in earnest now, pelting their flesh with icy droplets that brought them both scrambling to their feet. With Babette's precious cargo sheltered protectively under Lane's arm, they ran to the Jeep, where Hunter was just levering Babette back upon her belly. Unmindful of the rain, the loggerhead immediately began a methodical march back to the sea.

"We're going to make a run for my place," Lane shouted to Hunter over the noise of wind and rain. "Want to come along?"

"You two go ahead. I've got a couple of things to take care of and then I can get home. Sandy's probably starting to worry by now."

He thanked Lane for his help and the two men sealed their new friendship with a final handshake. Hunter's roughened fingers reached out to pat Maggie's cheek. "I'll call you when Babette's brood hatches."

She nodded, and then Lane was pulling on her hand, urging her to hurry.

The rain had packed the loose, shifting sand into a solid surface that made their flight easier than they both expected. The wind was ferocious. It threatened to separate them, but Maggie hung on tightly and followed Lane's lead. To escape the slashing rain, she lowered her face and allowed Lane to pull her along, offering up a swift prayer that the man's sense of direction wouldn't be totally inept for once. His fingers were a warm, firm lifeline, guiding her around debris blocking their path, tugging her upright when she stumbled and seemed destined to fall. Palm fronds slapped against her legs, then danced away to pirouette down the beach. Icy needles of rainwater stung along the backs of her calves and arms. Just when Maggie began to fear they might be running aimlessly, the apartment door was suddenly before them and they fell inside.

They stood a moment in the dark, their breath coming in quick little gasps of sound, the rain puddling off their bodies and upon the hardwood floor in tiny rivulets.

"Catch your breath," Lane advised. "I'll get the lights."

She waited patiently while he found one of the lamps, switched it on, then retrieved a handful of towels from the hall closet.

She caught the fluffy towel that Lane tossed her way and pressed it to her face. It smelled of fabric softener and the familiar scent of her mother's homemade rose sachet. Pulling its nubby softness over her head, Maggie began toweling her hair dry, then jumped visibly when she felt Lane's hands close over hers. He rubbed the towel along her scalp with brisk efficiency while she remained perfectly still and quiet. Finally, using the dangling corners as a lever, he forced her head up and tossed back the edges obscuring her vision.

His eyes were dark with desire, and Maggie bit her lip nervously, trying to slow the erratic thumping of her heart. She was shivering, and she knew she couldn't chalk it up entirely to being chilled.

He chuckled softly. "God, you look like a half-drowned kitten."

"Lane, I . . ."

"Shh," he said, placing a warm finger upon her cold lips. "It will be all right. I promise."

His lips took hers, whispering over her mouth gently, locking the breath in her throat. Her body pressed willingly against his, and he responded with a low growl of pleasure at the contact, threading his fingers through the silky wetness of her hair. She spread her hands along his back, distantly aware of the play of muscles there beneath the shirt plastered to his skin.

She was aware of little else because Lane's mouth had taken full possession now. Her lips parted and his tongue was exploring, teasing. Its velvety softness delved deeper and deeper, until she felt a dizzying sweetness melt her insides. Timid at first, then with increasing boldness, Maggie allowed her own tongue to meet his, imitating his movements in a way she hoped would please him.

Eventually, his mouth slanted away from hers, and she drew a quick, shaky breath as Lane scorched her flesh with his lips, placing nibbling kisses along her cheeks, her brow, the curve of her neck. His touch seemed alternately to chill and then burn. She shivered deliciously as he nudged away the collar of her soaked blouse to trail his tongue across the hollow of her throat.

His fingers twitched apart the buttons of her blouse with one hand, peeling its dampness away from her skin. "You need to get out of these wet things," Lane whispered against her flesh. "You'll catch cold."

"I seem . . . to be warming up," Maggie replied dreamily as his tongue found a sensitive spot beneath one ear.

Lane gave a low, rumbling laugh. A drop or two of rainwater lay poised at the tip of her earlobe, and he captured the moisture with his tongue, taking a moment to suckle the flesh above it.

Her shorts and panties slid down her legs to become a sodden mass at Maggie's feet, though she was hardly aware that he had helped her slip out of them until she felt the chilly air against her flesh. In another moment her blouse joined them on the floor and she was naked. Yet the thought was only mildly unsettling.

Lane draped a towel around her body, and with another he began to stroke the wetness from her skin. His touch was a balm, a delightfully peculiar sensation shimmied along her nerves. The warmth of Lane's strong fingers seemed to seep right through the fluffy material—massaging, stimulating. It was a lazy, sensual feeling against her flesh.

Lane worked the towel over her body slowly, and, adrift in the pleasure of his touch, Maggie squeezed her eyes shut, allowing him free passage. She felt weightless, made of less substance than spun sugar. She couldn't fathom a feeling more delightful then this, but even as she had the thought, Lane's knowledgeable fingers were showing her how much more there could be.

He parted the material that covered her, his hand settling along her stomach. She gasped, the muscles contracting as he toweled gently, his fingers making ever-decreasing circles, until she began to imagine there was no barrier of cloth between his hand and her flesh. Her entire being seemed centered and focused on that small, mesmerizing movement just above the naval. A tingling weakness seemed to radiate from that marvelous point of contact.

In the next moment, the sensual warmth of the feeling seemed to increase, and, dimly aware something had changed, Maggie opened her eyes. Lane had lowered himself to his knees in front of her, and where the towel had once stroked, his mouth now moved with deceptive slowness. She moaned as his fingers slid along the slight curve of her rib cage, down the hollow of her spine to cup her buttocks. He squeezed and kneaded gently, and she surged convulsively against him, filling his mouth with her flesh. His tongue swirled and dipped over her velvety skin, and Maggie's spine went taut. Unaccustomed to such intimacy, her fingers settled upon Lane's shoulders, plucking at the damp material of his shirt.

"What are . . . you doing?" Maggie choked out.

"Warming you, sweetheart," he said, and the low,

husky vibration of those few words against her abdomen made her squirm with pleasure.

On the pretense of drying her legs, Lane's hands slid up and down their length. His movements were deliberate and unhurried as he enjoyed the tightening shift of each muscle, the fragile turn of her ankles. Such long, beautiful legs she had. Like most of the rest of her, they were tanned a golden-honey color, yet there was none of the leathery toughness about Maggie's skin that afflicted so many sun worshippers. Her flesh was soft and supple. Touchable.

When his lips touched the edge of satiny curls that hid her womanhood, and his hand stole to the inside of her thighs, Maggie's reaction was instant and uncontrollable. She clenched against his invasion.

Lane lifted his eyes to hers, keenly aware of her sudden confusion. The light from the single lamp he'd lit had turned her features golden, and in the midnight shadows of her eyes he watched myriad expressions drift through their depths—shy pleasure, surprise, fear. He wished he could make this easier for Maggie. He was torn between sympathy for her and the most potent desire he'd ever felt in his life.

"Maggie," he whispered. His voice was very gentle, and his gaze probing. "Share this time with me, love. Don't turn away from it."

Tiny shards of apprehension pricked her consciousness, but Lane's hands had magic in them. They no longer drifted over her blindly, but with purposeful intent, his fingers caressing the apex of her thighs, capturing pulse points until the fragile peace he'd induced earlier was shattered and her breath was coming in harsh, scant gasps.

Maggie's head fell back. Her long lashes fluttered down. She was oblivious to everything but the slow, sweet yearning within her body. "Yes . . ." she breathed raggedly. "Yes. Show me."

Her knees weakened and gave way, and Lane was there to slide his arm beneath them, sweeping her body close to his and stilling her groan of delight with another searing kiss. He carried her to the master bedroom where the comfortable four-poster waited, laying her upon it with infinite care.

Maggie shifted her head upon the pillow.

Lane was beside the bed, his body turned from her as he slid out of his damp jeans and shirt with quick, fluid movements. He did not turn on the bedside lamp and the soft glow of light from the living room outlined his form as though his body had been tipped in gold. She was fascinated by the sight of him, the sleek, taut line of his back muscles, the creamy whiteness of his buttocks where no sun had found a home, the slightly furred thighs, so long and powerfully molded. He was beautifully proportioned. As dazed as his kisses had rendered her, she was still aware of how truly well-built Lane was.

Without full cognizance of her actions, Maggie's hand reached out to glide lightly down his bare hip. She felt muscles tense, then relax beneath her hand as Lane's head swung toward her.

"You're so beautiful," she breathed. "Like a statue of David I once saw in a museum."

He chuckled indulgently at her fancifulness and lifted her hand to his lips. Without ever taking his brown gaze off her face, he planted a kiss in the center of her palm. "Not a statue, sweetheart," he murmured. "Just a man. A man who needs you so much . . ."

Where his kiss had fallen, his tongue now bathed, and Maggie shivered at the warm, tickling feel of it. He feathered kisses along the length of her arm, stroking his tongue across the fragile flesh at the inside of her wrist where the slight tracing of blue veins lay, the soft crease at the bend of her elbow. Her bones turned to water.

The bed sagged under Lane's weight and she stiffened slightly, avoiding his eyes. He was stretched out beside her, naked and wanting. She could sense the hot, urgent need of his body, and a surge of pure excitement leaped within her. As yet she was too unskilled to know how to fill that need, but soon, very soon, Lane would show her the way.

In the next moment, Maggie fully expected Lane's body to cover hers, expected his warm heaviness to press her into the mattress. She thought the act of lovemaking little more than a quick coupling, a hastily sought release. She had not counted on Lane's skillful handling.

Bracing himself on one elbow, he allowed his fingers to trail through the dark-gold silk of her hair, enjoying the way it curled around his hand, crisp and clean and still slightly damp from the rain. He tugged gently at the knotted towel covering her until it slipped out of harm's way. His eyes leisurely traveled the length of her. Her skin was lustrous in the velvet half-shadows, the slight curves of her body as exquisitely molded as he had known they would be. She was quite still now. He could feel the crackling tension within her, could see the thrillingly uneven pattern of her breathing. He felt a rush of compassion for her, even as he experienced an intoxicating flush of desire tighten his loins.

His fingers skimmed across the surface of her breasts. His touch was practiced, eliciting a response he knew would come eagerly. He rubbed the pink nipple until it peaked generously, and Maggie drew a deep, sudden breath. The movement caused her flesh to fill Lane's grasp.

"Lane?" Maggie whispered hoarsely.

"Mmm?" His lips began their remembered magic, fastening upon one breast to leech all resistance from her body.

"Should I . . . do anything? To help, I mean." Her voice shook slightly as his mouth trailed fire.

He lifted his head. Amusement flitted in eyes heavy-lidded with passion. "Do you think I'm in need of assistance?"

Her gaze touched his, then danced away in embarrassment. "No . . . I just didn't want you to have to do all the work. I'm not very experienced in this sort of thing, but I'm willing to help out."

Laughing deep in his throat, Lane said, "There will be

plenty of chances to be democratic. For now, just relax. Believe me, I'm enjoying this as much as you are.''

"Oh."

"You *are* enjoying this, aren't you?" His mouth teased her nipple to life again.

"Oh, yes!"

Enjoying it? A throbbing need was growing within her. She felt herself rushing headlong toward some unknown, vital wanting. A small part of her was still fearful and nervous, yet more and more Maggie was being swept up on a rising tide of passion that left her panting with anticipation.

When Lane's hand delved once more between her legs, Maggie couldn't stop herself from arching toward the contact. His fingers stroked with tantalizing adeptness; to her surprise she felt herself grow unexpectedly warm and moist, the ache within her consumed by an unknown fire. Maggie's cry of pleasure was devoured by Lane's lips. He lingered there, their breaths mingling. He whispered love words in her ear, allowing his mouth to wander across her jawline, along her cheekbone, as though he craved the closeness of her flesh.

She was scarcely aware of the moment Lane's weight shifted, when his knowledgeable fingers were replaced by his questing manhood. Gently he urged her thighs to part, and she conceded easily. He entered her slowly, expecting the barrier of her virginity and finding it. He was fighting to maintain control now, but when he would have continued a cautious exploration, Maggie's hips arched forward convulsively and he was suddenly plunging through the guardian of her desire.

Over the sting of pain, her eyes found his. There was apology and concern in their brown depths, but when he would have spoken, Maggie silenced him with a kiss of her own. "It's all right," she whispered close to his ear. "It's fading already."

And surprisingly, it was. The stretch of burning was melting into a strange and wonderful warmth, a warmth that tingled and spread as Lane began to move within her. She gave herself over to the delicious age-old rhythm of lovemaking, instinctively urging him on with movements closely matching his. A wondrous sensation was escalating inside her now, and Maggie clutched at Lane's back, her fingers seeking purchase, a place to ground herself to keep from being flung outward. She had not expected this wild and unthinkable loss of control over her own body. Her senses were ricocheting crazily, seeking, stretching as their bodies gloriously merged. And when her body finally attained that mysterious pinnacle of fulfillment, a small, ragged cry escaped her lips, and Maggie feared she would faint from the sheer joy of it.

Under Maggie's bewitching spell, Lane's own throaty sound of satiated ardor was only a heartbeat behind hers. Shudders quaked through his limbs, his breath was scraping harshly in his windpipe, and when his gaze met hers, the hunger in his eyes had been replaced by a dark, dazed pleasure. Etching every detail of Maggie's body into his mind, Lane's ecstasy peaked and his head fell forward to find a cushion in the hollow of her throat.

His body was heavy atop hers, but she didn't care. Their heartbeats indistinguishable, the contact seemed right and good somehow. While their lungs worked for air, Maggie's hand curled around Lane's back, stroking the smooth, muscled expanse now slightly damp with sweat. She traced the long, hard curve of his spine with her fingertips, thinking how foolish she had been to be so fearful of this man. How could she have wasted the precious little time they might have together?

Lane's hands drifted upward to find Maggie's brow. He did not lift his head, but his fingers sifted through her hair languidly, over and over again, like a mother intent on soothing a fretful child.

Spent and trembling, their bodies still molded tightly together, it was a long time before either of them could speak.

NINE

They made love once more before the storm abated that night.

Afterward they lay together in warm intimacy, their bodies a slick tangle of arms and legs. They were quiet, neither of them anxious to disturb the shared contentment between them. They listened to the rain patter off the sea grapes just outside the bedroom window and watched the lightning illuminate the room with its eerie pearl-gray strobe.

Nestled in the shadows, the two lovers touched and teased, their earlier passion heightened by a comfortable satisfaction in each other, as well as healthy lust. Lane's mouth was tender upon Maggie, his hands relearning the lush curves of her body once more with such gentleness that she felt tears clog her throat. He pulled her close so that her head was pillowed at the joining of his arm and shoulder. The warm, male scent of him filled her nostrils, and Maggie brought her hands to his chest, sorting through the crisp dark hair there, settling the pads of her fingers over his breastbone to absorb the beating of Lane's heart—no longer pounding crazily with a passionate madness, but with a slow and steady rhythm that was almost lulling.

"Lane?"

He mumbled a sleepy response.

"I guess this makes me a woman now, doesn't it?"

He began to laugh, a heavy, rolling chuckle that made her hand bounce upon his chest. "Sweetheart, if you aren't, you've just done one hell of a good impersonation."

She punched him playfully. "Don't laugh. You know what I mean."

He twisted his head to look down at her. Her features were barely discernible, but he knew her brows were knit together and that she had caught her bottom lip between her teeth in that funny habit she had whenever she was confused or frustrated or just plain scared. An aching tenderness for her threatened to overwhelm him as he kissed her temple. "My sweet Maggie Rose, how can you doubt it for a moment?"

"I just don't want to disappoint you." Her voice held all the no-nonsense practicality of a schoolmarm. "I know you've probably . . . dated hundreds of women."

Lane smiled into the darkness. "Perhaps not hundreds."

"It's very important to me, Lane," she said softly, and turned her face into the hard wall of his shoulder.

She made no sound but he sensed her withdrawal immediately. His hand found her heated cheek quickly. "Maggie, what is it?" A tear slid beneath his thumb and he smoothed it away with a gentle touch. "Sweetheart, tell me. What's upsetting you so?"

She was appalled by her lack of control. "You'll think I'm such an idiot, but I can't help it. I want it to be special between us. I don't want to be just one more woman you've . . . you've enjoyed. Another notch on your bedpost."

"I don't even *have* a bedpost," he countered patiently. "But even if I did, have I ever led you to believe I'm the sort of man who keeps score?"

"Yes."

"Oh."

He couldn't argue that point further. When he thought

back over the last week, Lane admitted that he'd been pretty cocky with Maggie, pushing a little harder than usual, trying to shock, trying to confound her so she forgot that sheltered, innocent upbringing and those starchy moral codes of hers and just weakened—weakened and gave him what he'd wanted from the first moment he'd laid eyes on her.

Jesus, he felt like the Big Bad Wolf! No wonder Maggie was scared to death she'd be just another sexual conquest.

"Maggie, please." His lips descended to the top of her head, nuzzling, winnowing through the golden silk. "Don't cry. I never meant to play so unfair with you. You couldn't possibly be like any other woman I've ever known. And I mean that as a compliment." He thought of those women—sleek, flashy, assertive—and knew he wouldn't trade one moment of time with Maggie for an eternity with any of them. In the quietest, most serious tone he had ever used with her, he said, "Believe me, little love, you are *very* special to me."

She tilted her head upward, trying to read his expression through the shifting shadows. "Do you honestly mean that?"

His mouth blended with hers as he bestowed a kiss that spoke of desire too long denied. "Does that answer your question?" The shimmer of unshed tears turned her eyes to diamonds. The look she gave him was so trusting, so eager to be convinced. Concern darkened his eyes. "Why is it so important to you, Maggie?"

She sat up slowly, clutching the sheet to her bare breasts like the prim maiden she had been only hours before. Her head swiveled away from him, her attention seemingly fixed upon the moon shadows dancing along the wall. Bathed in the predawn light, her features were ethereal, a merciless taunt to Lane's senses. He watched her slim, lovely throat spasm as she swallowed hard. Her sigh was a whisper of sound in the stillness of the room.

He levered himself on one elbow. "Maggie?"

She didn't look his way. But in a moment she responded

quietly. "It's important to me because . . . I'm horribly afraid I'm falling in love with you."

He was silent while the news penetrated. Love from Maggie James? It wasn't much of a bulletin, really. He'd known it in his heart from the moment she had agreed to share his bed. Someone with Maggie James's values didn't give of herself freely unless there was some deeper commitment, some emotional involvement to make sex outside of marriage acceptable to those antiquated principles of hers. There were those in this day and age who would call such thinking silly and old-fashioned, but there it was nonetheless. Maggie was wearing her heart on her sleeve for him to see, to crush or enfold as he chose.

The funny part was, Lane realized suddenly, that there really *was* no choice. It had been made a long time ago.

His gaze swept lovingly over her features again. He could see the pulse quivering in her throat and he wanted to press his lips to it, taste the pulsating velvet of her once more. But he couldn't. Not yet. Not now. She was too vulnerable, struggling hard to justify new emotions. The compulsion to take her into his arms was powerful, but to do so would only unbalance her, so he clamped down hard on the flickering fire heating his blood.

Maggie stirred fitfully, and there was panic in the quick glimpse she gave him. Lane knew she was already regretting the freedom of her tongue, envisioning his rejection. "I'm sorry. I wasn't trying to put you on the spot."

"No, it's all right," Lane reassured her. He inched upward until his back rested against the headboard. Locking his arms across the broad expanse of his chest, he said, "I'm curious. Why does the idea of being in love make you so afraid?"

Maggie pulled her knees up and wrapped her arms around them. "I've thought I was in love before."

"Ah, yes. The infamous Tom Hadley."

Maggie nodded.

"Care to talk about it?"

She shrugged and rested her chin on her knees. "Not much to tell, really. I was in love, he wasn't."

"Come on, Maggie," Lane urged. "Don't you see you've got to get rid of all that?" He reached out and seized the lumpy impression of her foot under the sheet, giving it a firm shake. "Talk to me, damn it."

She was silent a long minute before she finally acquiesced, nodding limply. In a low, precise voice, Maggie said, "Tom came into my shop just before last Christmas. He and a bunch of his friends were here for a couple of weeks before heading back to college. While they were in the shop he broke one of the pieces I had taken on consignment from another artist. When I saw he was going to walk out without paying for it, I stopped him." She glanced his way and her lips twisted into a bitter smile. "I'm afraid I gave him quite a tongue-lashing."

Lane grinned. He could see her doing it. "Poor guy."

"You don't really understand the love-hate relationship we have with off-islanders. Admittedly, we need the revenue they bring, but they also litter the beach with beer cans, race their cars over the dunes, and kill the wildlife by speeding along the roads as if they didn't have a care in the world. Every year we spend months cleaning up after the messes they leave. Anyway, I was pretty short on patience that day and I really let him have it. At first I could see he was furious with me. After all, I embarrassed him pretty badly in front of his friends. But then, he gave me the most beautiful smile, handed me a hundred dollars to pay for the sculpture, and asked me out on a date."

"Smart fellow."

"I'd have been better off if he had just slapped me and walked out the door. For the next two weeks he wined and dined me, and it didn't take long for me to convince myself we were in love. I couldn't believe my luck. Here was this great-looking, sophisticated guy seemingly in love with *me*. A little hick-from-the-sticks nobody who was so gullible . . .'' She broke off, shaking her head in self-disgust. "God, I still can't believe I was such an idiot."

The words were clear and unemotional, but though the time for tears was past, Lane could hear the hurt in Maggie's voice, the ache of remembered folly. "Go on," Lane pressed gently. "Let it go, Maggie."

She took a deep breath, lifted her chin, and gave Lane a direct look. "The day before Christmas I went to the market and overheard a couple of Tom's friends talking. They were laughing over the 'little joke' he was playing on me. It seems Tom had made a bet with a friend he could have me in bed by the time they left the island. Five hundred dollars to humiliate me for being what he referred to as 'a driftwood beach bum who didn't know her place and needed to be taken down a peg or two.' A fitting punishment for having insulted him in front of his friends. Pretty clever, huh?''

Lane didn't speak. He didn't move. He couldn't. The anger was bubbling through his blood so hot and furiously that his usual ready address failed him. Silently he cursed the bastard who had managed to do such intrinsic damage to someone so undeserving. The man had single-mindedly tried to break Maggie's spirit; he had put the wariness in her eyes, and Lane realized how easily he could hate Tom Hadley.

"Needless to say," Maggie said, her voice straining to keep the bitterness out of her words, "I ended the relationship immediately. I heard that Tom left the island the next day. I suppose he was five hundred dollars poorer for giving up so easily."

"Maggie . . ."

"So you see," Maggie said quickly, afraid that when Lane spoke, his voice would be tinged with pity. She didn't think she could bear that. "Here I am, back in the same boat, when I promised myself I would never, *ever* let someone sweep me off my feet again."

She raked a hand through the silken tumble of his hair.

"I want to be cautious and sophisticated, but instead I end up behaving like a lovesick teenager."

Rigid with barely leashed rage, Lane was quiet for a long moment. When he continued to say nothing, Maggie looked at him, a nervous expression lining her features. "Say something!" The words thundered from her.

Lane sat up straight, allowing his arms to dangle over his knees. "Maggie, I'm sorry. Really I am. But let me tell you something. *You're* not the one who's got a problem. That poor son of a bitch Hadley's the one who needs his head examined. We should pity him. Although," Lane added thoughtfully, "if I ever run into the guy, I'd be sorely tempted to rearrange his face for him." He shrugged his shoulders. "So you made a mistake. People a lot more worldly than you do it all the time. The trick is not to doubt yourself afterward. Your heart got the jump on your head—is that so bad? Do you want to go through life analyzing everything people do or say, looking for hidden motives all the time?"

She pillowed her cheek in one hand, resting her elbow on one knee, as though giving the matter serious thought. After a moment or two, Maggie slanted a look his way. "You think I'm a flake, don't you?"

He grinned and eased himself across the distance separating them. One hand slid up the back of her neck, diving into her hair, and with a playful tug, he used a handful of it to arch her head back so that their faces were nearly touching. "I think you're a generous, caring person who worries too much about some pretty foolish things."

He took the gentle curve of her sweet mouth, nipping at its lush fullness as he tipped her slowly backward to the mattress, his forearm supporting her descent, their bodies at right angles to each other.

The sheet slid away slowly, leaving her naked to the waist, but Maggie made no move to retrieve it. Close above her, Lane's eyes grew nearly black with passion as his gaze roved over her face, his free hand running lightly over her breasts. "Love's not horrible, Maggie. And you don't have to be afraid,'' he said softly. ''Not of me.'' His voice filled with such fierce tenderness that the blood set up a wild coursing in her veins once more.

She felt herself spiraling down as his tongue shot deep inside her mouth, chasing away the last vestiges of her fears. With Lane conquering the secret places of her body once more, her worries seemed silly and groundless. Lane Stafford could never be like Tom Hadley. Not ever.

It was only later, much later, that Maggie would remember that her admission of love had brought no echoing response.

The next few days were the happiest Maggie had ever known.

She and Lane spent every available moment together, as though both were secretly aware that time was slipping away from them. Maggie didn't know what would happen when it came time for Lane to leave; she refused to think about it. Obviously they would see each other again, especially if their plans for the restoration of the inn were successful. But the thought of being separated at this point in their relationship, even for a few weeks, was too awful to contemplate.

The weather changed drastically, releasing its hot stranglehold on the state. The rainy season began in earnest. It poured most afternoons, powerful, sudden storms soaking everything in sight and then disappearing as quickly as they had come, leaving Caloosa Key fresh-scrubbed, but steamy.

Lane and Maggie barely noticed. They strolled along the deserted beach hand in hand, exclaiming over sunsets and occasionally splashing into the gulf for a quick swim. Lane took Maggie to dinner at the Italian restaurant in town. The next day Maggie showed him how a true islander hunted stone crabs for supper, an excursion which Lane maintained was barbaric and nonsensical as long as there was a market on the island but an endeavor in which he nevertheless excelled and the results of which he heartily devoured. Together they pored over their notes on the inn. Maggie even attempted, to no avail, to teach Lane how to throw pots. Every time she tried to bring her hands around his to guide them upon the spinning clay, he invariably found her movements a sexual invitation and took Maggie into his arms. Not one pot was ever formed.

They made love often. Maggie bloomed under Lane's tutelage. He was a skillful and considerate lover, sometimes taking her with a playful ferociousness that left her quivering with excitement, other times draining her will as he gently explored, until her slowly budding desire soared beneath the fire of his fingertips. Not every moment was spent in wild passion. Sometimes they laughed or talked quietly, and each day brought a greater understanding of each other's needs and desires.

They were openly affectionate with each other, and it quickly became obvious to Robbie that something was going on between the two. Ever cautious of appearances, Maggie never allowed Lane to spend the night at Banyon House, though Lane suspected the boy knew the true situation since he was quick to find excuses to leave them alone. They were both relieved to realize that Robbie seemed genuinely pleased with their new relationship.

Robbie proved just how perceptive he was one hot afternoon as he and Lane stood waist deep in the gulf. Lane had gamely agreed to try his hand at sailboarding, a sport Robbie had mastered years ago, and was eager to demonstrate. Maggie stood on the beach, shading her eyes against the brilliant sun sparkling off the water and occasionally calling encouragement.

The sport called for a great deal of upper-body strength and concentration on balance. While Lane wasn't hopeless on the board, neither did he seem to be a natural, much to Robbie's disappointment.

Lane knew why he couldn't seem to keep his attention on the board and what he was doing. Every time he had the hang of it and the board took off in a skimming slice across the water, he'd happen to glance toward the shore and there was Maggie—following his progress along the beach in a slow jog, her body scantily covered by a simple white bikini, the twin mounds of her breasts bouncing slightly with each footfall. She was driving him crazy!

Cartwheeling over the sail in a perfect comic's pratfall, he took another header into the drink and came up sputtering.

"You okay?" Maggie hollered from the beach.

Lane squeezed saltwater out of his eyes and gave her a thumbs-up sign.

"Wish I'd had a camera for that one!" she called, laughing.

Robbie swam up beside him. He didn't attempt to hide his disappointment and disgust. "You're not paying attention to the wind shift."

"Right," Lane agreed, and his gaze touched briefly on the shore, where Maggie was bending over to retrieve a shell. Jesus, what a sight!

Robbie caught Lane's glance and said with some asperity, "You're supposed to be listening to me, not gawking at Maggie."

Lane sluiced water off the surface of the board, then fixed the boy with a meaningful look. "Rob, another time I think I'll get the hang of this just fine. But right now what I'd really like to do—and don't take this personally— is tie you to this board and let it sail off to Mexico. I've got other ideas in mind at the moment, and in a few years you'll understand what they are."

Robbie liked Lane too much to take serious offense. "Are you in love with my sister?" he asked in his usual blunt manner.

"Kinda looks that way, pal."

"Then why don't you ask her to marry you? Then you two won't have to keep sneaking around. You can just be together *all* the time."

"Well . . ." Lane began to explain, then subsided.

Well *what*? Why *didn't* he just marry her? More and more he was aware of time growing short. In a few days he would have to put the beautiful warmth and brightness of this time behind him and return to Chicago. Even if he managed to pull off the near-impossible feat of convincing Jerry to restore the inn, a real worry, but one he never shared with Maggie, even if he came back to Caloosa Key to handle that restoration, eventually his future would take him out of Maggie's orbit forever.

The thought filled him with aching despair. Before Maggie, he'd been fully satisfied with his life, sure of where he was heading in his career. Now he couldn't imagine a life without Maggie James in it.

But as much as he was coming to enjoy the slow, uncomplicated pace of island living, his family, his work, his entire future lay in Chicago. He couldn't stay here forever. So what alternatives did that leave? He wasn't willing to settle for a long-distance love affair, a few stolen days between projects that took him to California or Texas or New York.

Which meant the only answer, of course, was to take Maggie back with him. Convincing her to come to Chicago wasn't going to be easy. He could imagine her reaction to the Windy City, how foreign it would seem to a woman raised on sun and sand and saltwater. There was Robbie to think of, too. He would live with them, of course, but could he adjust to the public-school system in Chicago? Leaving behind his friends and that ridiculous menagerie of pets?

It might take all the powerful persuasion he could bring to bear. But they *could* work it out.

The ease with which he accepted the idea of marriage surprised him a bit. He'd always thought the road to life-long commitment would be traveled slowly, and only after months of careful consideration. He'd savored his freedom, liked playing the field. He hadn't expected the sensible, unswerving plans for his future to be derailed by an unshakable passion for someone he'd known less than a month.

Love was a funny thing. It stubbornly refused to follow

timetables or agendas. It couldn't be pigeonholed or manipulated or organized. And it damn sure didn't give a person much warning.

But no matter how poorly it fit his plans, Lane couldn't deny it any longer. He loved Maggie Rose James and he wasn't going to settle for an affair or a meaningful relationship or having a "significant other" halfway across the country. He wanted permanence. He wanted a lifetime of waking up beside the same woman. He wanted kids. And he wanted all of those things with a funny, complicated little islander who knew how to catch her own dinner and allowed skunks in her house and could quicken his pulse with a soft smile.

Lane's gaze traveled to the shore once more. Maggie saw that he was looking her way and her mouth tipped up at the corners. "Giving up?" she called tauntingly.

"No!" came his immediate response. Then, under his breath, he added, "Not a chance!"

That night Lane was different.

Maggie sensed something the moment he came through the screen door, one hand curled around a bottle of the finest wine the island market sold, the other clutching an object in the tail of his shirt. He laid it gently on the kitchen counter, revealing two small eggs, still warm from the nest.

Robbie was excited over Lane's find. "Where'd you get them?"

"Up in the cupola at the inn. When I came back from town I thought I saw something climb over the railing from the rooftop. I investigated and caught your friend Roscoe in the act of stealing them out of the nest. Some unwise mother had made a home along one of the baseboards up there. I was afraid to leave them for fear one of the raccoons would come back, so I figured I'd bring them to you and you'd know what to do."

Robbie was a flurry of activity. He took charge, and before dinner was placed on the table, he had created an impromptu home in the garage for the latest additions to his collection.

While Lane uncorked the wine, Maggie checked the casserole in the oven, listening to Robbie scurrying through the house, collecting items for a makeshift incubator. "He won't be able to sleep until those two hatch." She tipped a knife into the center of the pot pie's crust and added in mock reproach, "Two more mouths to feed. Thanks a lot."

Lane said nothing and she glanced his way quickly. Their relationship was peppered with a lot of good-natured bantering, and Lane's lack of response surprised her. But he seemed totally absorbed in removing the cork from the wine bottle. Perhaps he hadn't heard her.

Maggie tossed the oven mitts on the counter. "I have some encouraging news. One of the undersecretaries of the State Preservation Society called today. She's interested in lending her support to get the inn restored. Seems she stayed there once when she was a little girl. Isn't that great?"

Again no response.

It seemed so uncharacteristic that Maggie went to him, touching his sleeve to draw his attention. "Lane, did you hear me? I said—"

"Yes, I heard," he interrupted absently, his mind obviously fixed upon the task at hand. "That's great, Maggie."

The corkscrew bit through the bottom of the cork, and Lane tugged upward. But instead of popping out cleanly, it broke off, leaving the obstruction still in place.

If Lane's behavior moments before had been unlike him, his reaction to the recalcitrant cork was completely unexpected and, to Maggie, a shock. With an oath, he angrily tossed the corkscrew on the counter. The wine bottle followed; he slammed it upon the Formica so hard that Maggie was surprised the glass didn't shatter. Resting his hands upon the rim of the countertop, Lane stared at the wall. "I hope you like bits of cork in your rosé," he said harshly.

Maggie was stunned. Lane's anger was rare to her, and the circumstances hardly warranted such a strong reaction. She glanced down at his hands. The knuckles were white, his fingers almost a death-grip. She wasn't afraid of him in that moment, merely afraid *for* him. Maggie's insides twisted. This Lane was alien to her, someone she'd never met before. She wasn't sure how to approach the problem. She wasn't even sure what the problem was.

"Lane, what is it?" she tested carefully. "What's wrong?"

Some of the anger seemed to leave him. Standing beside him, Maggie could see the fight drain out of his body. His fingers relaxed and his shoulders slumped slightly. It was a moment or two before he looked at her, but when his gaze met hers, Maggie felt dizzy and slightly breathless. There was a bleakness in the look he gave her, a finality that had no business there and which Maggie prayed was a trick of the light. Her brow knit in confusion and her heart began to pound quickly, and in that moment, she *was* afraid.

But as quickly as the last, another transformation took place. Lane's eyes became objective, his thoughts hidden away. He smiled at her. It was the familiar, teasing grin of the man she'd fallen in love with.

"I'm sorry, sweetheart," he said gently. "I didn't mean to frighten you."

She squeezed his arm. "You couldn't. But tell me what's upsetting you."

She watched his eyes slide away from her, and Maggie wanted desperately to believe there was no deception there, that Lane was merely embarrassed by his outburst.

"There are so many things I want to say to you, Maggie." Lane's voice was a whisper of sound, as though he said the words for his own benefit. "Time is getting away from us. I can't stay here forever."

Relief trickled through her. So that was it. Time. Robbing them of precious moments together.

Standing on tiptoe, Maggie brought Lane's head down

to hers. His body was disturbingly taut, and she rubbed her hands along the tops of his shoulders in an attempt to massage away some of the stiffness. She nipped playfully at the corners of his mouth, brushing her lips across his in a possessive brand that a month ago she would have considered bold and wanton. "All the more reason why we can't waste a minute." Her lips stretched into a secret smile. "Are you really hungry?" she asked close to his ear.

He shook his head.

"Then why don't we take that bottle of wine and a blanket and go for a long walk on the beach." She kissed the slight indentation in his chin. "I'll show you how to make the best use of the time we have left."

They left the casserole warming in the oven and a note for Robbie, who would probably not leave his latest patients until his stomach protested the lack of nourishment.

The weather cooperated beautifully. The evening was balmy and bugless, the stars a glorious diamond-studded canopy above their heads. They found their favorite spot on the shore, a half-moon curve of sand sheltered by a wide stand of strangler firs. The scent of night blooms was a heady, potent pull upon the senses.

Lane spread the blanket upon the sand, which was still warm from the intense heat of the day. With the moon silvering their bodies and the breeze gently ruffling their hair, they sat side by side, scarcely touching as they listened to the soft gurgle of waves lapping at the shore. They watched the lights of ships move along the horizon, and Lane, who had done very well in college astronomy classes, pointed out various constellations, making up silly names for the ones he couldn't remember. They laughed softly, sometimes reaching out to touch each other with tentative, featherlike strokes, a finger trailing along a bared thigh, a hand brushing away grains of sand from a moonlit cheek. Often there were long stretches of companionable silence, a quietude neither of them felt compelled to break.

After a time some of the tension seemed to leave Lane, and his previous black mood slipped away. He was still slightly distracted, but he was able to laugh more often, and the tightness no longer corded the muscles along his shoulders. The beauty of the night was working its magic upon him, and Maggie was relieved to see him gradually respond to her teasing persuasion.

At last Lane sighed heavily and said, "God, I'm going to miss this place."

There was a note of such wistful anguish in his voice that Maggie looked at him quickly. His features were indistinct in the moonlight, but the thought came to her suddenly. *He's already saying good-bye.*

She came up on her knees to face him. With a faint smile upon her lips, Maggie shook her head. "You'll never be far away from it." Her hand reached out to cover his heart. "The island's a part of you now. In here."

Lane lifted her hand to his lips, lightly placing kisses across each fingertip. "Not just the island, Maggie. There's so much more. So much I want to say to you. We need to talk—"

"No." She halted him by slipping her hand out of his grasp and pressing her fingers to his lips. "Not yet. There's still time."

Maggie refused to allow the enchantment of the evening to dissipate. The future was an uncertainty. But whatever problems had to be dealt with in their relationship, for now, he was hers. *Just a little longer*, she begged silently. *A day or two more. Then I can face the reality of whatever comes afterward.*

"Besides," she continued in a softly lilting voice, "I have a couple of presents for you. Hold out your hand." In spite of the poor light, her eyes held his in an embrace that promised much. Lane felt a quicksilver heat skitter along his veins.

She reached into the basket they had brought, then placed a tissue-wrapped object into Lane's outstretched palm. He removed the paper carefully until the gift was exposed.

The egret he had admired in Maggie's shop.

In the moonlight it gleamed a milky white, almost eerie in its stark beauty. Lane was quiet, admiring once again the skillfully formed curves of the figurine as a fine edge of joy cut across his senses. An awesome gladness was gathering within him, laying all the devils of uncertainty to rest.

Maggie sat silently, waiting for his response. When it did not come, she lost a little of her new-found confidence. Had she overestimated the statue's appeal? "I've others you might prefer . . ." she began nervously.

"No." He looked at her sharply, his face somber a moment, then lifting in an infectious grin. "You know this is the one I want."

Their thoughts merged, remembering.

Embarrassment brought a searing blush to Maggie's cheeks, and she was glad for the diminished light. She continued brightly. "You won't be able to look at it without thinking of Caloosa Key."

"And other things," Lane added with a devilish laugh. He tipped toward her. "Now let me thank you properly."

He reached out for her, but Maggie placed a restraining hand upon his chest. "Wait. You'll spoil my second present."

In a voice rough with passion, Lane growled, "I'm not sure I care."

"How ungrateful you are!"

"Not ungrateful. Merely impatient."

His knuckles traced a pattern along the satin angle of her jaw.

"But I think you'll like this present even better," Maggie said, with a kittenish purr of delight. Her fingers stole along his knee, as light as fairy wings upon Lane's warm flesh. "I've been giving this a lot of thought, and it occurs to me that every time we . . . make love, you're the one who pleasures *me*. Not that I mind that," Maggie said reasonably, but don't *you* ever want to be the one who's pleasured?''

Lane smiled. ''I assure you, I get a great deal of pleasure.''

Under lowered lashes, Maggie favored him with a teasing glance. Her fingers reached out to slide under Lane's T-shirt, brushing across his taut stomach. He drew breath sharply, and she felt the fluid ripple of strong muscles tighten against her delicate, searching touch. ''But wouldn't you like to see how much I've learned?''

Her unexpected boldness shocked Lane into silence, and Maggie took quick advantage of the moment. She pushed his shirt upward until most of Lane's chest was exposed, at the same time gently pushing him down upon the blanket. Lifting herself over him, Maggie shrugged out of her blouse, her bared breasts exposed to the cool evening air, the nipples responding immediately.

Watching her, Lane was speechless. In the silver light she was beautifully unreal. A sea nymph come to shore to cast a spell upon him. Was there ever a more willing victim?

Her mouth descended to his waist, charting a slow, teasing course upward along the furred expanse of his chest. Her breath stirred the fine, dark hairs, exploring the familiar sinews that responded to the lightness of her touch with an undisciplined quiver. Deliberately Maggie allowed her ivory breasts to press against him, her movements designed to ignite the source of his passion.

When her lips closed over one pap and Maggie suckled the nub seductively, Lane could barely contain his response. With a low groan, he plunged his hand into her hair, pulling her head gently back until she was forced to meet his gaze. ''Sweetheart, do you have any idea what you are doing?'' he demanded to know in a voice very nearly out of control.

''Not really. I'm making most of this up as I go along,'' she replied mischievously. Her eyes were wide with deliberate innocence, but there was a merry twinkle in their sapphire-shaded depths. "Let me know if I'm getting warm."

"*You're* warm, *I'm* on fire."

A smile blossomed upon Maggie's lips. "Shall I stop?"

"No." He shook his head roughly. "God, no."

Encouraged, Maggie's hand dipped low to the front of Lane's shorts. His body jumped at the contact, but emboldened by this sudden, heady power over him, Maggie quickly stole through the barrier of clothing to find the essence of his maleness. The ragged sound of his breathing drifted into the darkness as her fingers stroked and tightened around him. She could feel his heart pounding across her breasts and a wicked smile curved her lips. Her grasp, so untutored only a month ago, toyed with the fullness of him. She was delighted to discover she could arouse Lane as easily as he had excited her in the past week.

What little restraint Lane had managed to exercise vanished, and he rolled her body under his, his hands framing her face as he pinned her to the blanket. "Enough!" he growled. His breath was coming hard and fast.

"But I haven't finished," Maggie pouted in mock distress.

"I'm the one who'll be finished if you don't stop," Lane said, and his mouth closed upon hers with such hot, urgent intensity that she forgot her newly discovered power and surrendered to the intoxicating honey as their mouths blended together.

His kiss turned sweet, his tongue probing the inner recesses of Maggie's mouth until she felt as though his touch had flicked upon her very soul. She responded in kind, savoring the soft, warm sensations her exploration could create.

When Lane drew back at last, they were both gasping for air. "No matter how much you've taught me, there's always one more lesson to be learned," Maggie said with a soft sigh of disbelief.

Staring down into her eyes through the darkness, Lane's face suddenly lost its playful look. Lightly his fingers trailed along the clear, clean cut of her jaw. "You're the one who's taught *me*, Maggie. So many things . . ."

They came together in an unrestrained excitement, the rest of their clothing quickly discarded upon the edge of the blanket. With a passionate madness, Lane drove into Maggie, moving so strongly within her that she thrashed frantically beneath him, impaled by a sweet havoc that threatened to overwhelm. Incoherent whimpers of delight escaped her lips as her body unconsciously fueled his driving assault. Their bodies met in a raw, exquisite agony, moving in perfect counterpoint.

Maggie's cry of pleasure echoed Lane's—a shared bliss.

And for just a few brief moments, time obligingly ceased to steal away from them.

TEN

As always, the aftermath of their lovemaking was a quiet, reflective exploration. They relearned the contours of each other's bodies once again in gentle ways—nibbling kisses in the soft hollows of a dozen secret places, a hand sliding over the flare of a hip, a gaze that touched seductively, then danced away.

They redressed unhurriedly, the only sound in the stillness their slight, muted breathing. What would it be like, Maggie wondered, to go to bed every night and wake up every morning beside Lane? No more stolen hours. No quick kisses in dark corners. The thought was appealing. Was it such an impossible dream?

"What are you thinking?" Lane asked as he pulled his shirt over his head.

She couldn't voice her heart. Lane's lovemaking unfettered the woman in her, but not enough to dismiss years of strict upbringing completely. A declaration of love had already been made. Perhaps unwisely. But to suggest a deeper commitment was unthinkable; her feelings were too fragile to bear rejection. Besides, no man liked to be pushed into marriage, her mother had counseled years ago. No matter how times changed, Maggie couldn't bring herself to reveal the true direction of her thoughts.

She tossed her head, a flash of silver in the moonlight. "I was just thinking, we ought to drink that wine," she improvised, striving for a light tone. "Especially since you made such a superhuman effort to open it."

Lane reached out to give a lock of her hair a sharp tug. "Witch."

With a laugh, Maggie retrieved the wine and two glasses. His earlier incompetence conquered, Lane removed the cork with a flourish and poured a generous amount into each glass she held.

They took their first sip in silence. Maggie let the wine slide down her throat slowly. She wasn't much of a connoisseur, but the rosé seemed unpleasantly bitter. Resisting the temptation to make a face, she offered Lane a vague smile.

The corners of his mouth lifted, and he held the goblet skyward, absorbed in angling the glass until it caught the meager light. After a quiet moment or two, he said succinctly, "I don't believe I've ever had a more horrible wine than this."

There was a second or two of silence, then they both burst out laughing.

"Thank goodness," Maggie said. "I thought I was just unschooled in how good wine should taste."

"Trust me," Lane remarked with a lift of one eyebrow. "This ain't it."

"Oh, I don't know," she teased lightly. "I think the bits of cork add something."

He threw her a scathing glance. "There's *no* cork in the wine."

"Yes, there is. In fact, there's a tiny bit stuck at the corner of your mouth."

Leaning towards him, Maggie lifted a finger to that spot. With a light touch she flicked away an imaginary speck, then allowed her fingertips to trail along the curve of Lane's bottom lip.

His mouth stretched lazily, but the look he gave her

was warm and intense. "Maggie . . ." His voice was a husky murmur. "Maggie, you play with fire, sweetheart."

She grinned, then gave a little gasp of surprise when Lane's head dipped suddenly to capture the tip of her finger with his teeth. He savaged it playfully, then pulled it further into his mouth, laving with his warm tongue. Maggie giggled, delighted by the teasing, sensual feeling that inflamed her senses and set the pit of her stomach aquiver.

They might easily have allowed their leashed desire to soar once more, but in that moment, Maggie heard Robbie calling their names. The budding passion eva, rated.

"Your brother has the worst timing of anyone I've ever met," Lane observed with a rueful laugh, but there was a slight edge to his voice and his eyes remained solemn, as though he truly regretted the interruption.

"At least he's smart enough not to make a personal appearance," she said as she began gathering remnants of their tryst. She called an acknowledgment to the boy, and Robbie replied that Lane had a telephone call from Chicago. Jerry Carlisle.

Maggie looked at Lane expectantly, but he offered no comment to that news. They trudged back up the beach, their fingers linked. As they walked side by side, Maggie sensed an immediate tightening within Lane. She could feel the stiffness running through him and wondered at its return. Curiosity made her cast a probing glance his way. "Lane, is there something you're not telling me?"

"No."

His response was so uncommunicative that Maggie fell silent and said no more. She felt a trace of nervousness sketch along her veins. Was he already anticipating a difficult time persuading Carlisle to restore the inn? No. She wouldn't borrow trouble by starting to doubt now. Besides, Lane was as committed to the project as she. She believed and trusted in his ability to persuade.

Robbie was waiting for them at the back steps. He had little interest in Lane's call, but he was anxious for both of them to admire his handiwork in the garage. He clutched at his sister's arm impatiently. "Mag, come see what I've rigged up for the eggs."

Before she could respond, Lane's hand fell on her shoulder. "You two go on. I'll join you in a minute. Jerry's probably just wanting to know when I'm coming home."

In spite of her growing anxiety over Lane's moodiness, Maggie gave him a smile of encouragement and followed in Robbie's wake.

A few minutes later, she left Robbie in the garage trying to raise the base of the nest nearer the bulb he had rigged to keep the eggs warm. He needed an extension cord, and Maggie was sure she had a spare one in a kitchen drawer. If she could find it.

Lane's voice filtered to her from the kitchen, still engrossed in conversation with his friend. The words were low, indistinct, and Maggie wondered if he had broached the subject of the inn with Carlisle. Her stomach fluttered with the nagging uncertainty she'd been striving mightily to hold at bay. *Please, Jerry Carlisle, just hear him out.*

Not wishing to disturb Lane, she entered the room quietly. He was turned away from her, one hand raking through his dark hair in a distracted manner, and something in his stance suggested discouragement. Her heart triphammering, Maggie stopped to listen.

"I've done as much as I'm going to do, Jer," Lane was saying. "Find someone else." There was a pause while Jerry pressed home a point. "It doesn't matter now. You'll have the resort you want. Maggie James won't be able to stand in your way. No matter how much she wants to." Another pause. "Yes, I'm sure." He listened for a long minute, then shook his head. "No. She trusts me. She thinks I'm going to help her get the damned place restored." There was a self-deprecating note in his voice. "No, of course not. The place is unsalvageable. I recommend that it be torn down immediately."

The conversation continued along those same lines, but Maggie scarcely heard. Frozen in misery, she stood in numb silence, aware only that the earth had shifted and the bottom had just dropped out of her world.

Lies.

All of it.

He'd never intended to help her. He'd never intended to convince Jerry Carlisle. All he'd ever intended was to have his own way. She had been a willing dupe, and the thought left Maggie's stomach coiled in knots of bitter self-hatred.

Fool.

Idiot.

She felt as though something had suddenly died within her. Hope for their future. Faith in her own judgment. Love. In that moment Maggie despised herself almost as much as she hated Lane.

Her chest ached. Breathing had become almost impossible. She took a quick, anguished breath, and perhaps Lane realized that he was no longer alone.

He turned, his eyes catching hers immediately. He was still, watching her, and for a moment Maggie could read nothing in his face. She knew her own features must be paper-white, with every word she had heard written upon them, and in a moment Lane read the truth there. His eyes widened. He stopped listening to Carlisle and whispered her name. Once.

Maggie couldn't speak, but life returned to her numbed limbs. She turned and ran.

She pounded out the back door, her destination unknown, her only thought escape. Reaching the beach, Maggie began a stumbling run along the shoreline, mindless of the driftwood that threatened to trip her and broken shells biting cruelly into her bare feet.

A hand dragged at her arm, bringing her up short, and Maggie whirled to face Lane. She jerked out of his grasp and backed warily away from him, splashing into ankle-deep water. Her chest heaving with unreleased sobs, she stood still, watching him.

"Maggie, you don't understand . . ." he began.

"No, don't! I don't want to hear anymore lies. Just leave me alone."

"It isn't what you think. If you'll just let me explain . . ."

"I don't need an explanation, I might be a first-class idiot, but there's nothing wrong with my hearing. Or are you going to deny what I heard?"

In spite of the white-hot rage that flamed within her, a small part of her begged denial. *Tell me I'm wrong. Tell me I'm crazy. Just don't let me have been wrong about you.*

"No. I'm not going to deny what you heard."

A sharp, stabbing disappointment knifed through her, and Maggie felt broken inside. "You told Carlisle that the inn should be torn down."

"Yes."

She leveled an icy stare in his direction. "Then we have nothing further to say to one another."

"The hell we don't," Lane countered, his patience overtaxed. "And by God, you're going to listen."

She moved suddenly, splashing out of the water to slip around him. His fingers snatched at her arm once more, jerking her around. His hand shook her arm angrily, but she refused to acknowledge him. "Damn it, Maggie. Listen."

Don't, an inner voice warned. *Don't listen. He'll make you believe again.* She kept her face averted, staring down the dark, deserted shoreline.

"I was going to tell you tonight," Lane explained, his voice low and harsh, "but the timing never seemed quite right. I knew what your reaction was going to be, so I was waiting for the right moment. Hell, maybe I was a coward trying to avoid an unpleasant task. Don't you think I know by now what that old relic means to you?"

Maggie refused to comment.

"The report on the samples I sent to the structural engineer came back today. They were conflicting. The evidence suggested major structural damage due to water, but there was no moisture present. So just before I came over this evening, I paid another visit to the inn. It was there all the time, Maggie. The drought dried out and hid a lot of what's wrong, but now that it's raining every day, the place is holding water like a sponge. Damage like that makes restoration impossible. I'm not just talking about costs here. It's dangerous. I couldn't in all good conscience recommend saving it."

Maggie turned to look at him, night shadows dancing across her features. Her eyes were hard and emotionless. "I don't believe you. I think you've been lying to me from the beginning. I heard you. Jerry Carlisle wanted you to win my trust, and that's what you did, isn't it?"

Lane stiffened. Not many people dared to call him a liar. "Yes, Jerry felt it would be a good idea to have you on his side," he said angrily. "But I told you before, I don't work for Jerry. Whatever's happened between us has happened because *I* wanted it to. No one's dictated my actions."

"It all comes down to the same thing, doesn't it?" she asked, a bitter curve to her lips. "You got what you wanted."

"Yes."

No denial. Not even remorse. Tears welled in her eyes. "You bastard," she whispered raggedly.

"If you won't listen to reason and you won't listen to the truth, then listen to a few hard facts. Yes, I got what I wanted. What I wanted from the first moment I saw you. I've never denied that. I'm a normal, healthy male, and I used every bit of expertise I could to get you in my bed. I'm *glad* it worked. And so are you, if you'd stop and think about what we've shared this past week or so."

"No," Maggie exclaimed with a violent shake of her head. "It's over."

"The hell it is."

"I hate you," she hissed.

Fire flashed in Lane's eyes and a shiver of apprehension slid down Maggie's spine. His grip on her arm tightened as he pulled her down the beach. She began to struggle violently to free herself, but Lane's hold was unbreakable. His profile was a stony mask as he stalked along with Maggie in tow.

He stopped in front of their private spot, where earlier they had lain intertwined. "An hour ago, you and I made love here," he snapped. "Did you hate me then, Maggie? Were all your responses faked?"

Flushing scarlet, she muttered with cutting sarcasm. "I know only too well how I responded, and why. I'm a hopeless romantic who has a tendency to confuse the magician with the magic. It's stupid, but it's not fatal."

"So you're just going to pretend nothing ever happened between us?" he demanded. His features were drawn in hot rage, and Lane realized his heart was banging so loudly, he could hear it pounding in his ears. He felt icy-cold and realized he was scared. Terrified because Maggie was slipping away from him and he couldn't seem to do anything to stop her. Jesus! *How has it come to this?* he wondered frantically.

Maggie's eyes were bleak, but her response was clear and measured. "No. I can't pretend. But I can try to forget."

Lane's temper reached new heights. "You little idiot. Do you think it's that easy? There's more here than that. Do you think in six months you'll have forgotten what I look like? How it feels when I touch you? You won't. Because I won't let you. Tonight you told me the island was a part of me now. You're right. But you're a part of me, too, Maggie. The best part. I'm not walking away from that."

His words had the power to move her, but Maggie refused to allow a weakening of her resolve. Deliberately she looked away, shutting Lane out. Her entire body exhibited a frigid disdain for anything he had to say.

Lane witnessed the death of something deep inside her

and desperation filled him with a vague sense of impending doom. "Maggie . . ." Her name was a plea. "Don't do this to us."

"There is no *us*," she replied coldly, her voice filled with unshakable conviction. Her indigo eyes were glitteringly hard.

Lane took a deep breath, trying to master the raveling edges of his self-control. "Can't you see what you're doing here? The inn's just an excuse you're using to protect yourself. It's an easy way out of this relationship—a relationship that scares the hell out of you."

She said nothing.

"I know you've had a shock," Lane said, his voice sounding suddenly tired and hollow. "You need time to adjust to the idea of losing the inn. I'm willing to give you that. I'm flying back to Chicago tomorrow." When she made no comment to that news, Lane gripped her chin between his fingers and brought her head around. He regarded her with weary regret for a moment, then shook his head grimly. "You're a stubborn woman, Maggie James. Give up the inn. It's over. But *we're* not."

Angered beyond sense, Maggie lashed out at him. "You can't *make* me love you!"

Lane laughed harshly, and with a tender sweep of his hand, he tilted her face upward so their eyes met. "Sweetheart, I already have."

His mouth found hers unerringly, the feel of his lips hard and compelling. Tangling his hand in her hair, Lane forced her head back until her mouth parted slightly. His tongue plunged ruthlessly, a quick rape of the senses. But before Maggie could respond he was already pushing her away, releasing her with a contemptuous movement.

"See if that's one of the things you can forget," he challenged in a low, bitter tone.

With the back of her hand pressed shakily against her bruised lips, Maggie watched as Lane stalked back toward Banyon House.

*   *   *

Maggie was miserable.

Oh, she tried. She really did. But no matter how hard she fought to resurrect her anger toward Lane, within a week of his departure it had evaporated. Left in its wake was the sharp pang of sadness and regret.

Lane was right, of course. About everything. Her fears, her unwillingness to take a chance on love. He hadn't lied or used her, she knew that now. His concern for the inn had been too genuine to be subterfuge. Remembering his excited interest, the hours he spent poring over records of the inn's history, Maggie felt hot shame steal over her. How could she have made such an unworthy accusation?

In her most optimistic moments, a flicker of hope continued to burn within her. Lane would call. She would beg forgiveness. And in that practical no-nonsense way of his, he would tell her it was about time she came to her senses. He would pull her into his arms and kiss her; her mouth would open willingly, so willingly. . . .

But the month of July faded and Lane did *not* call. Each passing day twisted a knife blade of anguish into her heart as her worst fears came to fruition.

She lectured herself sternly. Why should he call? It was over. The man had had enough of her seesawing emotions and had put the unfortunate incident behind him. He was getting on with his life. Who could blame him? She had allowed her fears to blind her to the truth of his love, and if what they had once shared now seemed irrevocably destroyed, Maggie admitted that she had no one to blame but herself.

With the simplistic logic of a child, Robbie encouraged her to call Lane and apologize. Maggie loved Lane—Lane loved Maggie. It was a pretty obvious solution to the problem.

"I can't!" Maggie told him for the third time in one day.

"Why not?"

"Because . . ." The words settled.

Because she didn't want to have her worst fears confirmed once and for all. She didn't want to hear his voice, polite but distant, telling her perhaps their breakup had been for the best. The hurt would be unbearable, crushing any faint illusions she might harbor.

But July slid into August and the truth was painfully clear. It was finished. Even Robbie stopped pestering her to contact Lane, recognizing a bitter fact of life—some things just didn't turn out the way you wanted them to, no matter how badly you might wish it.

They got on with the business of their lives. Maggie sculpted in her shop almost every day, creating such a ridiculous surplus of inventory, her shelves were crowded and unappealing. The garden was tended mercilessly, the grounds surrounding Banyon House were raked and planted. She replaced screens and painted the porch railing.

She was tired.

And lonely.

And her heart, never a very reliable organ, refused to put the past behind her and ached with the tender remembrances of what might have been.

Lane was miserable.

He should never have given Maggie time to think things over. That was the problem with the woman. She thought too much. It wouldn't help; it could only prolong the agony of separation. But he'd been so frustrated and furious with Maggie, he hadn't known what else to do.

He returned to Chicago grim and dispirited.

He threw himself into his work, but his concentration was shot. Worst of all, the sleek, cool lines of his designs no longer pleased him. They seemed lifeless, impersonal. Lane found himself recalling the pleasant, jumbled clutter of Banyon House, and more and more, the thought of the haphazard architecture of the island brought a faint smile to his lips.

Chicago itself seemed alien to him. The city no longer seemed exciting or glamorous. It was muggy and crowded and too noisy. He remembered too well the quiet peace of Caloosa Key, the tang of salt breezes, the warm sand squeezing up between his bare toes. He knew he was being foolish, drawing comparisons where none should be, but he couldn't help himself. He discovered he missed the island and its unique, antiquated way of life.

He wondered if Robbie had managed to hatch the eggs he'd found. He hoped so. If need be, he knew the boy would sit on them himself to save them.

Most of all, he missed Maggie. He missed the way her hair tumbled around her shoulders in charming disarray. He longed to hear her laugh, to touch her, to see her smile at him with honeyed sweetness. His recollection of her was a weakness, a narcotic in his blood. Since returning to Chicago, his life was not his own.

He couldn't go on like this, Lane told himself. The uncertainty of the future was driving him insane! He wanted to pick up the phone and put an end to this once and for all, but he couldn't. Time. She needed time. He'd pulled the rug out from under her. Now he had to give her a chance to get back on her feet.

He was behind his desk at his office. Jerry Carlisle sat across from him, and Lane was suddenly aware the man had spoken.

"What?"

"Come back to earth, Staff. What does that thing do, put you in a trance?"

Lance glanced down at his hands, surprised to find the clay egret in his grasp. He didn't remember picking it up, but he realized the feel of it brought an odd sort of comfort to him. His fingers paused to memorize once more each hardness and curve before he placed it back upon the desk.

"Sorry." His smile was mechanical. "You were saying?"

"I was saying, I want you to join my party on the boat this weekend."

"No."

"Why not?"

"I've got . . . plans."

"Like what?" Jerry pressed.

Lane's brow arched at his friend's inquisitiveness. "Since when do I need to report my actions to you?"

"Since you've cut yourself off from your friends and family the past three weeks. Ever since you got back from Florida you've lived the life of a monk. No parties, no poker games, and your cleaning lady says there hasn't been one overnight guest, either. *Very* unlike you. Even your secretary says you've become a grouch."

"Are you through, Sherlock? Or would you like to tell me what I had for lunch today?"

"Pastrami on whole wheat," Jerry said with a broad grin. "Impressed?"

"Very. Is there a point you're trying to make here?"

Jerry leaned forward in his seat, his features suddenly serious. "Just one. Call her, Staff. You're not going to be sane again until you do."

Most of what Jerry knew about Lane's relationship with Maggie was guesswork. He didn't know the particulars, but they had been friends long enough so that Jerry was pretty adept at filling in the blanks. "You don't know the whole story," Lane said.

"Don't have to. I know when someone's miserable. That's you, pal. Call her," he repeated.

"I can't."

"Why not?"

"Because it's too soon."

"Too soon for what?"

Too soon to find out if I've been kidding myself. Too soon to find out it's over. To Jerry he said, "Too soon to push her into making a decision about us."

Jerry scoffed at that answer. "I've never known you to be such a coward. She's just a woman, Staff. A shy country maid who'd probably jump at the chance—"

"Don't!"

Jerry's eyes narrowed at the sudden tight note in Lane's voice. Lord, his friend was worse off than he'd thought. "You've got it pretty bad, don't you, pal?"

Lane dropped his mask for a moment. There was weary resignation in his expression. "I've known that for a long time. The problem is convincing the lady she's no better off than I am."

In the end, he took the coward's way out.

One of his firm's projects in Finland was having difficulty, and it was suggested that Lane fly over and straighten it out. It was on the tip of his tongue to refuse, but in the moment when he would have spoken, he found himself agreeing to go instead.

The assignment seemed a blessing in disguise. It would allow him to stay busy—too busy to dwell upon the problem of Maggie. It would give her time to adjust, and it would distance him from friends and family, who were quickly becoming well-meaning pains in the neck.

But the problems in Helsinki offered him no relief from the turmoil in his mind. In the cold and dreary city, the warmth of Caloosa Key seemed more desirable than it had in Chicago. The difficulties with construction were time-consuming, but there were too many free evenings spent in his hotel room. In the dark, late hours of the night, Lane's mind replayed every moment of his time spent on the island. And sometimes he could not shake the fear that he had lost Maggie forever. That she was never, ever going to be his.

In the darkness of his room, Lane's eyes drifted to the bedside nightstand to find the white blur of the egret. Stuffing it into his briefcase and carting it halfway across the world had been an uncharacteristic, sentimental thing for him to do. Lane smiled, thinking how Jerry would chide him if he knew. He didn't care. The sight of it pleased him enormously. Its serene and regal beauty was his only tangible link with the one person he most wanted to be with. It reminded him of shared passion, beautiful moments where the ugliness of mistrust had no place in their relationship.

Lane sighed into the darkness. *Ah, Maggie, how could you doubt me? Don't you know how much I love you?*

A sudden thought snapped into his brain and Lane shot upright in bed. *Did* Maggie know? He loved her, and he had told her so, hadn't he? He focused his mind on those three small words, striving to remember having said them aloud, angered when he realized he could not. He wracked his brain, re-creating conversations, but not once could Lane recall actually saying the words to *Maggie* that seemed so obvious to *him*.

Stafford, you idiot! No wonder the woman doesn't trust you.

He wanted to snatch up the telephone that very instant and tell her. Make her realize once and for all what he'd known all along. His hand actually touched the receiver, but at the last moment he suppressed the urge. When he told her, he didn't want to be half a world apart. He wanted to be close, kissing close. With delights of Maggie's ripe, warm body pressed up against him, the clean, feminine scent of her filling his nostrils, her pliant mouth opening beneath his. She would surrender meekly to the primitive need enslaving them both.

And *then* he would tell her.

And show her. In a dozen secret ways.

Yes, that was the way to let a woman know you loved her.

For the first time in weeks, a feeling of confidence and strength came to him and his despair lessened. He fell asleep, dreaming of the loving union that would soon take place between him and Maggie. And in those dreams, he never once considered that those simple words might bring him anything but the most welcome response.

Two weeks later, Lane returned from Finland, a man of renewed conviction. The long, bleak nightmare of separation was over. He felt strong and invincible and ready to do battle if need be.

He went directly from the airport to his office, giving the senior partners of the firm a brief but concise update on the situation in Helsinki. They seemed pleased with his report, and the moment they left his office, Lane was thumbing the intercom button.

"Yes, Mr. Stafford."

"Alice, would you call the airline and book a flight for me to Fort Myers, Florida? The first one out. I'll need to pick up a rental car, too."

"I'll try, sir," his secretary's voice came back with brisk efficiency, "but that may not be possible."

"Why not?"

"Because of the storm."

"What storm?" Lane asked sharply.

"There's a tropical storm down there right now. It hasn't been upgraded to a hurricane, but I believe all flights to that area have been placed on hold."

His stomach roiled unpleasantly. "See what you can do, Alice."

He had to go up and down the dial before he found a radio station broadcasting a weather report. Tropical storm Deborah was ten miles off the west coast of Florida and expected to do little damage, but residents had been advised to prepare for severe winds and rain. The weatherman seemed to regard the storm as more of an inconvenience than a threat, but Lane's gut had not stopped quivering since Alice had given him the news.

He didn't know why he was edgy. Certainly Caloosa Key had survived worse than this. Maggie and Robbie were probably experienced in this sort of thing; no doubt they had buttoned themselves down pretty tightly. Banyon House was old, but had managed to stand up under more severe tests. He realized his vague feeling of unease had more to do with the inn than with the cottage. A good blow and the place was destined to come down like a house of cards. He'd been right in sanctioning its destruction, and he wondered with frantic suddenness if his recommendation had been carried out. He didn't like to think of Maggie and Robbie going anywhere near the inn, even if it *had* been demolished into a pile of huge matchsticks. That wasn't likely, he reassured himself, trying to calm jagged nerves. He told Maggie it was dangerous. She wouldn't willingly put herself or the boy at risk. Still, he didn't like it. Not a bit.

He instructed his secretary to get Jerry Carlisle on the phone, and in fifteen minutes he had located him on the tennis court.

"This better be important, Staff," Jerry told him. "I'm about to ace the competition."

The wait had stretched Lane's nerves taut. He wasted no time in preliminaries. "Jerry, did you raze that inn on your property on Caloosa Key?"

"I assume my construction crews took care of it. The board's still fighting over the designs you gave me, so I haven't had much time to follow what's happening down there."

"Can you find out? I need to know, Jer."

Alerted by his friend's tone that something was clearly wrong, Jerry said, "Give me ten minutes."

It was the longest ten minutes of Lane's life. He paced his office, his eyes black with turmoil, an icy numbness clenching his heart in a viselike grip. He told himself his worries were foolish and misplaced, but every time he had himself half convinced, he would remember Robbie's penchant for exploring the inn property and Maggie's tendency to seek solace there.

Lane's insides wrenched and he ground his teeth in frustration. "Damn it, Jerry! Call!" he swore savagely.

If anything happened to Robbie or Maggie, it would be his fault. He hadn't warned them sufficiently. He should have made sure that miserable wreck was destroyed.

Unable to wait any longer, Lane gave his secretary instructions to contact Banyon House. The first conversation with Maggie since he'd left the island—this was hardly the way he'd hoped to reestablish the relationship! The niggling panic clawing at him might very well prove groundless, but, if not, he wanted them to stay as far away from the place as possible. This time he'd make sure

Maggie listened to him. After he was certain they were safe, he'd worry about love.

The call from Jerry came through. Lane snatched the receiver, offering a silent prayer.

"The construction foreman down there says it's been raining too much to chance bogging down his equipment. It's been rescheduled to come down next week if this storm doesn't set them back."

"Christ!"

Jerry's voice was low and serious. "What's going on, Staff?"

"You'll think I'm crazy."

"I already know you're crazy. Try me."

Briefly Lane explained his fears; the sixth sense that nagged at him wouldn't let up. Voicing his concerns aloud made them sound foolishly unfounded, but the hairs on the back of his neck wouldn't stop prickling.

"So call her," Jerry advised calmly. He considered Lane's fears the overprotective worry of a man deeply in love. "If she won't listen to you, tell her I'll sue the socks off her if she or her brother step one foot on that property."

Lane grimaced. Maybe he *was* overreacting. "I've got a call in to her now." At that moment, his intercom buzzed. "Hold on, Jerry." He pressed the button that connected with his secretary. "Yes, Alice."

"I'm sorry, Mr. Stafford. The telephone lines are down on the island. I can't get through."

The breath stilled in Lane's lungs and his nerves flared with the first real terror he had ever known.

ELEVEN

The phone lines to Caloosa Key were down, but that was hardly a concern to the residents. Storms were a way of life on the island. Most of the locals regarded them as inconvenient, but almost a mixed blessing. The winds often cleared away dead limbs and debris, improved fishing, and brought die-hard shellers exciting new specimens as the waters receded and left hundreds of tiny sea creatures behind on the shore. Residents were seldom evacuated unless the storm was upgraded to a hurricane, and if the truth were known, some of the islanders regarded a tropical storm as a challenge to their adaptability and would not have left Caloosa Key unless *forced* to do so.

With Robbie's help, Maggie taped windows at the shop and Banyon House. They sorted through the jumbled mess in the garage until they located their ancient camp stove, and stockpiled supplies of candles, kerosene, and water. Robbie made sure all his animals were present and accounted for, secure in the safest corner of the garage. He cleared the ground around the house of any large limbs that might become dangerously airborne while Maggie stored away the porch furniture and latched all the storm windows tightly.

Mostly, they waited.

* * *

The storm came, the wind rattling the windows in their casings and howling under the eaves. Maggie's real concern, the tin roof, echoed hollowly with every lift of the wind, but it remained in place. She was relieved to see the cottage was more solidly built then she'd expected. They could hear the once-calm gulf pounding waves hard upon the shore, but the cottage was built high and far enough away that they did not expect to be flooded.

When the slashing rain slowed to a drizzle, Robbie scurried to check his pets while Maggie tried to get an up-to-date weather report on the television. A few minutes later, her brother came back from the garage, his eyes bright with anxiety.

"Roscoe's gone," he told Maggie.

"How?"

"I don't know, he just is. I've got to find him." The boy started to move toward the door, but Maggie captured his arm quickly.

"Hold it. You're not going out yet. Not until the storm passes completely."

"It's not raining hard."

"No, but listen to the wind. It's still kicking up out there. Roscoe can take care of himself."

Robbie was beside himself with worry. He was sure the raccoon was in horrible danger, a miniature Dorothy spinning off to Oz. Maggie did not agree. Roscoe was a clever beast and had probably found a quiet, dry corner to hole up. She suggested that possibility to her brother and reminded him that there was hundreds of other wild animals on the island that would see the storm through in fine shape.

But Robbie wasn't buying it. He paced and fretted, glancing out the back door every few minutes in the hopes of finding his pet huddled, wet and miserable, on the steps. Watching the boy's movements, Maggie was going insane.

The sudden thought came to her that if Lane were here,

it would be different. He would find a way to divert Robbie's attention, to convince him Roscoe was safe. The man had a way with her brother that made her almost envious. He was—

Stop that! she scolded herself. *He's not here, and that's that. You promised yourself you wouldn't think of him anymore.* But sometimes she couldn't help it. She still missed him so much.

Patience was a virtue Robbie practiced little. He pleaded and cajoled, threatened to throw a tantrum, and made promises he could not possibly keep. In another fifteen minutes Maggie was exhausted from arguing with him, and Robbie was quick to press his advantage. She gave in at last.

"All right. We'll both go. But you'll do as I say. Got it?"

The boy nodded eagerly. They put on raingear and rolled up the cuffs of their pants. Robbie scooped a warm blanket out of the closet in case the raccoon really *was* hurt and needed medical attention.

The rain was slight, but the wind tossed it every which way. In minutes they were soaked to the skin. The wind had not lessened as much as Maggie would have liked. It pushed and pulled at them, toying with their hair and clothing until they both resembled scarecrows set out in a field. The low spots of the property had become miniature lakes; Maggie grimaced as she splashed through what remained of her garden. The small plot of land was three inches under water.

They searched the compound around the house first. Under the porch steps, in the bushes, the interwoven branches of the banyon tree. No Roscoe.

"I'll bet he's around the inn," Robbie said after they had abandoned all hope of finding the beast in their own backyard. "I see him heading that way all the time."

Maggie shook her head. "We're not going over there. Lane said the place is dangerous." She wasn't sure she heartily accepted that verdict, but she was learning to live with the thought of the inn's destruction. She had not visited the place once since Lane's departure. Even her walks along the shore were planned in the opposite direction of the inn.

"Let's just check out the grounds," Robbie pleaded, and then before his sister could voice an objection, he took off down the path leading to the inn as though all the hounds of hell were after him.

"Robbie . . . come back here!"

Maggie charged after him, leaping over the debris blocking her flight, splashing mud and water all the way to her thighs. If she ever caught up with that boy, she was going to wring his neck!

She reached the edge of the inn property, cold and slightly out of breath. Robbie was nowhere to be seen. She blinked in surprise at her first sight of the inn. After what Lane had said, she expected to find it a shambles. The wind had pulled loose some shingles and part of the cupola railing was missing, but the place looked the same as ever. Worn, but lovingly familiar. No chance to save it? None, according to experts who should know. She swallowed despair and looked away.

"Robbie!" she called. "Come here this instant!"

"Mag! I've found him. Come quick."

She ran around a corner of the inn, pulling up short at the sight of Robbie and Roscoe. The boy had his hand outstretched, but the raccoon had pressed himself into a corner of the building and seemed unwilling to come forward. Through the drizzling rain, Maggie could see the pink tinge of blood seeping down the beast's front leg.

Uneasiness crept through her. Roscoe might have been raised from a baby, but he was still a wild animal. She didn't want to rely on his behavior remaining predictable. Her hand reached out and pulled Robbie back. "Wait. Let's not scare him."

"He's hurt, Mag," the boy cried.

"I know," she replied, trying to calm his fears. "But

I think we should be careful. Roscoe may not want much to do with us right now. Give me the blanket.''

"What are you going to do?''

"I'm going to try and throw it over him. If he bites, he'll get a mouthful of wool instead of me. You stay back.''

She approached the small animal slowly, the blanket stretched in front of her like a matador's cape. Roscoe regarded her warily. He seemed frightened, but, thankfully, not hostile. Maggie never took her eyes off the raccoon, prepared to jump back if it suddenly attacked.

Roscoe had other ideas. He didn't want to be stuffed into a blanket; he wanted to be left alone. He ignored Maggie's softly crooning voice and turned his back on her. In spite of his injury, he agilely climbed upon the rose trellis that covered one wall and slipped up into a small, sheltered corner of gingerbread trim decorating the building.

The overhang was too far above her head for Maggie to reach. Roscoe regarded her with a bright-eyed satisfaction, as though perfectly aware of that fact. Maggie captured her bottom lip with her teeth. She was silent for a long minute, thinking how best to approach the problem. The wind howled suddenly, cutting through her wet clothes and making her shiver.

To hell with Roscoe. He wasn't seriously hurt, and when he felt like coming down, he would. As far as Maggie was concerned, he could stay up there as long as he liked. *She* was going home to dry off. And so was Robbie.

She turned around to tell the boy that, but her brother was nowhere in sight. "Robbie?''

"I'm here,'' the boy called over the wind and rain.

She looked up and he was just coming over the slight incline of the roof, his blond hair whipping madly in the wind but a wide grin on his face. Her heart plummeted to her toes. "Come down from there.''

"In a minute. I climbed up the trellis on the other side,

just like Roscoe. Throw me the blanket. I'll sneak up from behind and catch him before he knows it.''

Maggie shaded her eyes against the sting of icy raindrops. ''No. Come down, Rob,'' she commanded in the calmest tone she could manage. She didn't want to frighten Robbie into making a misstep, but she was terrified by the sight of him on the roof. The pitch wasn't steep, but one wrong move could send him sliding off the side of the building. Lane's words rocketed through her brain. Water damage. Dangerous.

Even as she had the thought, Robbie's foot slipped on a wet shingle and he fell heavily. Maggie choked back a cry, frightened, then awash with sudden shaking relief when no harm seemed to have been done.

Robbie picked himself up, embarrassed more than anything else. ''I'll be careful,'' he said with a weak grin.

Later it seemed as though the entire sequence of events happened in slow motion. One moment Robbie was smiling down at her. The next there was a groan of protest even the racket of the wind and rain could not drown out. The roof was sliding, caving in, and Robbie was scrambling for a foothold, his features pinched and white with stunned surprise. The walls creaked and swayed, colliding with each other. Maggie was vaguely aware of her own voice, screaming for Robbie to jump, her arms stretching to catch him. The raccoon leaped past her, into the open air, and then she, too, was flinging herself backward to avoid being captured in the wreckage. Something struck her hard in the ribs and her side flared with hot pain as the breath was knocked out of her.

She landed in the mud and came up on her hands and knees, struggling to remain conscious. Her hair was hanging in wet strings over her eyes. With a muddied, trembling hand she pushed the sodden mass out of her face and looked up where Robbie had been . . . and screamed.

He wasn't there. The *roof* wasn't there. The entire wing of the inn had collapsed upon itself and now lay in a jumbled pile of beams and plaster that still sifted and trickled.

Maggie pushed herself upward, ignoring the stab of pain in her side and the cold nausea threatening to overwhelm. She was sobbing her brother's name and a litany of prayers: *Please, God. Please. Help me. Oh, God!*

"Robbie! Where are you? Answer me!" she begged.

She scrambled over the wet and rotted wood, plucking away bits of debris with shaking hands. Her breath was coming in harsh, panting sounds of terror and anguish. Splinters gouged her hands as Maggie dug amid the wreckage, trying to find some sign of her brother.

"Maggie?"

A cry of relief broke from her lips as she heard Robbie's trembling inquiry. He was alive! *Thank you, God. Thank you!*

Favoring her side, she inched under a canopy of fallen beams toward her brother's voice. Rainwater runneled down the rubble to slide beneath her clothes. Maggie realized suddenly she was shivering with cold, but drenched in sweat. When she came in contact with Robbie, she was so achingly glad that she burst into tears.

"Don't cry, Maggie. I'm all right."

"Are you sure?" she demanded, running her hands over him. "Do you hurt anywhere?"

"Just my arm." His voice was surprisingly calm. "I can't move it."

Fear slid down Maggie's spine once more. Robbie's arm was twisted away from his body, buried under a pile of debris. Her fingers inched down his shoulder as far as they could go, tugging gently. When her touch brought a small whimper of pain from him, she stopped. Robbie's arm was firmly pinioned by the wreckage.

"Do you think you can scoot yourself out from under this mess if I lift these beams off you?"

"Yes."

She gave him her most encouraging smile, but the moment Maggie tried to lift the beam that had Robbie trapped, she caught her breath in a sharp, agonized gasp and doubled over in pain.

"What's the matter?" Robbie said quickly. His features had gone paper-white.

It took a moment for the red haze in front of her eyes to settle. "It's just a bruise," she reassured him. "But I don't think I can lift these. I'll have to have help." She looked at her brother worriedly and wiped mud off his cheek with a loving hand. "Can you lie here quietly for a few minutes while I go into town? I promise I'll be back with help soon."

The boy nodded. "I'm okay. Are you all right, Mag?"

"I will be as soon as we get you out from under this mess."

Tears welled in the boy's eyes, sliding down the sides of his face to mingle with the rain. "I'm sorry."

She touched his face again. "It's all right, honey. Everything will be fine. Please don't cry. I love you, Robbie."

"I love you, too, Mag." He sniffed loudly. "Is it okay to be scared?"

Scared didn't begin to sum up her feelings right now. "Sure it is."

The boy grimaced. "I guess I'm in big trouble, aren't I?"

"The biggest."

He smiled weakly at that, and Maggie took a few more moments to reassure him before she left.

She levered herself off the ground, gritting her teeth against the white-hot pain that clawed at her. Dizziness enveloped her, but she fought against its disorientation, knowing she could not give in to it. Her right leg had begun to burn, and with some surprise, Maggie noted blood seeping through her torn pant leg, a sticky wetness pooling in her sneaker.

As fast as the pain would allow, Maggie raced back to the cottage. The wind seemed stronger now, fighting her headlong flight, or perhaps she was physically less able to withstand its buffeting. The garage doors were closed, with the drop latch secured across them to keep out the storm. With a grunt of pain, Maggie threw the latch upward and finally managed to swing the doors wide on their hinges. She yanked open the door of the station wagon, but the moment she slid behind the wheel, she realized her mistake. The keys were in the cottage.

Of course they were! *Think, Maggie! Stop panicking and think what you're going to do. Into town. Find someone. Robbie. Please, honey. Don't be badly hurt.*

The pain knifed into her side once again, and Maggie leaned forward to rest her head and arms across the steering wheel. Rainwater ran across her cheeks to drip off the end of her nose. Her breath was rasping loudly in the shadowy stillness of the garage. Spots danced across the inside of her eyelids. She tried to take several calming breaths, realizing that if she passed out she could hardly do her brother any good.

A hand settled on her shoulder, and Maggie jumped a little. She tilted her head, blinking several times in stunned surprise and confusion. Lane? How could that be? He was thousands of miles away in Chicago. He *couldn't* be here beside her. She must be hallucinating. *Oh, stupid. Stupid. How can you be indulging in fantasies at a time like this!*

"Maggie, damn it. Talk to me," the hallucination demanded.

She stared at him hard. "Lane?"

"Yes, sweetheart. I'm here." His hand reached out to smooth tangled strands of hair out of her face. "Tell me what's happened."

Maggie clutched Lane's arm; her eyes widened with the sudden realization that Lane truly *was* here on Caloosa Key. "Oh, Lane, thank God. The roof caved in and Robbie's trapped. I couldn't lift it. You've got to help him."

"All right, Maggie. Stay calm. Are *you* okay?"

"Yes. Just help him."

"You stay here and rest. We'll have him out in no time."

"Wait. I'm coming with you."

He didn't waste time arguing with her. By the time she had gotten out of the garage, Lane and another man were already disappearing down the path leading to the inn. She followed as quickly as she could, vaguely aware that her strength was nearly gone. *Just a little longer*, she told herself. *Robbie will be free and then you can give in.*

She reached the place where the west wing of the inn had been, and Lane and the stranger were already lifting debris. Lane was issuing instructions to the man with him. Evidently he didn't want some beams lifted before others, since to do so might create further collapse. Occasionally he called encouragement to Robbie, who seemed less frightened now that rescue was close at hand.

When Maggie tried to maneuver down to her brother's side, Lane picked her up bodily and carted her out of harm's way. She squirmed against him for a moment, then subsided on a gasp of pain when her struggles brought the knife blade slicing deep into her side.

He grabbed her face between both his hands. "You stay put," he commanded. "I can't worry about both of you right now, and you'll only get in the way. Understand?" She nodded, and he frowned at the sight of shock and pain in her bright blue eyes. "What's the matter with you? Are you hurt?"

"No," she lied. "Just get Robbie out. I'm so scared, Lane." She clung to Lane's arm in a childlike plea, craving reassurance.

"Everything will be fine, Maggie." His fingers whispered against her jawline. "He'll be out of this mess in another minute. Just rest." His lips touched hers briefly, a cold contact quickly gone.

She watched him hurry away, thinking how unbalanced the world seemed. She closed her eyes a moment, wishing the darkness would stop cartwheeling. Her leg throbbed in swollen agony. The rain was a light drizzle now, a soft gray mist against her cold skin, but she felt chilled all the way to the bone. She realized her mind was wandering, spinning cobwebs, and Maggie tried to focus on Lane, his movements an economy of motion.

He looked fit, the way she remembered. She was inordinately glad to see him, even if he didn't love her. What had brought him back? she wondered, her hand unconsciously fingering the spot where he had touched his lips to hers.

Another minute and Robbie was free. Maggie watched Lane scoop her brother out of the wreckage and set him on his feet. He wobbled a moment and cradled one arm, but he seemed to be in one piece.

Maggie rose slowly, finding the movement almost beyond her capabilities. Robbie was suddenly beside her, hugging her fiercely with his good arm. They were both sobbing with relief, and over the boy's head, Maggie's eyes met Lane's.

"Looks like a simple fracture," Lane answered her unspoken question. "We'll have him at the hospital in Fort Myers in twenty minutes."

"How?"

"Dave's gone to rev up the copter now. Didn't you notice we had landed on your front lawn?"

Maggie shook her head slowly. Rising had brought spots dancing in front of her eyes. Lane's voice seemed to be oscillating in and out. She was catching only half of what he said.

She swayed on her feet, and Lane steadied her. "Let's go. Your sister looks done in, Rob. Can you manage to walk?"

The boy looked affronted at the idea he might have to be carried. "I'm okay. I never had a broken bone before. Will I get a cast?"

"Probably." Lane glanced down at Maggie, who was clinging to his soaked shirtfront with a death-grip. "Maggie, you still with us, sweetheart?"

She frowned up at him. "You're all wet."

He grinned. "This island plays hell with my wardrobe, doesn't it?" His gaze slid over her cold, wet features.

"This isn't how I planned our reunion, but it doesn't seem to make much difference now. I've missed you, sweetheart." His lips took hers in undemanding but comforting pressure. "I love you, Maggie Rose. Tell me we can work things out."

She blinked in confusion. "What?" she mumbled, her mind shutting down in a fog of pain and cold. It seemed very important that she stay alert right now, but for the life of her, Maggie couldn't seem to manage it. She shivered, and the movement brought the hurt screaming into her brain. She whimpered against it.

Lane looked down at her hard. She was deathly white and her wide, blue eyes were unfocused. He glanced down at her leg and saw for the first time the dark stain of blood through the mud that flecked her pants. "What the hell . . . ?" he murmured, tightening his hold.

She slumped against him, unconscious.

For Lane, the next thirty minutes were a blurred nightmare.

He carried Maggie's cold, still form to the helicopter, Robbie following closely in his wake. The boy's voice held a hysterical edge as he questioned Lane frantically. He had never seen his sister completely helpless before, and he was scared. Lane tried to be calm and reassuring, but his own heart was drumming a mad tattoo.

He helped Robbie into the copter's front seat, then slid himself and Maggie into the rear compartment. As soon as they were settled, Dave lifted off. Robbie issued a squawk of fear as the wind buffeted them, but Dave reached over and touched the boy's good shoulder in reassurance.

"Don't worry," he said. "This wind is nothing compared to what I flew through in 'Nam. Have you studied Vietnam in school, son?"

The boy shook his head, and Dave launched into a series of war stories deliberately designed to distract Robbie from his fear for his sister and a bumpy first flight in a helicopter. Lane thanked him silently, making a mental note to see to it that Jerry Carlisle's pilot got some kind of bonus for his help here. He wasn't sure how he would have managed without him.

He looked down into Maggie's pale face. It looked like marble—smooth and cold and lifeless. He cradled her fragile framework against him, stroking his hands along her arms, trying to force warmth into her unresponsive limbs. Maggie didn't stir.

He ripped open the tear in her pants, his mouth forming a grim line as he noted the jagged tear in the fleshy part of her thigh. The cut would need to be stitched, but it did not seem life-threatening. It seeped blood, and it seemed likely she had lost quite a bit. As quickly as he could manage to in the cramped quarters of the helicopter, Lane ripped off the bottom of his shirt and wrapped it tightly around Maggie's leg, forming a crude tourniquet. Through all his ministrations, she remained ominously still.

Robbie swung his head around. His eyes had a desperate look to them. "Did she wake up?"

Don't make a muddle of this, Stafford, Lane warned himself. The boy was scared to death. "No, but that's all right," he said, straining to keep terror out of his voice. "She needs the rest."

His hands traveled gingerly over Maggie's inert body, searching, yet afraid to find, greater injury. When his fingers trailed across the rock-hard heat of Maggie's side, he knew he had found it. Lifting her blouse, he nearly gasped aloud at the sight of the ugly, purpling bruise that marred her flesh. Fear jolted him. Internal injuries.

No, his mind screamed dully. *No, no.* He stared hard at the spot, willing it to disappear. *Just a bruise, a bruise. It's going to be all right, Maggie. Do you hear me? I love you, sweetheart. Don't do this to me.*

He felt ice-cold, near to being physically sick. He gathered Maggie close, pulling her back against him to kiss the moisture from her finely drawn cheeks. The inside of the helicopter blurred in his vision, and Lane realized he was perilously close to losing control. He couldn't allow that. Not with Robbie here, hurt and scared to death and depending on him to be strong. Lane clamped down hard on his ricocheting emotions.

They were suddenly setting down at the hospital heliport. There was a flurry of activity in the soft rain as briskly efficient attendants went about the business of saving lives. Stretchers were positioned. A white-coated orderly levered Robbie out of his seat carefully.

Maggie was lifted out of Lane's arms. He felt immediately bereft and made a sudden movement to recapture her, then subsided as he realized he had to let go. His limbs felt as cold and achy as an old man's, but he ignored the feeling, his eyes riveted on Maggie's still form. Against the white sheet and the gray light, she looked dead already. *I love you, sweetheart. Please stay with me.*

He followed in the attendant's wake, a fist of fear clenched tightly in the pit of his stomach.

She woke slowly and opened her eyes. Her eyelids seemed too heavy, disconnected from her brain; she had to fight to keep them open. Maggie tried to focus on her surroundings. She was aware of warmth and soft light, the faint click and hiss of machinery. The unpleasant smell of medicine.

Her brain began to reconstruct, bits of memory filing neatly into place. A hospital. Of course she would be in a hospital. She had hurt herself. Hadn't she? As if to remind her, pain throbbed along her right side, but it was a healing hurt, not the knifing agony of before. She turned her head slightly, relieved to find she still had the ability to do so.

Her gaze skated over a man's still form positioned in a chair at the side of the bed. Lane. His head was cradled in one arm that rested against the mattress. His other hand held hers in a loose grip. His clothing was dirty and a mass of wrinkles. Flecks of dried mud matted his rich brown hair. He was asleep.

She frowned, struggling to remember, and her hand moved reflexively in his.

He came awake instantly and shifted his head toward her. When he saw she was conscious, his tired eyes brightened and a smile stretched his lips. "Hello, sweetheart," he whispered. "How do you feel?"

She swallowed. Her throat felt dry and scratchy. "Hurts," she murmured hoarsely.

He touched his lips to the back of her hand. "I know it does, but you'll feel better soon. The doctor says you'll be up in a week."

"What's wrong . . . with me?"

"You broke two ribs, and one of them punctured a lung. There's a gash on your thigh, but it will hardly leave a scar." His hand sifted through her hair, stroking it away from her forehead. "You scared the hell out of me. Why didn't you tell me you were hurt?"

Memory returned in a rush. "Robbie. Where is he?"

"Robbie's fine. He's down on Pediatrics under observation for the next couple of days. He's got a broken arm and a few bumps and bruises, but he'll be up and about in no time."

"I want to see him." She moved in agitation, then subsided as the pain nagged at her side.

"Relax," Lane commanded in a soft voice. "In a few days I'll bring him up here to see you."

She seemed about to protest further, but didn't. Her weakened condition made her feel helpless and afraid. Her emotions close to the surface, tears of frustration slid down the sides of her face. "You're always telling me what to do," she accused petulantly, like a thwarted child.

Amused rather than angered by her words, Lane used his fingers to erase the wetness from her cheeks. "And you're always not doing it." His lips followed the pattern of her tears. "Just rest, Maggie," he whispered close to her ear. "When you feel better, we'll have a nice long talk, you and I."

His voice was lulling. She *did* feel tired, barely able to

keep her eyes open. Her lashes fluttered. Half asleep, she frowned at Lane in confusion. "I dreamed . . . you said you loved me," she said in a voice cracked with exhaustion.

His deep chuckle vibrated near her ear. "Not a dream, sweetheart. Reality." He deftly caught her mouth with his, a brief, warm communication of his love. "Beautiful reality."

He wasn't sure Maggie heard. She was already fast asleep.

Two days later Lane entered Maggie's hospital room to find her propped up in bed, her hair pulled neatly back from her face, captured in a blue ribbon. She still looked tired, but there was color in her cheeks, and the smile she gave him was nearly radiant.

Robbie sat on one end of the bed in a pair of Spiderman pajamas, his injured arm encompassed in a huge cast already sporting several signatures. He looked at Lane anxiously. "How are my animals?"

"They miss you," Lane said, depositing a box of personal items in a nearby chair. He held up a finger covered by a Band-Aid. "Roscoe sends you his best. Miserable creature."

"Then he's all right."

"You'll see for yourself soon enough. The doctor's discharging you today. I've brought some clothes, so how about getting changed?"

The boy hopped off the bed with an excited whoop of pleasure. He was eager to get back to the island, back to his animals and friends who would listen wide-eyed to his tale of how he had fallen through the inn roof and lived to tell about it. He gave Maggie a quick kiss, grabbed up the tidy pile of clothing Lane indicated, and left the room.

Lane positioned himself close to Maggie's side and captured her hand in his. "And how are *you* feeling today?"

"I feel good." She gave him a wistful half-smile. "I wish *I* could go home."

"You will soon. You have to. I'm not sure I can manage Robbie all by myself."

"He's very happy to have you back here."

"I'm happy to *be* back," Lane replied quietly.

Maggie looked away, her gaze settling on a pulled thread in her blanket. "Who was the man with you that day?"

"Dave Byers. He's Jerry Carlisle's corporate pilot. I called in a favor and Dave flew me down here in the company jet. There were no boats going over to the island, so Dave suggested a helicopter. It took some talking and all the cash we had with us, but it worked."

"I never got a chance to thank him."

"You will someday."

She gave him a hesitant glance under lowered lashes. "I never thanked you, either."

Lane grinned. "*That* you'll definitely do—soon."

Maggie sighed and laid her head back against the pillows. She stared up at the ceiling. "You were right about the inn."

Lane's hand found her cheek. "I swear to God, Maggie," he said softly, "I never wanted to be."

She looked at him. "I believe you." A long silence engulfed them. At last, in a voice that trembled a little, Maggie asked, "Why did you come back here?"

His thumb slid under her jawline, gently stroking for a moment, then tilting her face until their eyes were in direct contact. He thought she seemed scared and uncertain, but her features were so achingly familiar to him, so cherished, that Lane felt a knot of emotion clog his throat. "I came back because I knew something was wrong the moment I heard about the storm. It kept nagging at me until I had to come down and see for myself. It's a damn good thing I did."

That wasn't the answer Maggie really hoped to hear. Her bottom lip disappeared between her teeth. "Oh. A premonition."

"Something like that." His hand slid down the curve

of her throat, trailing over her collarbone that lay exposed beneath the voluminous folds of the hospital gown. "I also came back because I couldn't face another day without you. I gave you as much time as I could. Hell, I had to leave the country to keep from turning up on your doorstep. I hope you've adjusted to the idea, sweetheart, because, like it or not, I love you and I'm never going to let you go."

Maggie's mouth formed a little O of surprise. "I thought you hated me."

Lane smiled, and he drew her close. Careful not to harm her tender side, he cradled her in his arms. His mouth drifted over hers, warm and gentle, but with an underlying hunger that sent tiny shocks tingling down Maggie's body. Her lips parted invitingly as she was filled with the same sweet yearning he always evoked in her. She yielded eagerly, and Lane groaned in frustration, longing to taste the honeyed sweetness of her so long denied, yet knowing Maggie was still far too fragile to withstand the powerful need threatening to override his control. He forced himself to pull away, but he could not let her go completely.

He looked down into her wide eyes and smiled lazily. "Did that feel like hate to you, Maggie?"

"No . . ." Her voice was distant, soft and dreamlike.

"I didn't think so," he said with a low chuckle.

EPILOGUE

The Gulf of Mexico lapped at his ankles, a cool, gentle wash across his bare feet. He took a deep breath, savoring the scent of salt and seaweed. The night was balmy; the wind teased his hair and plucked at his clothing like the grasping hands of small children. Soft laughter from the shore drifted toward him on the breeze and Lane smiled. He wriggled his toes in the sand, thinking how different his life was now, how completely changed in less than a year.

He supposed he should return and join the others, but there was still time. Time to enjoy the quiet peace, the gentle compelling rhythm of small waves nipping at the shore. An infinite rightness filled Lane's heart. This is where he was meant to be. On Caloosa Key with Maggie. Loving Maggie. Always. He felt good. Strong. He was happy.

He felt her approach, knowing it would be Maggie before he ever turned his head. In the moonlight, her body was etched in silver. He returned her smile, loving his wife so much that he thought his heart would burst from the sheer joy of it.

She slid into the warm circle of his arms, and nuzzled

his ear. "You're missing the performance," she crooned softly. "Babette's nearly done."

"Hunt and Robbie can manage without us."

He traced a languorous pattern with his lips across one of Maggie's brows, placed his lips against the pulse pounding at her temple, nibbling kisses down the column of her throat. His hands stole under her T-shirt to capture her unbound breasts. With slow, erotic movements his fingers grazed her rose-tipped nipples, delighting in the feel of the silken texture of her skin.

She moaned at the contact, lifting her arms to bring her fingers spreading through the thick richness of his hair. As always, his hands were quick to touch off lightning currents of arousal with.... ...r.

She loved him so much. Sometimes Maggie was afraid she loved him *too* much. She didn't want to stifle him. To have him one day regret the changes he'd made in his life.

"Lane . . ."

"Mmm?" His mouth had found a delightful indentation near her collarbone and he nibbled it playfully.

"Are you ever sorry you gave up everything in Chicago?"

His mouth stopped moving and he pulled away from her, just far enough to meet the shadowed sparkle of her eyes. "I didn't *give* up anything. I *found* everything. Right here with you. And Rob."

Her heart swelled as Maggie digested that statement. "Then your career—"

"What career? I was a successful architect in a *very* large firm. Setting up my own office here on the island was the best move I could have made. Here I make a difference. I help decide how fast or slow Caloosa Key progresses. I like that feeling." He trailed a finger down Maggie's nose. "I like working with you, too. My designs, your interiors. My clients are starting to think of us as a team."

Pleasure and embarrassment flooded through her. "I think we make a pretty *good* team."

"The best," Lane replied huskily, his mouth burning across her jawline with savage earnestness.

Maggie frowned with a sudden thought. "I'm worried about Robbie. How is he going to react to the idea of a baby coming?"

Lane sighed, realizing Maggie was not going to respond to his lovemaking until she had most of her questions answered. He settled for having her pressed up against him, exalting in the pleasure her nearness always brought him. "I think he'll be excited. Another little creature to fuss and fret over."

Maggie bit her lip. "I hope so. I just don't want anything to change . . ."

"You can't stop change, Maggie."

"I know," she replied softly.

He wondered if she was even aware her head had tilted unconsciously in the direction where The Caloosa Key Inn had once stood. It had been demolished shortly after Maggie's release from the hospital last year. Every beam and board had been cleared away; even the ancient swimming pool had been filled. Personally Lane was relieved to see the end of it. But Maggie had been quiet and withdrawn for days after its destruction, and he knew losing it had very probably broken her heart.

His hand stroked along her back with a gentleness borne of love. "You still miss it, don't you?"

She didn't pretend not to understand. "Sometimes. I know I shouldn't, because the miserable place could have cost me my brother's life. But the funny thing is, even though it's gone, I can still conjure up the memories. They couldn't be destroyed. They're still in my heart, and nothing can ever change that." Maggie looked up at him through her lashes. "Just like my love for you."

Lane smiled faintly, and his hands captured her face. A roguish gleam sparkled in his eyes. "What do you say we take a walk along the shore,'' he purred dangerously. ''Make a few memories of our own.''

Her fingers entwined with his, and Lane drew Maggie unresistingly down the starlit beach.